MORE THAN A KISS

Kate looked up and felt her face grow warm at the realization that she was standing directly beneath the ball of mistletoe hanging from the ceiling.

"I haven't seen one of those in years," Ethan murmured, slowly moving to her.

Kate knew she should step away, run away, yet was incapable of moving. "Connie saw one for the first time while watching an old romantic holiday movie," she said. "She insisted we had to have one."

"Then it would be a shame to waste it," he said, closing in on her.

Kate started to turn away, but Ethan lightly grasped her waist, holding her still. He lowered his head.

"Ethan." Kate's voice quavered and she drew in a quick breath, scenting the cold night air clinging to him.

"Merry Christmas, Kate," he murmured as his lips brushed hers.

Though his lips still held a chill from the outside, Kate felt a jarring charge of sexual electricity sizzle through her entire being. She curled her fingers into Ethan's chest and mindlessly arched her body against his, wanting more, so much more . . .

Books by Joan Hohl

COMPROMISES

ANOTHER SPRING

EVER AFTER

MAYBE TOMORROW

SILVER THUNDER

NEVER SAY NEVER

SOMETHING SPECIAL

MY OWN

Published by Zebra Books

JOAN HOHL

MY OWN

ZEBRA BOOKS
KENSINGTON PUBLISHING CORP.
http://www.zebrabooks.com

PROLOGUE

The scent of flowers permeated the air. The altar was adorned with tall white and gold tapers and garlands of white roses entwined in dark green ferns. Nosegays of dusky pink rosebuds and sprays of baby's-breath were attached by white satin ribbons to the endposts of each pew.

The church was full to capacity, the ladies dressed in their spring finery, the gentlemen attired in lightweight suits or sport coats. Though the children present were, for the most part, on their best behavior, an occasional murmur or restless rustle of movement could be heard above the combined voices of the choir singing a traditional love song.

As the last strains of music faded, the formally attired groom and his men entered from a door to the right of the nave.

The organist struck a signaling chord.

The groom, his attendants, and the assembled families and guests turned to face the end of the center aisle as the organ boomed forth the wedding march.

Seated on the right—or groom's—side of the aisle with the members of the only family she had ever known, Kate Quinn didn't see the tiny flower girl and four bridesmaids in their dusty pink gowns. Nor did she see the beautiful bride, resplendent in stiffened white silk and lace, walk down the white runner on the arm of her father.

Kate's attention was riveted on the solemn visage of the handsome groom, Ethan Winston, her best friend.

Ethan. The cry inside Kate's head was wrenched from the depths of her heart.

A flood of memories brought a rush of tears to her eyes, blurring her vision so that all she could see was the edge of his face. But the inner images of Ethan and their past were clear, bright as the spring morning.

Kate had been eleven, Ethan sixteen, the first time she had seen him. Thirteen years had passed since that fateful day, and yet her memory of it was as sharp, as vivid, as if it had been just yesterday.

Oblivious to her surroundings, she did not notice the beginning of the wedding ceremony, the bride's father placing her hand into the safekeeping of the groom's palm. Nor did Kate see Ethan turn with his bride to face the minister.

Looking inward, Kate saw herself as a child, as she had been all those years past, uncertain, shy, scared about her future, her place in the new house she had come to live in with her mother and stepfather.

* * *

To that younger Kate, having lived every one of her eleven years in small apartments, the house itself had been intimidating, with its spacious rooms and half-bath on the first floor, four bedrooms and two baths on the second floor, and two big storage rooms on the third floor.

"Go, Katelyn," her mother had urged, sharing a smile with her husband of only a few days. "Go explore your new home, the yard, and the gardens."

Needing no urging, Kate ran outdoors to breathe deeply the fresh air, bask in the heat of summer sunshine, rejoice in what, at that young age, she considered the extensive lawns and gardens.

Having already seen the front lawn with its trees and shrubbery, she headed for the back of the house, thrilled with the width and depth of the property. There were flower beds ablaze with color, abundant with a variety of plants in full bloom. A hedge nearly as tall as Kate herself bordered either side and the back boundaries of the yard.

As she neared the far end of the yard, Kate heard a clipping noise. Curious, she wandered in the direction of the sound. She discovered the boy in the far corner, trimming the hedge with long-bladed clippers.

Either he was tall or standing on something, Kate figured, for his torso rose above the high hedge. He was young, though not yet a man, but a kid like her, just a few years older.

Shy, unsure, she moved closer, coming to a dead stop when he glanced over the hedge at her.

He was the best-looking boy Kate had ever seen. He had dark hair and even darker eyes, and when suddenly he grinned at her, her heart seemed to flip-flop.

"Hi," he said, his voice friendly. "You must be Katelyn, Mr. Gardner's new stepdaughter. Right?"

Tongue-tied, Kate nodded her answer.

"Thought so." He nodded, too. "I'm Ethan Winston." He indicated the house behind him. "I live next door. My parents and Mr. Gardner are good friends. I met your mother last week." He smiled. "That's how I knew your name."

"Oh," Kate said, suddenly recalling her mother mentioning that David Gardner's neighbors had two children, a son and a daughter, both older than Kate. "You have a sister, don't you?" she asked, hoping the girl would be a little closer to her own age than Ethan.

"Yeah." He nodded again. "Sharon, but she's away at college."

"Oh," Kate repeated, sighing in disappointment.

"Well, I'd better get back to work. See you later, Katelyn."

"Kate," she blurted out.

"Okay," he said, grinning once more. "I like that better, anyway."

Although Kate eventually met Sharon, a pretty young woman of eighteen, she had very little real contact with her, as the older girl was stand-offish, and in Kate's opinion, a little snooty. But she did see a lot of Ethan in those days. In truth, whenever he was around the house, she trailed after him like a devoted puppy. He tolerated her, teased her, and on one or two occasions took on the role of big brother, particularly when Kate lost her beloved mother three years later.

But even before that awful day, before she even turned twelve, Kate worshiped Ethan like a hero. By the time Kate was seventeen, Kate knew that she was in love with him.

"And now, by the powers vested in me . . ."

Hearing those fateful words, Kate blinked herself into the present.

"I pronounce you man and wife."

The statement was like a knife in Kate's heart. The pain of loss and bitterness seared her.

Ethan. How could he?

Staring at him, Kate saw Ethan gather the filmy bridal veil in his hands and begin to raise it above the beautiful face of his bride. Unable to bear watching him bestow the sealing kiss, Kate lowered her eyes.

How could he? Why had he led her to think, to believe . . .

A strong wave of anger and resentment surged through her, startling in its intensity. This minute, she could hate him, she *should* hate him, Kate fumed, raising her eyes just as Ethan lifted his mouth from his bride's.

She couldn't hate him, of course, because . . .

because he was Ethan, her friend, her hero, her . . .
Kate blinked the stinging tears that rushed to her
eyes.

It was done. It was over. Ethan had married another
woman—he belonged to another woman.

At that moment, all of Kate's secretly held hopes,
her cherished dreams, died an agonizing death.

The knell rang inside Kate's head.

Now I'll never have Ethan for my own.

CHAPTER ONE

Katelyn Quinn needed a cigarette.

The wedding was over. Ethan Winston, the man Kate had loved for years, and the man she believed, for a few short weeks, was falling in love with her, had married another woman.

Hurting inside, fighting to maintain her composure, Kate moved slowly with the crowd up the white runner to the front of the church, where the bridal party had lined up to accept the congratulations and well-wishes of respective family members and friends.

When at last she stepped into place before Ethan, Kate stuck out her hand to grasp his, and muttered the expected congratulations.

"I hope you'll be very happy."

"Kate." Ethan's voice was low, urgent, anxious.

Beginning to tremble, knowing she had to get out of there, Kate released his hand, stretched her quivering lips into a brilliant smile, and rushed on to the glowing, laughing bride to offer her good wishes.

The bride gave her a vague smile, and a quick, "Thank you" before shifting her gaze to the woman behind Kate.

Outside the church, certain that she'd receive frowns if she dared light up a cigarette not to mention shocked expressions from her family, Kate drew a deep breath of the mild spring air, and turned her attention to her excited, chattering half sisters.

"That was so beautiful," said Connie with all the dramatic feeling of a ten-year-old.

Her sister, a more worldly twelve, nodded in agreement. "Even nicer than Sharon's wedding . . . Not as . . ." She paused, as if searching for the right words. "Not as fussy."

Change pretentious to fussy, Kate thought, secretly agreeing with the assessment, and sharing a smile between the girls. "The gowns were lovely, weren't they?" She was making conversation for the sake of the youngsters, for in truth, with her attention centered on Ethan, she hadn't noticed the designs of either the bride's or bridesmaids' dresses.

"I liked that pretty kinda almost purple color."

"Rose," Mandy clarified for her younger sister. "It's called dusty rose."

"Whatever." Connie shrugged, unconcerned. "Didn't you just love the bride's gown?"

"Her name is Paula." Mandy shook her head in impatient exasperation.

Connie heaved a meaningful sigh. "I knew that."

"I thought Ethan looked a bit strained," observed David, the girls' father and Kate's stepfather.

"Maybe he was excited," Connie suggested.

"Maybe he was nervous," Mandy offered.

Or maybe he was feeling a twinge of guilt. Kate didn't voice the thought, probably because she seriously doubted its validity.

The girls chattered on, drawing their father into their minute-by-minute rehash of the entire proceedings.

Would this never end?

On the verge of tears, despairing her weakness, Kate stood in the midst of the laughing, bantering crowd bunched outside the church entrance, little netting packets of rose petals clutched in their hands, eagerly awaiting the emergence of the wedding party.

"I think they're coming out now," said a middle-aged woman positioned close to the large open double church doors.

Unwilling to witness again the radiant face of the bride—even more so, the groom—Kate glanced down, startled to see she had shredded the tiny packet of rose petals clutched in her trembling fingers. Lowering her hand, she concealed the ruined packet behind her skirt, letting the petals slip through her fingers, slowly drifting to the ground. Doesn't matter, she mused. She didn't want to throw the petals anyway. She wanted to throw stones.

Ashamed of the violent urge, Kate forced herself to look up and smile, hoping she appeared animated.

Heads down, laughing, the newlyweds and their attendants dashed through the shower of fragrant petals to the streamer decorated limousines lined up at the curb.

Soon the limos pulled away, horns blaring. The crowd slowly began to disperse. Herding Mandy and Connie before her, Kate led the retreat to the church parking lot.

"What's your hurry, Kate?" Mandy demanded, panting to keep up with the headlong pace of her half sister.

"Yeah, anyway," Connie grumbled, her shorter legs pumping to catch up.

"Uh ... I ..." Groping for a credible response, Kate shot a glance at David, noting his lack of color, the evidence of fatigue around his eyes and mouth. "Your father is looking tired," she said, disgusted with herself for using David and a his declining health for an excuse. "I think he needs to rest."

"Oh." Connie peered at her father, her small faced puckered with concern.

"Are you okay, Dad?" Mandy asked in alarm.

"Yes, I'm fine." David smiled, a gentle, tender smile that tugged at Kate's heart, and her conscience. "But Kate's right, I could do with a little rest."

They reached the car. "I'll drive, you relax," Kate said, sighing with relief as she slid behind the wheel of the roomy Lincoln.

"You've had to play chauffeur to me for a lot of social events lately, haven't you?" David murmured, settling into the soft leather seat beside her.

Unusually subdued, the girls scrambled into the back, buckling their seatbelts quietly.

Kate turned her head to give David a genuine, caring smile. "I don't mind," she assured him. Her smile widened. "Matter-of-fact, I like driving this car," she confessed. "It's a nice change from my little puddle jumper."

Connie giggled, delighted by Kate's use of the description she had given the seven-year-old compact.

"You could have one of your own, or any other bigger car of your choosing," David offered, not for the first time. "All you need do is say the word."

Kate concentrated on pulling into the line of vehicles exiting the lot before replying. "Now, David, we've been through this before. I'm perfectly happy with my own car," she said, inching up two car lengths.

It was the simple truth; Kate was happy with the car. It was small, easy to handle, and she liked the splashy red color. But, more importantly, she had made the payments on the car with money from her salary, giving her a sense of accomplishment.

"Besides," she went on, inching up another car length, "it gets me where I need to go. . . ." She flashed a grin at him. "And with a lot better gas mileage, I might add."

"I can't argue with that." Chuckling, David shook his head in defeat and tilted it back against the headrest.

"Are you really okay, Dad?" Mandy insisted, her voice tight with renewed anxiety.

"Yes, love, I'm okay." His voice was stronger—and only Kate saw the effort it took him to reassure his daughter.

"We're still gonna be able to go to the reception, aren't we, Daddy?" Connie asked hopefully.

"Yes, sweetheart." David sighed. "We have a couple hours until the reception starts. By then, I'll be rested and raring to go."

The reception. Kate suppressed a shudder. The very idea of attending Ethan's wedding reception made her feel ill. Desperate, she scoured her mind for an out.

"Oh, good," Connie said with heartfelt relief. "I didn't want to miss it—especially since Mandy and I couldn't go to Sharon's reception."

Though subtly worded, the invitation to Sharon's large and elaborate Valentine's Day wedding had clearly indicated the bridal couple's wish to have no young children in attendance at the reception.

So, scratch any hope of an out, Kate thought, since Ethan's wedding reception did not exclude any children. Her spirits hit rock bottom.

They arrived home to a lunch of soup and sandwiches prepared by the housekeeper, Helen Detrick, the pleasant woman David had hired ten years ago to help with the housework and the care of Mandy and the new baby, Constance, after the death of his wife, Maureen, Kate's mother.

In her late-forties at the time, recently widowed and childless, Helen doted on the girls, Kate, and even David, as much as he'd allow. Now nearing sixty, Helen was like a member of the family, a surrogate grandmother, as well as a dear friend.

As usual, the girls consumed everything set before them; Helen always teased that they ate like starving truck drivers. The minute they finished, they excused themselves and took off after their own pursuits.

"Change your clothes if you're going outside to play," Helen called after them.

"Okay," Mandy yelled back, noisily clattering up the stairs after her sister.

Her appetite lost, Kate dawdled, picking at her food. David bypassed the sandwiches, but managed half his soup and a cup of coffee before getting up from the table.

"We have several hours before we have to leave for the reception, so I think I'll have a nap. As usual, the soup was excellent, Helen," David complimented her as he left the kitchen to go to his room.

"I'm worried about him, Kate," Helen said, a frown scoring her lined brow.

"I know." Kate sighed. "So am I. Despite the medication the doctor prescribed, he seems to be sinking deeper into depression."

"If he's even taking the medication," Helen said at the doorway. "I'm beginning to wonder if there's some other medical problem he hasn't told us about."

"I've been wondering the same," Kate said, made anxious by hearing her own fears echoed by the other woman.

"He looks tired, more tired than usual. Maybe he should skip this reception," Helen suggested.

"I'm sure he should," Kate agreed, getting up to clear the table. "But he won't. The girls are looking forward to it so much—their first wedding reception—and he doesn't want to disappoint them.''

Shaking her head, Helen shooed Kate away, and proceeded to clean the kitchen herself.

Effectively dismissed and needing to be alone, if only for a few hours, Kate left the kitchen, heading for her room on the pretense of taking a rest and then freshening up before it was time to leave for the reception.

Needing a cigarette almost as badly as she needed to be alone, Kate glanced longingly at the sliding glass patio doors on her way to the stairs. She hesitated, fingers tightening on her handbag which contained the secret package, but shook her head and moved on.

Mandy and Connie might come bursting onto the patio and catch her in the act. Kate didn't want to set a bad example for them.

Besides, she had indulged too much lately, she chastised herself. She had smoked two just yesterday, had been smoking two, sometimes three a day ever since the invitation to Ethan's wedding had arrived.

Normally, Kate could not be described as a regular smoker by any stretch of the imagination. She had never even tried smoking until she was in her freshman year of college. A classmate had offered her one, claiming it would calm her nerves when she was stressed about mid-year exams.

Since then, Kate rarely smoked more than five or six cigarettes a week. One pack might last her up to a month or more; hardly anyone's notion of a heavy habit.

But these were not normal times. Throughout the past several weeks, she had a valid reason for feeling nervous, uptight, stressed.

And weepy.

With a last, longing look at the patio doors, Kate started up the stairs. In the next moment her longing changed to relief as Mandy and Connie came tearing down the stairs.

"Don't run on the stairs." She might as well have saved her breath; the girls were down and dashing for the patio doors. "And don't get dirty."

"Okay," they called in chorus, not bothering to glance back.

"We're only going to sit on the glider!" Mandy yelled just as the doors slid shut behind her.

Thankful she had held out against temptation, Kate continued on to her room. As soon as she shut the bedroom door behind her, her facade of composure cracked, revealing her pain. Shoulders drooping, she slipped out of her shoes, removed her dress, hung it on a hanger, and pulled on a robe. Feeling depressed, near tears, she sat on the bed and stared out the window, seeing nothing, feeling too much.

God . . . she needed a cigarette.

Sighing, she opened the drawer on the nightstand and removed a journal, the first in a series of three spiral notebooks in which she had been keeping a record of events since the day she moved into her stepfather's house.

Smoothing her hand over the bright red, frayed cover, she opened it to the first page, the first sentence scrawled in her then still childish handwriting.

Mommy and David got married today.

Reading the words brought a wave of memories, flooding her mind with images, and her eyes with tears.

CHAPTER TWO

Kate's father had died before she was born, so she had no actual memory of the man, Colin Quinn. But she had an image, a candid photograph of him and her mother, Maureen, taken by a friend on the day they were married.

The enlarged photograph, encased in a silver frame set dead center on the nightstand, was one of her most cherished possessions. The color photo depicted a sun-drenched, desert landscape and a young couple, smiling happily for the camera. The man was sandy-haired, ruddy-checked, with laughing blue eyes and an attractive, pleasant face. He was attired in the uniform of the United States Air Force. The woman appeared to be barely out of her teens, more than pretty, with russet hair, hazel eyes, and a creamy, soft-looking complexion. She was wearing a lightweight, sleeveless white summer dress.

Less than a year after the photograph was taken, the plane Colin Quinn was test piloting malfunctioned, spinning out of control before crashing into the rugged mountain terrain of Nevada. There had been no survivors. Maureen had been in the third trimester of pregnancy.

Both Colin and Maureen had been orphans, wards of the Philadelphia child welfare system, with no known relatives, raised in foster care. They had met while attending the same high school, and were drawn to each other by their similar backgrounds, as well as a strong mutual attraction.

Falling deeply in love, the young couple had been determined to create their own family, and a better life. To achieve those ends, Colin enlisted in the Air Force after graduating from high school. He married Maureen two years later, after she completed high school.

Barely twenty, suddenly alone and pregnant, devastated by the death of her husband, Maureen returned to Philadelphia, the only home she had ever really known.

Maureen kept the memory of Colin Quinn alive for her daughter, who inherited her own russet-colored hair and her father's blue eyes.

Still, secretly, Kate always longed for a father, for a natural family of her own.

For as long as she could remember, Kate and her mother had lived in a small apartment in Philadelphia. Frugal with the life insurance money paid to her by the U.S. government, Maureen invested in their future, first by opening a small mutual fund account, and second by taking courses a few evenings a week, to acquire a licensed practical nursing certificate while a neighbor babysat Kate.

By the time Kate was ready to enter the first grade, Maureen was ready to enter the work force, securing a position at a highly accredited Philadelphia hospital.

A few months before her eleventh birthday, her mother began seeing a man she had met at the hospital who had gone to have a minor walk-in procedure. His name was David Gardner, and as Kate later learned, he was divorced and without children, a circumstance he sadly regretted.

David was in his early forties, nice-looking, though to Kate's young eyes, he appeared to be an older man. By the standards she was used to, he also appeared to be financially well-off, maybe even rich.

David was kind and generous to Kate, and seemed not to resent sharing much of his time with Maureen in the company of her child.

And so, soon after her eleventh birthday, Kate was not too upset when Maureen told her she had agreed to marry David, and that they would be moving to his house, which was located in one of the upscale sections of mainline Philadelphia.

When David and Maureen returned from their weekend honeymoon, they collected Kate from the neighbor who had watched her. Taking along some of Kate and Maureen's belongings, the three drove to the house that would now be their home.

The house looked like a mansion to Kate. Used to the confining small rooms of an apartment, she was awed by the size of David's house, actually not a mansion, but large by any standards with its many spacious rooms, its two-and-a-half bathrooms. But Kate immediately fell in love with her white and pink bedroom, perhaps because it was the smallest of the bedrooms and felt cozy and secure to the anxious girl.

The next day, still feeling a little lost in the unfamiliar house, Kate was more than happy to follow her mother's suggestion to run outside and explore the patio and the extensive yard and gardens.

It was while Kate was in the backyard that she met the boy next door, a fateful meeting that would impact the rest of her life.

His name was Ethan Winston, and he was the best-looking boy Kate had ever seen.

Ethan.

Sniffing, Kate made a sound of impatience and swiped a hand across the tears running down her cheeks. Reaching for a tissue, she blew her nose. Another tissue dried her eyes enough to read the next passage she had written.

I really, really like Ethan. He is so nice.

Though she groaned in protest, chastised herself for being a fool, and a weak-minded fool at that, once again the floodgates of memory sprang open.

CHAPTER THREE

Tall and lean, loose and lanky, Ethan Winston had dark hair and eyes, and flashed an engaging grin that made her feel warm and good all over.

Friendly from the first, Ethan told Kate that he had a sister, Sharon, who was two years older than he, and away at school.

Within days of their first meeting, Ethan took Kate home to meet his parents. His mother, Virginia, was a soft-spoken, sweet-natured woman. Kate immediately liked her, thought it impossible not to like her. Ethan's father, Mark, was a different story. He was taller than Ethan and quite good-looking, but reserved, straight-laced, and somewhat autocratic, due, no doubt, to the fact that he was the senior partner in a prestigious Philadelphia law firm which had been established by his grandfather.

Kate eventually met Sharon, but the older girl paid

scant attention to her, considering herself much too mature for the eleven-year-old child. Though she tried, Kate really couldn't like Sharon, and felt guilty because of it. It wasn't until much later that she realized Sharon considered Kate beneath her, a "nobody."

At sixteen, Ethan exhibited less pretension. In fact, to Kate's surprise, he seemed to genuinely like her . . . in a brotherly fashion.

Before long, she was trailing after Ethan whenever she caught sight of him around the house. He teased her, sometimes scolded her, but patiently tolerated her dogging his every move. Over time, his nature much like his mother's, he proved himself the kindest, gentlest boy she had ever known.

Naturally, before that summer ended, Kate worshiped Ethan as a hero. He knew it—how could he not know it?—and accepted it with a grin as he tousled her nearly waist long, spiral-curled, always unruly mop of russet hair.

"Oh, it's Miss Fuzzywig," he'd say in his usual greeting to her, grinning every time she'd fall into step at his heels. "Want to help me skim the pool?" he'd ask, inviting her to join him, or to weed the flower beds, rake the autumn leaves, or help with whatever chore he happened to be doing.

And, of course, Kate was always willing and eager to tag along, just to be near him, to hear him laugh, sometimes sing, to ruffle her hair, and call her Miss Fuzzywig.

Ethan had always been there for her. He listened and understood, calming her fears when she confessed her uncertainty about fitting in at her new school. He helped her with her homework. He rejoiced with her when Maureen gave birth to Amanda a little over a year after her marriage to David. And he had shared her loss, comforting and consoling her when, two years later, Maureen succumbed to a blood clot the day after delivering another daughter, Constance.

At fourteen, teetering on the threshold of womanhood, the shock of suddenly losing her mother devastated Kate. Numb with grief and disbelief, she had run weeping from the house into the cool autumn late afternoon.

Ethan found her in the patio curled up and shivering in a corner of the brightly flowered, cushioned glider.

"Kate."

That's all he said, just her name, his voice soft with affection and compassion. Shrugging out of his nylon sports jacket, he sat down next to her, gently drew her into his arms, and draped the jacket over her shoulders. Still without speaking, holding her tight, secure, he stroked her arms, her back, and smoothed her long cascading mass of hair while wrenching sobs racked her slight body and tears dampened his sweatshirt.

When the worst of the weeping at last subsided, she accepted the hankerchief he shoved into her hand, wiped her eyes, and blew her nose. Lifting a trembling hand, she touched the wet spot on his sweatshirt.

"I'm . . . sorry," she said, sniffing.

"Don't be an idiot," he gently chided. "It'll dry."

They sat quietly for a few minutes, Ethan moving

the glider slowly back and forth with his foot. It was then that the full realization of her situation struck Kate.

"I'm an orphan, Ethan!" she cried out of fear. "Though David talked about adopting me, with Mom getting pregnant so soon, then the excitement when Amanda came, and then Mom getting pregnant again, he never did get around to it. What's going to happen to me? Will I have to go and live with foster parents, like my mom and dad did?"

"C'mon, Kate, now you're really talking like an idiot," Ethan scolded her. "You know as well as I do . . . or at least you should . . . that David's not going to let that happen. He loves you. This is your home. Your sisters are here."

Despite having lived three years in her stepfather's house, Kate knew very little about his financial situation. Before they had married, her mother had told Kate that David was part owner of a company called Technologies of Tomorrow. Kate figured out for herself that David derived a substantial income from the business because, while not in the least lavish, their lifestyle was definitely comfortable.

But it wasn't her physical comfort Kate feared losing, so much as it was her sisters, the sense of belonging somewhere, to someone, the security of . . . home.

"But . . . will they let him keep me?" she'd anxiously asked, meaning the authorities.

"Of course. My dad will see to it," he'd assured her with conviction. "He'll arrange for David to either adopt you now, or be named your guardian."

"Truly?"

"Truly."

As it turned out, Ethan was right. David was appalled when he learned of Kate's fears. Right after Maureen's funeral, he spoke to Mark Winston about setting the wheels in motion to have himself named as Kate's legal guardian

It was almost the same as having a father of her own. Almost.

Moisture blurred her vision, swirling the entry Kate had made in her journal that long ago day.

Some hero Ethan had turned out to be.

Heaving a sigh, Kate lifted a hand to swipe the fresh stream of tears from her face, blew her nose, then speared her fingers through her now shoulder-length hair that neither time nor uncounted hair products had tamed.

Telling herself to leave memories where they belonged, in the past, she set the notebook aside, and rising, left to go to the bathroom to clean her face and bathe her red-rimmed eyes with cold water.

Returning to her room, she put on her dress, smoothed the crisp sheath over her hips, stepped into her shoes, and went to her dressing table to brush the unruly russet mass and apply concealing makeup to her tear-ravaged face.

Like it or not, she had a wedding reception to attend. Now, more than ever, Kate hated the thought of seeing Ethan with his beautiful new bride, but she really had little choice in the matter. Her half sisters were excited about going, and Kate didn't have the heart to disappoint them. Besides, David had insisted they all attend both the ceremony and the reception, not only for Ethan's sake, but because he and Ethan's parents had been close friends for so many years.

Poor David. Shaking her head, Kate turned away from the dressing table to sweep an encompassing glance over her form reflected in the long mirror attached to her closet door, examining her dress for creases or wrinkles.

Kate's glance was cursory, as she really wasn't seeing herself, her attire; instead she saw the sad, drawn face of her stepfather, the man who had always treated her as if she were one of his own.

David and Maureen had been so very much in love. During the too brief years they had been together, the house rang with laughter and the joy of life. Maureen's sudden, unexpected death devastated both Kate and David. But, where Kate found solace with Ethan, the spark, the light of joy died inside David.

Though he still went to his office every day, gave the same amount of attention to his daughters, as the years passed, he depended more and more on Kate.

Not that Kate minded; she didn't. Besides feeling indebted to David for everything he had given to her, a home, as well as clothes and an abundance of materialistic things, both necessary and frivolous, she genuinely cared for him.

Poor David, she thought again, concerned, heaving a sigh. Though his doctor proclaimed him physically fit—at least, *he* maintained that his doctor proclaimed him physically fit—lately, Kate was having serious doubts—and emotionally he was just a shadow of . . .

Kate's troubling thoughts scattered at the sound of a quick tap against her bedroom door.

"Kate, are you almost ready?" Mandy called. "Dad said to tell you it's time to leave."

"Coming," Kate called back.

Dismissing the image in the mirror, Kate turned, worked her lips into a smile, and crossed the room to swing open the door. Stepping into the hallway, she firmly pulled the door shut, closing her memories inside the room.

"Did you sleep?"

"No." Her smile softening, Kate smoothed a wayward lock of hair, the exact dark chocolate brown color as her father's, from Mandy's cheek. "Did David?"

The girl raised her bony shoulders in a "Who knows?" half shrug. "He said he did—and he does look better, not so tired and washed out."

"Good, I . . . ," Kate began, only to be drowned out by a high-pitched call from the foot of the stairs.

"Mandy," Connie yelled. "What's taking so long? Daddy's in the car already. Isn't Kate ready yet?"

"We're coming," Mandy yelled back, giving Kate a wry look that revealed a maturity beyond her twelve years.

But though Mandy was mature in so many ways, she was still just a child, Kate mused, smiling as Mandy skipped to the car, excited about attending her first wedding reception.

Kate again took the wheel to play chauffeur.

The reception was held at the country club, and

though as hastily arranged as the wedding, given the short notice, the banquet hall was as elaborately decorated as the church had been, with masses of flowers, garlands of greens and white and dusty rose ribbon streamers and bows looped around the edges of the white clothed tables.

It was a crush, a sea of faces, individual voices blending to create a din of animated speech and laughter.

For the first couple of hours, Kate caught only glimpses of Ethan, as the happy couple and their attendants performed all the required rituals. And with the enactment of each one of those rituals, Kate suffered a knife-sharp pang of loss and rejection.

She was disgusted with herself for harboring a love for Ethan that even his cruel use of her had not killed. She was equally ashamed of the sick jealousy she felt for the beautiful blond bride. A friend of his sister's, Ethan had met Paula several years previously, then became involved with her when she had been a bridesmaid in Sharon's wedding a mere three months ago.

With David engaged in conversation with another man seated at the next table, and the girls off somewhere with other neighborhood youngsters, Kate excused herself their table on the pretense of "mingling" and made her way to a far corner of the room.

Standing at one wide window, almost hidden by the drapes, she stared morosely out at the golf course, desperately wanting a cigarette, and blaming the sparkle of golden late afternoon sunlight for the sting in her eyes.

Immersed in her unhappy thoughts, she started at a gentle touch on her arm, and ached with longing at the soft sound of a dear, familiar voice close to her ear.

"Aren't you going to dance with a friend?"

Despairing the shivery thrill his mere touch could draw from her, Kate dredged up a bright, if not deceptive smile, and turned to face the man she had always loved.

"Of course," she responded, cautiously moving into the inviting arms Ethan offered her.

It was bliss, it was torture, dancing with him, being so close to him. Unable to bear looking directly at him, Kate swept her gaze around the room, chattering inanities about how lovely the wedding had been, how beautifully the room had been decorated, et cetera, ad nauseam, until he ended her running commentary with one word.

"Kate." Ethan's voice was low and contained a strange aching note.

Her smile straining her jaw muscles, Kate reluctantly brought her wandering gaze to him. Shock rippled through her at the tautness of his face, the odd expression in his eyes. Instead of the picture of the elated bridegroom, Ethan appeared saddened, bereft, near despair.

Confused, hurt, and angry, Kate fought conflicting needs, one to raise her hand to his cheek, to comfort and smooth the strain from his face, another to lash out at him, inflict a measure of the pain he had caused her. She was spared the embarrassment of making an utter fool of herself when, at that moment, the music stopped and the dance ended.

A sad, heart-wrenching smile curved his lips. "In spite of everything that's happened, I hope we can remain friends." Remorse weighed his tone. "Can you find it in your heart to forgive me, be my friend again, Kate?"

Forgive him? How could she forgive his cruel betrayal? How could she not forgive him?

Kate longed to refuse, if only to salvage some of her pride, to hurt him as he had hurt her. But how could she, after all the shared memories, the years of loving him. *She couldn't.* It would be like denying her own existence.

She sighed. "Yes, always, but . . . ," she began, halting when she heard Sharon calling to him.

"Always," Ethan repeated in a whisper before stepping back away from her, to call over his shoulder, "Coming."

And then he was gone, swallowed up in the crowd of dancers mingling on the floor. There was no opportunity to speak with him again throughout the seemingly endless evening.

Later that night, after Kate at last regained the solitude of her room, she once again allowed the facade of serenity to drop, her rigidly held shoulders to droop. Tired, dispirited, she decided to exchange her finery for a nightgown. Discarding her clothes, she let the garments lie where they fell. Slipping into a wrap, she padded barefoot to the bathroom. After cleaning her face of makeup and brushing her teeth, she took a quick shower. Returning to her room, she made her way to the side of the bed.

There, on top of the spread near her pillow, lay her notebook journal. Chastising herself for her weakness, she crawled onto the bed, picked up the book, and began to skim the written lines, a faint smile shadowing her lips as she noted the improvement in penmanship from a childish scrawl to a maturing teenager's flourished script. Turning a page, she caught her breath at the entry.

I bought a special gift for Ethan. It seems like he has been away forever. I can't wait for him to come home.

Memories once again swept her back in time.

It was in the summer between her junior and senior years of high school, the year she had turned seventeen, that Kate realized that she didn't merely love Ethan, but that she was in love with him.

She had run to him with a gift to commemorate his graduation from college, and as she always did, threw herself into his arms for a welcome home hug.

Laughing, Ethan clasped her to him.

"Hi, Miss Fuzzywig, and how are you?" he said, loosening his hold to look into her up-turned face.

"I'm fine . . . now that you're home," Kate answered with innocent candor. "Oh, Ethan, I missed you so much."

His laughter faded. His expression grew serious. His dark-eyed gaze delved into the depths of her adoring blue eyes. "I missed you, too, Kate, more, I think, than I would ever have thought possible."

For long, breathless moments, they stared into each other's eyes. And then, slowly, almost reluctantly, he kissed her, not on the cheek, as he always had before, but on the mouth.

At first, his kiss was light, undemanding, more playful than serious. Then it changed. His arms tightened, crushing her to him. The pressure of his mouth against her closed lips increased as his tongue skimmed along the edges of her mouth. Instinctively, she opened to him, giving passage to his invading tongue as he deepened the kiss.

The kiss, her first real kiss, had a profound effect on Kate. Stunned, yet thrilled and willing, she arched into his hardening body. She felt the electric charge of physical attraction, experienced new and unfamiliar stirrings, deep, feminine, hungry stirrings of a sexual nature that were at the same time exciting and scary. From his avid ardor, the sudden tightening of his body pressing against her belly, she dared to believe that he felt the same exciting sensations.

How long the lovers' embrace might have lasted, Kate never knew, for the jarring sound of his father's voice calling for him startled them and they sprang apart.

For a moment, his breathing ragged, his expression stark, Ethan just stared at her, his eyes dark, clouded with aroused passion.

"Kate . . . I . . . I'm sorry . . . ," he paused, shuddered when the sharp, authoritative voice of his father rang out again.

Speechless, trembling, Kate stood there, watching as he pivoted, then sprinted away.

Next time, she told herself, her heart racing in time with his retreating footsteps.

But, to her dismay, after that too brief thrill of sensuality, Kate saw less and less of him. Though still outwardly friendly whenever they saw each other, Ethan held himself aloof, keeping his distance from her, almost as if he also had thought the kiss exciting yet scary.

But, through the ensuing years, there were moments when she caught him staring at her, his dark, intense gaze stealing her breath, warming her blood, stirring hopes of fulfilling her wish. Then he'd glance away, seemingly unconcerned, and her hopes plunged into despair.

A low moan shattered the quiet night. Tears blurring her eyes, Kate blinked herself from the realm of memory back into the present. Swiping her fingertips over her eyes, she opened the nightstand drawer and shoved the notebook beneath the other two inside.

She started to close the drawer, then compulsively pulled out the notebook on top. Blinking, she flipped open the cover, this one blue, and skimmed a glance over the page. Her breath catching at the sight of his name, she slammed the book shut and set it aside.

She and Ethan shared so many memories . . .

But now he was married, mere weeks after leading her to believe that every one of her dreams and hopes were soon to be reality.

This was his wedding night.

The thought gave rise to cringing mental images,

in detail, of Ethan and the beautiful Paula, entwined in a lovers' embrace in their wedding.

Whispering, "No, no, no," Kate curled herself into a fetal position. Hugging her knees, and burying her face into the pillow, she cried herself to sleep.

CHAPTER FOUR

Ethan Winston was a man with a problem; the problem's name was Kate.

Ethan loved Kate, had loved her like a younger sister almost from the day he met her while he was trimming the high hedge separating his family's property from that of his parents' friend and neighbor, David Gardner.

That he loved her was not particularly surprising to Ethan. With the possible exception of his sister, Sharon, everyone who met her, got to know her, loved Kate. Shy, sweet, yet tenacious in affection and defense of those she loved or cared about, her goodness and sense of fairness, her eagerness to please, made it nearly impossible not to love her.

As a young girl, Kate had been cute and appealing with her bright blue eyes the focal point of her small oval face, and her forever disheveled mop of long, tightly spiraled curls of auburn hair that grew even wilder, curlier, and frizzier in damp and humid weather.

Ethan had unmercifully teased her with the nickname "Miss Fuzzywig."

But that was when she was a youngster, skinny with bony arms and legs. That was then . . .

This was his wedding night.

Lying alone and awake in a center city Philadelphia hotel room bed, separated some two or so feet from the matching bed in which his pregnant bride lay sleeping, Ethan Winston reflected on the disastrous mess he had made of his life, and the events leading up to his present situation.

And his present situation was a monstrous mess of his own creation, his just rewards for rampant stupidity.

There was a soft rustle of movement from the next bed, from the woman with whom, earlier that day, Ethan had exchanged marriage vows aloud, in a church full of witnesses.

Ethan was committed to upholding his spoken vow of fidelity and support to his bride. Only he knew he had no intention of fulfilling two of the traditional promises; he did not, never had, or never would love her. And there would be no worshipping of her with his body.

It was a base form of that worship that had gotten him into this farce in the first place.

There came another rustle of movement, a soft

sigh. Ethan felt a pang of compassion, and glanced across to the other bed to note that she still lay asleep.

It had been an exhausting day for Paula. She had suffered a bout of nausea that morning, as she claimed she had every morning since agreeing to marry him and bear his child. Fortunately, the bout passed by the time she had to dress for the wedding . . . which was why they scheduled the ceremony for late in the morning.

The day had been long, as they performed every expected ritual, playing out the farce to the satisfaction of their respective, unsuspecting families.

When, at last, they escaped to this hotel room, Paula practically fell asleep on her feet in exhaustion. While she stood mute, nearly unconscious, Ethan unfastened the seemingly endless rows of tiny buttons that ran the length of her spine, dealt with the voluminous gown and yards of petticoat, peeled away the lacy teddy, and unmoved by the sight of her nude body, slipped the filmy virgin-white nightie over her head.

Past the point of making the necessary effort to remove her make-up, Paula dropped like a stone onto the bed, fast asleep within moments.

Ethan enjoyed no such luck.

Staring at the tiny pinpoint of red light blinking on the smoke alarm set high on the wall near the ceiling, Ethan winced at the image that rose to fill his mind.

Kate had looked so lovely today.

The thought hurt Ethan's heart, his very being. He could see her as clearly as if she were standing before him now, her hair framing her pale face, her tall, slender body sheathed in a crisp-looking spring dress in a shade of blue, matching her eyes.

Her eyes. Her eyes had seemed shadowed, evasive, faintly dark as though bruising had marred the tender skin beneath the lower lids.

"Kate." Murmuring her name aloud hurt even more, and brought forth memories, sweet and bitter.

Kate of the skinny arms and legs, the shy smile, the trusting blue eyes, the eager willingness to please.

With the clear sight of memory's eye, Ethan could see her as she had been, her coltish gait as she strove to keep up with his longer-legged stride, her long hair flying around her head, her soft, young voice, bombarding him with never-ending questions concerning every aspect of his life, chattering on about whatever happened that day that she believed might interest him.

"I got three A's on my report card." Her eyes and smile were bright with expectant praise.

He didn't fail her. "That's great. Congratulations, Miss Fuzzywig."

"You always get A's, don't you?"

"Well, mostly," he confessed.

"I'm going to be a teacher when I grow up." Her expression and tone were serious with intent.

It was not the first nor the last time Ethan heard the same declaration. He always responded in an equally serious manner.

"A commendable ambition. Teaching is an honorable and vital profession."

"And you're going to be a lawyer."

"Yes."

"Then you can be my lawyer."

"If you can afford me," he teased, laughing.

Strangely enough, throughout the years, he never resented or refused to answer her questions, no matter how personal, or silly, and the events of her days, large and small, interested him. Even though five years separated them, a considerable time gap between them, he genuinely enjoyed her company, and secretly reveled in her near slavish devotion to him.

He teased her unmercifully. Yet, as young as she was, Kate never took offense, and in fact appeared to bloom with his teasing attention.

The funny part was, Ethan continued to see Kate in that same awkward, gawky, endearing way . . . until she turned seventeen, the year he graduated from college.

Laughing, calling out her congratulations, Kate ran to him, graduation gift in hand, and in her usual impulsive way, launched herself into his arms, clasping him to her in a welcome home bear hug.

In that instant, Ethan's perception of Kate as the youngster she had always been suddenly changed. Her lushly matured curves were indelibly imprinted on his body and in his mind.

Why had he kissed her?

How many times had he asked himself that question?

Considering himself a fully mature man at twenty-two, and old enough to know better, the question tormented Ethan from the moment his lips touched hers, igniting a firestorm of desire in him, devastating in intensity.

Kate was like a sister to him—hell, if he were honest, Ethan had to admit, if only to himself, that he loved Kate more than he did his own natural, rather haughty sister, Sharon.

But his love for Kate was familial, tolerant and indulgent.

That one kiss, so innocently intended, turned his feelings into something else. The taste of her scrambled his thoughts, heated his blood, hardened his body in an instantaneous response unlike anything Ethan had ever experienced with another girl or woman, before or after the kiss.

Restlessly shifting on the bed in a fruitless attempt to alleviate the ache in his hardening body, Ethan fought to block the flow of memories.

He lost the battle.

It was electrifying. It was crazy. It was thrilling.

It was terrifying.

For, while Ethan secretly ached to experience the full spectrum of erotic passion with Kate, he was at the same time repulsed by his secret desire.

And it didn't help his conscience that his very proper father had unwittingly witnessed the kiss, ending it with his demanding call, proceeding to reprimand him for stepping out of bounds.

Kate was an innocent, his father reminded him— as if Ethan required reminding, with his conscience already racked with guilt. Even after his father finished scolding him, Ethan continued to excoriate himself for his mindless self-indulgence.

Kate not only trusted him, Ethan scathingly reminded himself, but considered him her ally, her staunchest supporter, her protector, her own personal knight in shining armor.

If he should betray her trust by awakening her sensuality, leading her along the path of sexual pleasure, he charged himself, who then would protect her from her protector?

Although his body burned to explore every erotic path with Kate, Ethan knew that he should not, could not, dared not, journey down that intriguing dark trail. He was five years older than Kate, five years more experienced, and he felt it his duty to prove he was five years older in wisdom, as well.

Chastising himself about allowing Kate her own years to grow and mature with the normal day-to-day experiences of budding womanhood, Ethan did the only honorable thing he could think of to do; he distanced himself from her, remaining coolly friendly, while holding himself aloof.

It wasn't an easy task Ethan set for himself. Being anywhere near her intensified the inner burning, tempting him to cast honor aside and damn the consequences. But he had held firm ... for her sake, even though he knew his new attitude hurt her. The sad reproach in Kate's beautiful eyes, the temptation of her pouting mouth, drove him to withdraw even further from her.

That fall, when Ethan returned to Yale to study law,

it was both agony and relief to escape the allure of Kate's tempting nearness.

He immersed himself in his studies, which he discovered he genuinely enjoyed. He dated several young women, and had sex with a few, to appease the normal sexual demands of his body, in hopes of quenching the fire of desire he felt for the one young woman he deemed off-limits to him—and his base desires.

Since their families were neighbors, and spent many holidays and family celebrations together, Ethan watched as Kate blossomed into a lovely young woman, mature and, he hoped, ready for an adult relationship. With almost boyish eagerness, he called her to ask her out, only to have his anticipation dashed when young Mandy informed him that Kate was out with her boyfriend.

When Kate made no mention of his call the next time he was in her company, Ethan presumed she wasn't interested enough to even ask.

Either he had let it go too late, or his timing was lousy. Whichever, Ethan felt he could not in good conscience intrude on her life.

After receiving his law degree, Ethan entered his father's law firm, specializing in estate planning and tax law, both of which he excelled in.

Soon after joining the firm, Ethan moved out of his father's house, into a center city apartment. He made the move for three considered reasons: to declare his independence, to be closer to his workplace and to distance himself from Kate, to quell the temptation to ignore his conscience and throw caution to the wind.

For some months, he had very little contact with Kate. He saw her only on the few occasions he attended mutual family gatherings.

Seeing her, being near to her proved to be more temptation than he wanted to deal with, so he began making excuses not to attend. By necessity, he chatted with her on the phone, on the rare occasions he needed to speak to David in regard to his estate planning which, at his father's request and with David's permission, Ethan had taken over.

Other than family gatherings during holidays and birthdays, when he knew Kate's family would be there, but he couldn't refuse to attend, he avoided any contact with her.

Naturally, he made other periodic visits to his parents' home when he was certain Kate wouldn't be there, primarily to visit his mother, as he saw his father every day in the office. Yet, as much as Ethan loved his mother, even those visits were harder and harder to bear.

It seemed that, inevitably, over the dinner table, or at some other point during his visit, Virginia would impart tidbits of information about the neighbors, information Ethan didn't particularly want to hear, most especially when it concerned Kate . . . which it often did.

Still, not wanting to be rude or hurt his mother's feelings, Ethan never conveyed his disinterest, but merely tuned out, smiling and nodding at intervals . . .

that is, until the mention of Kate's name riveted his attention.

"And, oh, yes," she said one rainy spring evening, "Kate made the dean's list again."

Ethan felt a surge of pride for her accomplishment.

"And Kate is student teaching now, you know," she said, on a bitter cold night in January.

Ethan hadn't known, hadn't allowed himself to know any more about her other than the bits and pieces so artlessly and innocently supplied by his mother.

But, of course, he couldn't help knowing Kate was in her senior year, and naturally would be student teaching. Ethan was heartened that she was working to attain her goal . . . although he never doubted for a moment that she would.

"And she works so hard, but then, as you know better than most, she always has, hasn't she?" his mother said on a sultry evening in midsummer.

Ethan frowned. Obviously, his mother expected an answer, a response of some kind, and, he was tuned out as usual, so he hadn't a clue as to what or whom she was next referring to. "I'm sorry, Mother, I'm afraid my mind was wandering," he apologized. "I missed what you were saying."

"Kate, dear," Virginia said, her soft voice edged with impatience. "I was talking about how hard she works, what with having taken on the responsibility of helping to care for her sisters, and the house, and excelling at her studies, she barely has time for herself . . . as you surely know."

"Yes," he dutifully replied, because he did know

that, from her own sense of indebtedness to David, and her devotion to him and her sisters, Kate never hesitated to perform any task, great or small. "She always was a willing worker."

She had eagerly agreed to help him at any task, as well. A tremor of regret and longing shivered through Ethan. An echo of her voice shivered through his mind.

I'm going to be a teacher.

He smothered a sigh. "And she was always determined to be a teacher," he finished.

Harder and harder to take, Ethan curtailed his visits to the house to the barest acceptable minimum.

It was after Kate graduated from college and accepted a teaching position at a local primary school that his father decided to ease into an early semi-retirement. David asked Ethan to handle his legal business.

Unable in good conscience to refuse David's request, Ethan had little choice in resuming minimal contact with Kate, as infrequently as when she answered one of his phone calls, or even less frequently if he had to stop by the house.

He was careful to keep their exchanges friendly, neighborly, but impersonal. It wasn't easy.

Then, in late fall, he learned from his mother, via Mandy, that Kate wasn't dating at all. Later, alone and in private, Ethan cursed a blue streak.

Once again, the timing was lousy, because he was involved with another woman, to the point of having her move into his apartment. He even toyed with the idea of asking the woman to marry him, simply because he reckoned it was time to settle down, start a family.

Toying with the idea was as far as it ever went, because, despite his genuine fondness for the woman, something inside him recoiled at the thought of stamping a seal of permanence to their relationship.

Eventually running its course, as both in the end admitted they had suspected it would, his relationship with the woman ended by mutual agreement a few months prior to his sister's wedding. Claiming she harbored no hard feelings, she moved out of his apartment.

Knowing Kate and her family would attend, Ethan looked forward to Sharon's wedding, hoping that this time . . .

Kate attended the wedding, but not merely with her family but a young man who gave every appearance of being a part of the family.

Dejected and dispirited, Ethan reacted in the most stupid way possible. First, he drank too much, which was unusual in itself, as he never overindulged, not even during his college years, when drinking to excess seemed to be the "in thing" to do.

Then, to compound his stupidity, he engaged in an irresponsible one night stand with one of his sister's bridesmaids, the beautiful Paula. Ethan had known Paula for years, since she was a close friend of Sharon's and had often been a guest in their home.

Paula also had too much to drink, drowning her disappointment over recently losing a part she had coveted in a play to be performed by a local repertory theater group. Paula, it appeared, had dreams of someday becoming a stage star, her name in lights on a Broadway marquee.

In addition to feeling dog sick with a hangover the next morning, Ethan felt foolish and ashamed when the drink and lust wore off. He felt even more foolish the next week, on learning from David that Kate and the man who had accompanied the family to the wedding and reception were simply friends, co-workers.

Elated, Ethan placed a call to Kate later that afternoon to ask her out, and to his utter relief, Kate accepted. They had four weeks together, seeing each other several times each week. Knowing he was rushing, yet wild about her, burning for her, he gave free rein to his desire one evening when she agreed to go with him to his apartment after dinner.

To Ethan's utter surprise—and shaming delight—Kate shyly confessed to still being a virgin. Though the knowledge hadn't cooled his ardor or his near desperate desire for her, it slowed him down enough to steer her gently, carefully, into the pleasures of physical intimacy.

Kate proved to be a quick and eager leaner. Their union was perfect, their climax simultaneous, and for Ethan more richly satisfying than any sexual experience he had ever had, or even fantasized having.

He knew he was in love with Kate, had probably been in love with her forever, and he loved it. He believed, hoped, and prayed that Kate loved him back.

Ethan floated in lovers' paradise for all of one week, planning the perfect moment to tell Kate how much he loved her, and to ask her to—please, God—marry him, share her life with him.

And then the bottom fell out of his world.

The killing blow came with a telephone call to his office from Paula.

"She says she must speak to you," Ethan's secretary said, adding, "she sounds very upset."

"Okay, put her through," Ethan instructed, struck by an odd sense of foreboding.

"I'm pregnant, Ethan." Paula didn't waste time on polite pleasantries but came straight to the point; he felt the news pierce his gut. "And you're the father."

"But . . . it's been weeks since . . ."

"I suspected sooner," she cut him off. "But I guess I've been in denial. I mean, really, even though we were too . . . ," she hesitated.

"Drunk," Ethan said.

"Well, yes," she snapped, sounding defensive. "So we drank too much and didn't take precautions . . . it was only that one time, for God's sake."

It only takes once. Lord, how many times had Ethan heard those old words of wisdom? Countless. And he knew they were sound. Still . . . there were natural doubts.

"You're positive?"

"Yes, of course, I'm not an idiot, you know. I didn't even depend on a home test. I saw an obstetrician."

"How can you be certain that I'm the father?" he asked, hope vying with incipient panic.

"Because I didn't have sex with any other man for several weeks before Sharon's wedding, and I haven't been with another man since then."

Feeling sick, trapped, remorseful for his own stupidity, Ethan closed his eyes, drew a silent, fortifying breath, and asked, "What do you want me to do?"

"Do?" she repeated. "I don't want you to do anything, other than pay for the abortion, that is."

"You want to have an abortion?" The relief he felt was intense; Kate would never have to know.

"Well, of course I want an abortion. You couldn't seriously think I'd want to have a baby?"

"I . . . er, couldn't know exactly what you wanted, could I?" Ethan asked, breathing easier.

"I've scheduled it for next week," she said. "Will you pay for it?"

"Yes, of course."

For all of one day, Ethan felt as if an unbearable weight had been lifted from his shoulders. He could get on with his life, ask Kate to marry him, have his children.

Then his conscience pricked, bursting his dreams. Although he longed to deny it, he believed Paula's claim that the child was his. Why would she lie about it, when all she asked of him, from him, was that he finance the abortion.

The child was *his* . . . his as surely as any child conceived with Kate would be his.

Ethan tried to convince himself, his conscience, that it wasn't the same. Knowing Kate, he felt certain she would want the child. Paula did not. That made it different.

But regardless the circumstances, the child was his, and no amount of rationalizing would change that fact.

In the end, his conscience won. So, accepting responsibility, he offered a deal, an alternative, to Paula.

If she would agree to marry him and give the child the legitimacy of his name, and live with him until the child was six-months-old, in return, Ethan would assume full custody and responsibility of the child, allow Paula to seek a divorce, and settle her with a substantial sum of money.

At first, Paula refused point blank.

Ethan argued . . . and then, he unabashedly pleaded.

Finally, with obvious reluctance, and numerous protests, Paula, to her credit, finally agreed, but on the condition that no one know the full extent of their situation and relationship.

While hating the deception, Ethan had little choice but to accede to her terms. Despising himself for the shock and hurt he knew he would cause her, Ethan ended his association with Kate with a telephone call.

Cowardly bastard.

Stifling a groan, Ethan blinked himself out of memory's grip. The red pinpoint of light on the smoke alarm blinked back at him.

The secret inner burning for Kate would pass in time, Ethan tried to assure himself.

So far, it hadn't—and he feared it never would. Having to see her, face her, talk to her at both the wedding and after had been sheer agony for him.

Holding her in his arms, wanting her, longing for

her, while maintaining a facade of neighbor and friend, had been both heavenly and hellish.

Somehow, Ethan endured the torture, remained silent while aching to blurt out the truth to her. It was not to be. He had done enough damage to himself, his sense of self-worth. He couldn't, wouldn't add the breaking of his word to his list of stupid mistakes.

Nevertheless, even as his wedding reception was winding down, and he had stood beside his lovely bride, accepting congratulations and best wishes from departing friends, his hooded, longing gaze clung to the slender, bronze-haired woman exiting the ballroom.

Ethan stifled a groan against the surge of despair welling up inside him, the rage of desire hardening his body, awareness making him weak with yearning, awakening his senses to erotic memories.

He could see her, her spiral curls a splash of russet against his white pillow case, her silky skin milky in the moonlight slanting through the bedroom window. He could smell her, the ellusive scent of her perfume, the more exciting, natural scent of her. He could taste her, the sweetness of her honeyed mouth, the slightly salty tang of her skin, the puckered buds of her nipples. He could feel her, her skin gliding against his, her arms encircling his taut neck, her hands skimming over his shoulders, down his chest, across his belly to grasp, caress . . .

Ethan clenched his teeth. But he could still feel her, the clenching thrill of being inside her, the soft, wet welcoming heat of her drawing him deeper, deeper.

He needed . . . needed . . .

Clamping his lips against a groan, Ethan crawled from the bed and stumbled to the bathroom. Breathing deep, fighting for control, he turned on the shower, full blast, ice cold, and stepped beneath the stinging spray.

What was done was done, and he had no one to blame but himself. Reliving the past led nowhere. Kate was lost to him. But at least sober and fully aware of what he was doing, he was protecting her.

Now, he owed his allegiance to Paula . . . for a certain period of time.

And he and Paula had a plane to catch in the morning for a two week stay in Bermuda, compliments of his father.

If he survived till morning.

Get hold of yourself, Ethan berated himself, beginning to shiver as goosebumps spread over his flesh. Shaking all over from the chill, a wry, dark-humored smile curved his numbing lips.

Ethan didn't know whether to laugh or cry. He laughed to himself . . . because he was long past the point of crying.

CHAPTER FIVE

Life goes on, and we don't always get what we want.
Song titles? Old sayings? Whatever, Kate adopted
them as her personal philosophy. Deciding it was time
to get on with her life, she stashed her notebook
journals in the nightstand drawer, and consigned her
seven year treasure chest of hopes and dreams to the
realm of mental fantasy land.

It was spring, a time of rebirth and new beginnings.
The flower beds bordering the house suddenly
seemed to blaze into vibrant colors, perky yellow daf-
fodils, white and deep purple hyacinths, pink and
red tulips. The flowering pear trees lining the streets
burst into tiny white blossoms that danced like a
shower of snowflakes in the frisky spring breeze. The
warm sunshine felt like a blessing.

Everything was so very beautiful, the warmth, the

color, the budding trees, it touched a chord in Kate, almost painful, but soothing.

She resumed her lifestyle as it had been before those weeks with Ethan. What had been was over, done, as much a memory as the last of the winter snow. At least, she told herself, she had put the past behind her, for good.

But it wasn't easy, and it didn't always work, because, for a few precious weeks, she had believed those hopes and dreams were within her grasp.

The nights were the worst. It was during the night, when she was vulnerable from fatigue, and the house was dark and quiet, that Kate battled the clawing demands of her body, weakened by awakened sensuality, and aching for the bliss of release.

She fought the one craving with another, by taking stealthy trips through the house to the patio.

Fortunately, during the daylight hours, Kate's mind managed control over physical desire. Having achieved the realization of her ambition to teach, at least the weeks following Ethan's marriage were busy for her.

Alone in her room one evening, Kate smiled at the pictures spread out on her bed. Two days before, she had assigned to her class a homework project of drawing pictures depicting their ideas of spring. The results were surprisingly good, some exceptionally imaginative.

It was at times like this, she mused, that she knew she had made the right career choice. She loved teaching, was genuinely fond of every one of her little students, but then, she always knew she would.

Hadn't she always told Ethan she would?

Ethan.

Kate sighed as his image took command of her mind. Such a short period of time had passed since she decided to get on with her life.

And yet, the mere thought of his name conjured his image, sending her mind traveling once again down the bumpy path of memory lane.

Earning her teaching certificate hadn't been easy for Kate. While she excelled in her studies, making the dean's list every one of her four years at the university, living at home and commuting daily to school, she also took on the additional responsibility of caring for her half sisters when Helen departed shortly after dinner.

That was before Helen had fallen on a patch of black ice on a sidewalk and fractured her ankle. Concerned about her being alone in her home, David asked her to move in with them while the bone mended. In the end, Helen remained. Giving into David's and the girls' pleas for her to stay on, Helen sold her home, invested the profit, and for all intents and purposes, ruled the roost.

But, before Helen became a permanent fixture, lending a respite for Kate, she never minded the extra responsibility. Apart from feeling a sense of loyalty and duty to David for his having sheltered and supported her, she loved the two girls, enjoyed their lively, if at times demanding company.

Still, even with her busy schedule, Kate managed to find time for an enjoyable, if limited, social life.

She made lots of friends, male and female, and dated occasionally. But she always drew the line at any hint of intimacy. Besides, none of the young men she met so far came anywhere near measuring up to Ethan.

Early in her junior year of college, Kate met a young man, a graduate student working for his master's degree, whose company she enjoyed more than any others. She began seeing him exclusively, not because either one of them were romantically inclined, but simply because they were so compatible.

His name was Edward, and he was a long way from home, with a special girl there waiting for him. By midterm, he became a regular visitor to her home, and Mandy and Connie referred to him as Kate's boyfriend, though he wasn't, not in the true definition of the term. Their association ended when she graduated from college and Edward finished his post-graduate work. Edward went home to marry his girl-friend.

Kate still cherished dreams of a home of her own, children of her own . . . Ethan for her own, even though her hopes grew dimmer with each passing year. Although she spoke to him a few times on the phone when he called to speak to David, she rarely saw him, especially after he moved out of his family's home, into an apartment of his own. When on the rare occasions they did meet, at family gatherings or holidays, while seeming more at ease with her, he still treated her like a sister, quite like he had always treated his own sister, with whom he had never been all that close.

And yet, there were moments, electrifying moments

for Kate, at those combined family gatherings, when purely by accident, he would brush against her and pull back, his expression stark, startled, as if he felt the same immediate shock wave of awareness and sensuality she experienced. And there was something about the look in his eyes at times, times when he watched her, an expression that spoke of hunger and longing, that kept her dwindling dreams alive.

Kate's dreams grew dimmer still when she was informed, smugly, by his sister, Sharon, that Ethan was currently involved in a relationship that gave all appearances of becoming serious and permanent.

Certainly, Kate had always known that Ethan had not, as she had, remained celibate. She realized that he dated women, went to bed with some of them. But as none of his affairs became meaningful, serious, she held to the hope that eventually, he would see her not as a friend or younger sister, but as a woman . . . the woman for him.

After receiving her teaching certificate, Kate accepted a position of kindergarten teacher at a local primary school. It was the perfect situation for her, as it was the school Connie attended, and was located a short distance from the middle school Mandy attended.

By any standards, Kate's life was full. She developed new friendships with several of the teachers at school. During the day she had work, which she loved, and in the evenings, she had David and the girls, and the occasional evenings and weekends out.

Over time, Kate became fast friends with two of those teachers in particular, one a man, the other a woman. It was actually a little strange, because the two were complete opposites.

The man's name was Jason Larson, and his personality was similar to Kate's: easy-going, polite, and usually quiet. Jason didn't make waves.

On the other hand, the young woman she befriended made waves as a matter of course. Her name was Carol Klinghoff, and though both attractive and feminine, she was fiercely independent, aggressive, and outspoken.

Though Jason and Carol tolerated each other when in Kate's company, the antagonism between them was obvious, as neither one of them bothered to hide it. Carol visibly bristled whenever Jason walked into the teachers' lounge when she and Kate were there, whereas Jason merely grimaced. More often than not, Kate found herself playing buffer between the two, but as she liked them both, she didn't mind. In fact, the situation did have its amusements.

Though Kate saw Carol often after school hours, for shopping excursions, dinner, or a movie, it wasn't until recently that she accepted an invitation to have dinner with Jason.

Jason proved to be good company, easy to be with and talk to, and Kate enjoyed herself. She didn't hesitate the next time he asked her out.

During this period, Kate saw little of Ethan. She did, however, talk to him a few times on the phone, when he called to speak to David.

It appeared that, as Ethan settled into his father's law firm, proving his merit with his growing expertise in estate planning and tax laws, Mark decided to cut back on his own work load, easing into retirement. When informed of Mark's plans, David chose Ethan to act as his representative instead of Mark.

Ethan's phone calls to the house were all business related. Whenever Kate happened to answer the phone, their brief exchanges, if a trifle strained, were always friendly in nature, never personal, the meaningless and banal pleasantries of old friends and neighbors.

Kate had been out with Jason several times when the invitation to Sharon's wedding arrived at the house. Both excited and apprehensive about seeing Ethan, yet not wanting to appear at the event like the love-sick-girl-next-door, which of course she actually was, she invited Jason to escort her to the reception.

During the week before the wedding, suffering nervous anticipation, Kate made far too many trips to the night-shrouded patio.

Ethan invited a member of the wedding party, a stunning blond bridesmaid named Paula, a friend of Sharon's, to be his date. Kate had seen her at the Winston home on several occasions. Admiring—and envying—the woman's ethereal beauty, Kate guessed her to be a few years older than herself, and possibly a year or so older than Ethan. He stayed close by Paula's side during the reception.

Her hopes and dreams diminishing, Kate could only feel relieved that Jason had accepted her invitation.

Then, out of the blue, a week after the wedding, Ethan had called Kate and asked her out on a date . . . a real date.

Kate was stunned, and excited. Her fantasy took wing, soared to new heights. Ethan wanted to date her, spend time with *her*. Perhaps good things did come to those willing to wait.

Their first date was a little awkward. Understandably. Kate was nervous; Ethan was reserved. For the first couple of evenings, after he took her home, Kate trekked to the patio to puff away her anxiety.

But slowly, over time, her nerves settled, his reserve melted. They began to laugh together, converse without strain. He was her best friend once more.

The first time Ethan kissed her, Kate surrendered to his mastery without a whimper. His kiss was everything and more, much more than she ever remembered or imagined, even in her wildest flights of daydreaming.

Kate went out with Ethan two, sometimes three evenings a week for three weeks. Their kisses grew hotter, the petting heavier. Passions running hot and close to the surface, nature took its natural course one unforgettable evening.

After dinner, during which Kate and Ethan picked at their food while devouring each other with smoldering eyes, Ethan suggested they scrap the movie they planned on seeing, and go to his apartment instead.

With a shameless lack of hesitation, fully aware of what to expect, Kate immediately agreed.

Kate barely got a look at his apartment, for Ethan pulled her into his arms the minute he closed the door. His kiss was everything she had ever wanted, and she surrendered to it, and him, without a qualm.

Without breaking the kiss, Ethan swung Kate into

his arms and carried her, breathless and clinging, into his bedroom. Placing her on her feet next to his bed, he immediately set to work removing her clothes. She did come to her senses long enough to tell him she was still a virgin.

The change in Ethan was electric, thrilling. His eyes, mouth, and hands gentled. Murmuring words she couldn't hear, he made sweet, tender, careful passionate love to Kate, making her feel special, fragile, while at the same time eager for each new and wondrous sensation. Finally, quivering, aching, it was she who begged him to free them both and consummate their union.

She felt bereft when he turned away for a moment, deserted. But then she heard the quick, unmistakable sound of tearing foil. As he turned back to her, she saw the tremor in his fingers as he unwrapped a condom.

The pain Kate felt when he finally entered her was nothing compared to the ecstasy of pleasure she experienced when his driving body sent her over the edge of fulfillment.

They spent their time together in Ethan's apartment over the next week, exploring the depths of erotic delights and their voracious hunger for each others' bodies.

With each passing day and night, Kate fell deeper in love with Ethan, and felt, believed, he was falling in love with her, though the words were never spoken.

Kate rationalized that it was too soon, too spontaneous for such declarations. Besides, she didn't need to hear the actual words when Ethan's tenderness, his gentleness, his passionate loving spoke more eloquently than words ever could.

She didn't need cigarettes, either. Kate hadn't made a trip to the patio since their third date.

Then, suddenly, without a warning, a clue to his motive, Ethan didn't call for nearly a week. Confused and hurt, Kate waited, wondered, held apprehension at bay. When at last he did call, she knew immediately something was wrong. His voice sounded strange, strained, almost forced as he apologized, saying only that he wouldn't be calling her anymore, that it had all been a mistake and just couldn't work between them.

Shock reverberated through Kate. A mistake? Couldn't work? She had thought it was working beautifully. She had given him everything of herself, her heart, her soul, her body. And she thought, believed . . .

Crushed, wounded, Kate was not able to reply. Afraid she'd break down, make an utter fool of herself, scream, rant and rave like a wild woman if she gave voice to her feelings, she gently hung up the phone.

Her emotions already shattered, Kate took some small comfort from the fact that no one, family member or friend, had known how intense and intimate her relationship with Ethan had become.

She had dreamed and hoped for Ethan's love for so long, and then it all happened so quickly, so unexpectedly; she wanted to hold it close, savor the sweetness . . .

The sweetness.

The sweetness turned to bitterness, but, thankfully, Kate alone tasted it. David, the girls, and Helen all believed that her relationship with Ethan was as before, two neighbors and friends, sharing casual evenings out. And she allowed both Carol and Jason to believe she was busy with family matters every time she begged off a movie or shopping excursion with Carol, or turned down the offer of a date from Jason. Neither her family members nor her close friends knew the extent of her involvement with Ethan.

Kate gave thanks for tiny mercies when she discovered the package of cigarettes she had stashed in her dresser drawer after her third date with Ethan. The package had not been touched since. Until now.

Two weeks later the wedding invitation arrived. It was addressed to David Gardner and family, requesting the pleasure of their company at the marriage of Miss Paula Sorrenson to Mr. Ethan Winston, to take place in one month's time.

David handed the invitation to Kate, requesting her to reply that they would be attending, and to purchase a suitable gift.

Stunned, Kate read, reread, and reread again the invitation. A mere two weeks had passed since Ethan's call to her. *Two weeks.* To Kate, the stunning implication was inescapable: Ethan had been seeing her, making love to her at the same time that he had been involved with, obviously deeply involved with, Paula.

How could he? Kate asked herself, hurt, shocked and bewildered. It simply wasn't like Ethan. It didn't fit his character. At least, it didn't fit what she had judged to be his character.

But there it was, in fancy gold script.

The message was clear, and devastating. Ethan had used her, played with her emotions, as well as her body, while he was seriously involved with another woman.

Kate decided she could not, would not, attend the wedding.

Of course, she did attend. Pride demanded she do so. To do otherwise would have sent a message she was unwilling to have Ethan receive. She also didn't want to upset David and the girls.

Kate bought the suitable gift. She even managed to smile while murmuring the expected words of congratulations, enduring the agony of being held in his arms while they danced.

And cried herself to sleep on his wedding night.

Square one. Kate's memories brought her right back to where she had started the day of his wedding.

Ethan was married, and that was that. No amount of despair on her part could change it. No amount of her tears could alter the reality. It was time, past time, to face cold, hard facts. Her dreams of having Ethan, his love, for her very own, were just that, dreams.

And what immature dreams they had been, Kate cynically chided herself. In fulfilling her childish fantasy, she had given herself, heart, soul, and body to Ethan, her hero.

Painful as it was, Kate at last faced the obvious conclusion: Ethan had used her for the intimacy—

the sex. Then he returned to the woman he really loved. Paula.

Some hero.

By all rights, Kate knew she should hate him. She didn't, but she should. But she didn't love him anymore, either . . . or so she assured herself.

So maybe now, she really could get on with her life.

CHAPTER SIX

The school year was winding down. Just a few weeks, less than a month remained until the start of summer vacation break. The weather was mild, some days hot. The students were showing obvious signs of restlessness, itching to be outdoors, to run and play.

This particular day was really warm, and Friday to boot. For Kate, just keeping her kindergarten class attentive for the shortest length of time was a major accomplishment. She was as relieved as they were to hear the lunch bell ring.

Following the last of the rambunctious students from the classroom, she started down the corridor to the teachers' lunch room.

"It's getting a little trying, isn't it?" Jason drawled, falling into step beside her.

Kate laughed. "More than a little . . . especially on such a warm summer-like day."

"Yeah, it is pretty warm, close to eighty degrees on the thermometer outside the classroom window." He paused a moment before casually adding, "It should be a nice evening, though. Don't you think?"

"Yes," she agreed, slanting a look at him, certain he was leading up to something.

They were nearing the teachers' lounge, and Jason put a hand on her arm to bring her to a halt. "Kate, I . . ." He paused again, then rushed on, "I have tickets to the Philly Pops concert this evening and . . . er . . . I was wondering if you'd like to go with me?"

Kate hesitated, feeling a twinge of guilt for his anxious expression. It had been months since she had accepted an invitation from Jason, ever since Ethan . . .

With ruthless determination she quashed that line of thought by reminding herself about her decision to get on with her life. And it was time, past time, to get out and about. She had always enjoyed Jason's company. Why not go out with him?

"Yes, thank you, I'd like that, Jason."

Surprise flickered in his soft brown eyes, causing Kate to feel another twinge of guilt.

"That's great." His normally quiet voice was rich with enthusiasm. "The concert starts at eight." Again he paused before rushing on, "How about having dinner with me before the concert?"

He looked so boyish, so eager. How could she refuse? Kate smiled. "I'd like that, too."

"Terrific." He looked as if he was ready to dance in place. "I'll make reservations for six-thirty, and pick you up at six. Okay?"

"Yes." Still smiling, suppressing a burst of laughter, she sent a pointed look at the lounge door. "But, right now, I think I'd like to sit down and have my lunch."

"Oh . . ." Jason flushed. "Yeah. Of course. And me. I'm sorry." Shaking his head, still holding her arm, he started for the door.

Kate spied Carol the minute they crossed the threshold standing next to a table at the far side of the room; she couldn't have missed her if she'd tried. Waving her arm, Carol called out, "Over here, Kate."

Taking a step forward, Kate slanted a curious glance at Jason when, instead of pacing beside her, he released her arm and looked around the room.

"What's wrong, Jason?"

He gave her a lopsided smile. "I'm feeling too good right now to exchange barbs with the school's resident witch," he said, shooting a baleful look at Carol. "I think I'll join Doug over there." He moved his head, indicating the middle-aged fourth grade teacher seated at a nearby table. "He may be a bit pedantic, but at least I won't have to don armor just to have a conversation with him."

Kate sighed, but accepted his decision. "All right. I'll talk to you later."

"Right." He turned away.

Kate crossed the room to Carol.

"The gutless one after you for a date again?" Carol sniped as Kate settled into a chair opposite her.

Accustomed to both Carol's acid tongue and her inexplicable antipathy for Jason, Kate rolled her eyes. "Jason is not gutless," she said in repressive tones.

"And yes, he did invite me to go to a concert with him this evening."

Carol's smile was downright nasty. "Was he crushed when you turned him down . . . again?"

"No, because I didn't turn him down," Kate mildly corrected her friend.

"Boy, you must be desperate," Carol ridiculed. "I thought you had given up on the boy scout."

Instead of a verbal response, Kate just smiled and shook her head, not for the first time wondering what it was about Jason that so antagonized the other woman.

To Kate's way of thinking, Jason could be described in one word, pleasant—in looks and demeanor. Jason was well-connected, well-educated, and well-mannered. He was one year older than she, and a year and a half younger than Carol. Surely that slight difference in age couldn't be the reason for Carol's superior, condescending attitude toward Jason, Kate reasoned. Could it?

"For awhile there, a couple of weeks back, I thought you had found a new, exciting guy," Carol said, giving Kate a probing look as they walked together to the fridge to retrieve their packed lunches, then on to the soda machine. "You were so . . . so up, happy, like a woman in love."

Ethan. *Damn.* How was she supposed to get beyond the pain of rejection, her humiliation if . . .

Stop it, Kate ordered herself, dredging up a hopefully serene and concealing smile for Carol.

"It must have been a touch of spring fever," she said, infusing a light note into her tone. It had been at the very beginning of April, and actually still pretty chilly outside when she and Ethan . . .

Clutching the cold soda can with trembling fingers, Kate turned away, on the pretense of going back to the table, but, in fact, to hide her reaction from her friend.

Carol was nothing if not persistent. "Well, it sure didn't last very long," she said, trailing after Kate and sliding into her chair at the table. "The last couple of weeks you've seemed really down, depressed. Are you?" Her voice, her expression revealed genuine concern.

"No, of course not." Wanting to reassure her friend—and end the topic of conversation—Kate managed a carefree shrug, and an excuse. "I suppose it was this sudden summer heat, just when I was enjoying spring." Yeah, right, she thought, cringing inside at the too vivid memory of that particular spring day, the mild breeze, the warm sunshine, the wedding, Paula in white. "Not to mention the effect of this warm weather on the students," she finished.

"Tell me about it." Carol grimaced, pulling her pretty face into a mask of disgust. "Those little darlings of mine are practically bouncing off the walls," she grumbled, referring to her class of first graders. "If I had that much energy, I could scale Mount Everest."

Relieved at having distracted Carol, Kate grinned at her as she pulled a ham and cheese sandwich from a brown paper bag. "I know what you mean. My kids can't seemed to sit still longer than two minutes."

"Umm," Carol nodded, and peered at Kate's sandwich. "What have you got there?"

"Ham and cheese on rye."

"What kind of cheese?"

Kate smiled. "Swiss."

"Mustard?"

"Yes," Kate said, laughing because she knew what Carol was leading up to. "What about you?"

"I've got tuna on white." Carol grinned. "Want to trade a half for a half?"

"Sure." The trade was made, a ritual they performed at least twice a week. They split and shared Kate's apple and carrot sticks and Carol's orange and celery sticks as well. The exchanges worked well for lunchtime variety.

"I'm thinking of joining a gym, taking some exercise classes," Carol said, frowning at her half of the ham and cheese sandwich. "Wanna come with me?"

"Why?" Kate laughed. "I mean, what brought on this sudden urge to join a gym?"

"I was going to ask you if you wanted to go shopping tomorrow." Carol grimaced. "I gained some weight over the winter and some of my clothes are a little tight. But, instead of shopping for clothes in a larger size, on the spur of the moment, while I was stuffing that sandwich into my face, I decided I needed to begin a regimen of some kind, watch my diet, work out, take off the pounds"—she grinned—"and get buff for a new swim suit."

Thinking that working out a few times a week might help keep her mind occupied, as well as her body,

Kate grinned back at her. "Okay, count me in. Did you have a particular gym in mind?"

Carol shook her head, and finished off her tuna sandwich before answering. "No. But I'll check around over the weekend, see what's available in the vicinity."

When the lunch period was over, Kate and Carol parted company in the corridor, Kate turning left to her classroom, Carol to the right.

"I hope you enjoy the concert tonight, anyway," Carol called after her in dust dry tones. "Too bad I can't say the same about your less-than-scintillating companion." With that final parting shot, and a pitying look, she walked away.

Shaking her head in bemusement at Carol's virulent disdain for Jason, Kate headed in the opposite direction. Within three steps, Jason was beside her.

"Are we still on for tonight, Kate?" He sounded uncertain, apprehensive.

Kate turned a puzzled glance at him. "Yes, of course. Why wouldn't we be?"

He shrugged, and gave her a relieved smile. "I thought maybe the wicked witch of the west might have talked you out of going with me."

"Honestly, Jason," Kate exclaimed, feeling trapped and harried by the two combatants, and impatient with playing the role of referee. "I thought you knew me well enough to know that neither Carol nor anyone else could talk me out of a commitment once I've made it. I don't play those kind of games."

"I do know that," he was quick to assure her, then

just as quickly reversed his assurance. "But, still, I was worried that somehow, she'd manage to . . ."

Kate silenced him with a fierce look. "She didn't, and couldn't. What is the problem with you and Carol? You are both seemingly nice, normal people. I just don't understand why you can't tolerate each other."

"She's a bitch."

"Jason!"

"Well, she is," he insisted, his tone harsh, his expression unyielding. "She's militant and nasty, and I suspect she gets off on putting others down, primarily men, and me in particular." His lips twisted with distaste. "She probably hates men, period."

"Oh, I don't think . . . ," Kate began.

But Jason went on, in a suggestive tone, "Maybe she prefers women."

His insinuation brought Kate up short. Her footsteps faltered. Her immediate response was to reject the idea as ridiculous.

"Really, Jason," she scoffed. "That's nonsense."

"No, it isn't," he persisted. "Just think about it—her hostility to men, her sarcasm."

Kate gave him a skeptical look . . . but her mind questioned the idea. Could it be true? It didn't seem possible. Other than her flashes of hostility, directed most noticeably at Jason, and her penchant for sarcasm, Carol always appeared so feminine. But, then, what did appearances have to do with anything? There were plenty of women, soft-spoken, feminine and beautiful, who unabashedly admitted to being . . .

The bell rang through the building, signaling the end of the lunch period, and Kate's contemplation.

"Gotta run," Jason said, striding away. "I'll see you this evening."

"Oh . . . yes . . . this even . . ." Kate's voice faded, a wry smile curving her lips. Jason was out of hearing range, swallowed up in the throng of noisy students streaming along the corridor to their classrooms.

Shrugging off her speculative thoughts about Carol, she hurried along to her own equally noisy classroom.

Still, at odd moments throughout the afternoon, Kate found herself pondering the possibility of Jason's being correct in his thinly veiled insinuation about Carol.

Kate couldn't believe it, didn't believe it, and wouldn't believe it, unless confirmed by Carol herself. And not once, in all the time they had spent together, sharing a meal, seeing a show, shopping, had Carol ever, by word or deed, given a hint of . . .

Besides, Carol had occasionally mentioned casual dates with several different men.

Not that it would matter one way or the other if Jason's insinuation proved true, Kate thought. She and Carol were friends. And Carol's personal life and sexual orientation was her own business.

More than likely, a simple personality clash explained her antipathy toward Jason.

So, forget it, Kate ordered herself, centering her attention on the lesson she was teaching to her restless class.

* * *

Kate greeted the end of the school day bell with a silent sigh of relief. With the promise of the weekend in which to recover, she managed smiles and pleasant words of parting for her young charges.

As usual, Connie was waiting for Kate beside her car in the teachers' parking lot.

"Megan Styer invited me to a sleepover tonight at her house," she announced, her voice high with excitement. "Can I go, Kate, please?"

"May I go," Kate automatically corrected, unlocking the car door for the girl before circling to the driver's side.

Connie rolled her eyes. "Okay, may I go?" she repeated dutifully. "Please, Kate," she begged, sliding into the passenger's seat and treating Kate to her best pleading look. "It'll be my first ever sleepover."

"I know," Kate said, settling into her seat and firing the motor. "And because it'll be your first sleepover, we'll have to discuss it with your father." Easing the car into the line of vehicles exiting the parking lot, she turned onto the road to the middle school.

"Daddy'll let it be up to you, anyways," she argued.

"We'll still discuss it with him," Kate said, knowing the girl was right.

"Oh, okay," Connie muttered, heaving a heavy, ten-year-old's dramatic sigh. "Megan only invited two other girls . . . and she only lives three blocks away from our house, you know."

"Yes, I do know," Kate replied, bringing the car

to a smooth stop next to where Mandy stood waiting by the side of the road. "And I'll be sure to relay that information to your father."

"And Megan said her mother said you should call her if you have any questions about it," Connie rattled on.

"Questions about what?" Mandy asked, getting into the back and slamming the door.

"About the sleepover."

"What sleepover?"

"The sleepover at Megan's house tonight."

"Megan who?"

"Megan Styer. Who else?" Connie demanded, loosening the seat belt and twisting around to ridicule her older sister. "How many Megans do we know, anyway?"

"Well, actually, three," Mandy retorted.

Kate swallowed a sigh. It had been a long, trying day . . . and obviously it wasn't over yet.

"What three?" Connie challenged. "Besides Megan Styer, that is."

"You wouldn't know them," Mandy said in superior tones. "They're older, middle schoolers."

Enough. "Connie, turn around and tighten your seat belt," Kate ordered. "And, Mandy, stop baiting your sister."

Connie frowned. "What's baiting?"

Mandy snickered.

Kate gave her a stern look via the rearview mirror. Mandy grinned in return. "Teasing," Kate explained to Connie, while shaking her head at Mandy.

"She's just jealous 'cause she's not invited to the sleepover," Connie said, smugly.

"Jealous?" Mandy ridiculed with a hoot of laughter. "Yeah, right. Like I wanna hang out with a bunch of silly ten-year-olds."

"You're only twelve," Connie shot back.

"But I'll be a teenager in a couple months." Mandy returned the fire. "And you, Megan and the rest won't. Besides, you don't even know if Daddy will let you go."

"He will if Kate says it's all right." Connie gave Kate her very best pleading look. "And you will tell Daddy it's all right. Won't you, Kate?"

There were times, few in number, but times like when she was very tired, discouraged—after having her heart and emotions trampled—that Kate felt overwhelmed with responsibility. This was one of those times.

She was twenty-four years old, within weeks of turning twenty-five. And for ten, almost eleven of those twenty-four years, Kate had tried her best to be both sister and mother to Mandy and Connie, and daughter and friend to David. She loved them all, very much. They were her family.

But . . .

Didn't she deserve some sort of life of her own?

"Kate?"

Apparently not, even though, she reminded herself, she did have a date with Jason this evening. That had to count for something, she supposed.

"Yes, Connie, I will tell your father it's all right," she said, smiling at the anxious girl, and the prospect of a night out herself. "But, the final decision is his."

Connie's anxious expression smoothed to one of complacency. "So long as you say it's okay, he'll let me go."

"Yeah," Mandy agreed. "Dad always goes along with whatever Kate says. It's easier that way."

Kate frowned as she made the turn onto the driveway to the garage at the rear of the house. Mandy was growing up so fast, she mused, and David's deteriorating health was becoming obvious, even to a twelve-year-old.

Although Kate hated the idea of prying into David's personal business, she was becoming seriously concerned about his lassitude. Like Helen, Kate was beginning to suspect he was keeping something from them. Despite her reluctance to do so, she made a mental note to have a talk with David about his physical condition.

"In case anybody's interested," Mandy said as Kate brought the car to a halt, "Dad already knows where I'm going after dinner."

"You're not goin' anywhere," Connie scoffed, scrambling from the car.

Mandy smirked. "Am too."

"Where?"

"That's for me to know, and you to find out," Mandy said, sashaying along the brick path leading from the driveway through the patio to the house.

"Kate!" Connie wailed in protest, charging after her grinning sister. "Make her tell."

Reflecting that family life was wonderful, when it wasn't driving her up a wall, Kate sent up a silent plea for patience as she trailed in the girls' wake.

"Mandy," she said, warningly.

"Oh, okay. If you must know, I'm going next door to play Parcheesi with Mrs. Winston." Laughing, Mandy dashed into the house.

"Parcheesi!" Giggling, Connie was right behind her. Like homing pigeons, they made a bee-line for the kitchen, and the after-school snack Helen always had ready for them.

"What's wrong with Parcheesi, anyway?" Mandy demanded. "I like Parcheesi."

Tuning out the girls' teasing banter, Kate followed at a slower pace.

Mrs. Winston.

Ethan Winston.

Until Mandy mentioned his family's name, Kate hadn't thought about him for ... oh, a couple of hours.

Damn. She wanted a cigarette.

Connie got what she wanted. After speaking with Kate, David gave his permission for her to sleep over at her friend's house.

Mandy got to go next door, to play Parcheesi with Mrs. Winston.

Helen got an evening all to herself.

David got peace and quiet.

But, though she enjoyed dinner, the concert, and Jason's company, and even the gentle but unexciting kiss he brushed across her mouth, Kate didn't get a chance to sneak a smoke until after he left her alone in the patio.

She only took a couple of drags on the cigarette, because it basted bitter, as unsatisfying as Jason's kiss.

The following weeks were busy one for Kate, so full that she was only occasionally tempted to indulge in her secret vice, like when Mandy innocently related some trivial bit of information Mrs. Winston mentioned about Ethan, and the night she awoke aching and yearning from an erotic dream about him.

The school year ended, to Kate's and every other teacher's relief, as the students had grown progressively more restless with each passing day.

Carol found a gym that suited her, and after checking it out herself, Kate agreed to a moderate three-days-per-week exercise program. Instead of a structured diet—which Carol confessed she probably would not stick to—they opted for a common sense approach of smaller portions and fewer desserts.

Working together, Kate and Helen made a production number of the advent of Mandy's thirteenth birthday, celebrating with a surprise party. All of her classmates and other friends attended, even Virginia and Mark Winston.

Kate's birthday, her twenty-fifth, was strictly a family affair. Mandy and Connie helped Helen prepare the birthday dinner, and bake and decorate the cake. It was a trifle lopsided, but Kate loved it.

When the meal was over, she was presented with four small giftwrapped boxes. Each one contained silver. There was a pair of silver hoop earrings from Helen, a silver neck chain from Mandy, and a matching silver bracelet from Connie.

The room grew quiet, seeming to shimmer with excitement and expectation when David handed the last of the small boxes to her. Aware of the four pairs of bright eyes watching her, not sure what in the world to expect, Kate's fingers began to tremble as she unwrapped and opened the little box.

Nestled in a bed of cotton was a set of keys.

Suspicious, almost certain she knew what the keys were for, she glanced at David.

"You didn't." Her voice was a bare whisper.

"Oh, but I did," he said, smiling while his daughters giggled. "It's in the driveway."

"C'mon, Kate," Mandy said. She took off for the door, her sisters right behind her. "Come look."

The car was silver. It was brand new. It was beautiful. Fortunately, it was a compact, not a luxury car.

"That is so too cool," Mandy said.

"And so not dorky," Connie opined.

"Well, I think that means the girls approve," David said, arching his brows at Kate. "What do you say?"

"Oh, David," she murmured, smiling at the girls, and blinking against a warm sting of tears at the same time. "I don't know what to say."

"Just say thank you," Helen said briskly. "Then come back inside and have another piece of cake."

"Me too," Connie cried, following Helen.

"And me," Mandy echoed, following Connie.

Laughing, tears running down her cheeks, Kate went Helen one better; she said thank you, gave David a kiss on the cheek and a big hug. Then casting a caressing look over the new car, her new car, she grasped David's hand to walk with him as they followed along behind the others.

CHAPTER SEVEN

The make-believe honeymoon that Ethan had been dreading was over.

Although he was glad to get back to his apartment, and to his office, Ethan had to admit that the wedding trip had not been as bad as he'd feared it would be.

Relieved of the stress of preparing for the event, and the natural advancement of her pregnancy, Paula's bouts of morning sickness subsided, then ended a few days after their arrival on Bermuda Island. Feeling better physically also had a beneficial effect on her emotionally, as well, and to Ethan's surprise, Paula proved to be a pleasant companion.

Determined to keep an impersonal distance between them, Ethan immediately upgraded their accommodations from the bridal suite containing one bedroom that his father had booked, to a two bedroom suite.

The arrangement worked out fine, allowing both Ethan and Paula the privacy of their own sleeping quarters, plus the added convenience of a comfortable sitting room and a small kitchen area complete with tiny sink, table and chairs, refrigerator, and automatic coffee maker.

Paula's appetite, practically nonexistent for weeks, became nearly voracious with the cessation of the persistent nausea and vomiting. Her vitality was restored, as well.

"Are we just going to sit here in the suite and brood for two weeks?" she asked the first morning she didn't lose her breakfast.

Seated at the table, a cup of coffee in one hand, Ethan glanced up from the file he had brought with him from the office. "What would you like to do?"

"Take a walk. Play nine holes of golf. Soak up some sun." Shrugging, Paula offered him a smile. "Since we're looking at being together for over a year, we might even talk, get to know each other a little better."

"Okay." Conceding her point, Ethan nodded, returned her smile, and slid the file back into his briefcase. "But, until you're feeling stronger, I suggest we start out slow." Finishing off his coffee, he stood and walked to the sink to rinse the cup.

Paula looked both relieved and eager. "Do you have anything particular in mind?"

Ethan glanced outside at the sparkling sunshine, the brilliant blue sky. "We could take that walk you mentioned, find someplace to have lunch . . ." He grinned. "We could even do a little shopping."

As if shopping was a magic word, Paula sprang up from the chair in which she'd been lounging, fairly shaking with anticipation, her eyes glowing, her grin flashing brighter than Ethan's. "When do you want to leave?"

Dressed casually in khaki slacks and a short-sleeved knit pullover, he ran a pointed glance over her neck to ankle, kaftan shrouded figure. "Whenever you're ready."

She headed for her room before he finished speaking. "Give me fifteen minutes."

Right. Keeping the wry thought and a tolerant smile to himself, Ethan refilled his cup, sat down at the table, and retrieved the file from his case, prepared to wait at least an hour for her to emerge from her room.

She surprised him. Although she didn't make the fifteen-minute time frame, she was close. She swept out of her room twenty-minutes later, looking both elegant and casual in crisp white shorts, a summer yellow sleeveless top and flat white sandals. In one hand she carried a wide-brimmed straw hat, in the other a pair of sunglasses.

"Ready," she chirped, her smile turning to a frown as she spied the file in his hand.

"So am I," Ethan said, replacing the file and getting to his feet. "I'll just stash my briefcase in my room and collect my sunglasses, and we're outta here."

And so they were.

That first time out, their walk was leisurely and rather short. Still, during their brief stroll, Ethan couldn't help but notice the looks, some sly, some blatant, as several men scanned Paula.

Acknowledging that Paula was a beautiful woman, with her blond hair gleaming golden in the sunlight, and her stunning face and gorgeous figure, Ethan could understand their interest and admiration, even the gleam of lust in their eyes.

He, himself, had admired her delicate beauty, had lusted after her curvaceous body. Under different circumstances, he might have formed an attachment with her . . .

But her hair didn't have a russet sheen. Her eyes weren't a particular shade of blue.

Her name was not Kate.

Ethan strolled on, unaffected by the covetous glances leveled at his wife by other men.

Other than breakfast or lunch, which they usually ordered in, throughout the rest of their stay on the island, they spent most of their waking hours outside the suite.

They took long walks. They went bicycling. They golfed. They sailed. And they talked . . . a lot.

"When you first told me you were pregnant," Ethan began carefully one morning over breakfast, "you said you knew the baby was mine because you hadn't been with another man for some time before we . . . er . . . were together."

"Yes." Nodding, Paula hesitated, staring at the croissant on her plate. "And not at all after that." She broke the roll, buttered it, slathered it with wild strawberry preserves, and frowned at it, as if wondering how it had gotten into her hand. Her lips tightened. "You see, about a month before Sharon's wedding," she muttered, sliding a quick look at him, then glancing away, "I was dumped by the man I had been with for some time."

"You were in love with him?"

"Yes, and I believed he loved me. At least, he claimed he did." Raising the roll, she took a vicious bite. "Turned out, he loved his career more."

Ethan frowned. "His career? I don't understand. What does he do that would cause him to dump you for his career?"

"He's an actor."

"I still don't understand," he confessed, confused as to what being an actor had to do with a man's love life.

Sighing, Paula proceeded to finish off her croissant before she explained, "Kenneth . . . his name's Kenneth, got a heads-up call from his agent, telling him about a part coming up for grabs on a nighttime soap. Ken flew to California to try out for the part." She glanced away, her lips tightening again, nails digging into her palm.

Reaching across the table, Ethan took her clenched hand in his, squeezing in encouragement. "Okay, I'm with you so far, and I get your drift. Something happened while he was out in make-believe land?"

"Oh, yeah," she answered. "The lead actress, who also happens to be the producer of the program, decided she wanted Ken for the role of her lover, on the set, and off. Getting the part was contingent upon his compliance.''

''He dumped you to crawl into bed with an actress for a part in the show?''

''He is very ambitious.'' Her tone dripped sarcasm. ''And she is beautiful . . . married, too.''

''Hey, nice guy,'' Ethan said in disgust. ''He dumps you and cuckolds another man in one fell swoop.''

''Yeah.'' Paula tried to appear careless and shrugged; she didn't quite pull it off. ''Look, lets finish up here and go for a walk or something. I need some fresh air.''

Ethan got the unspoken message; Kenneth's name was not mentioned again.

But they did have a discussion a few days later about Paula's plans to pursue her own acting career. She raised the subject one balmy evening after dinner, while they were ambling along the beach, playing tag with the waves.

''You do realize that I have no intention of putting my career on hold just because I'm pregnant,'' she said, lifting her ankle length skirt as she skipped at the edge of the water. ''Don't you?''

''I figured as much,'' Ethan drawled, unmindful of his rolled pants legs as he kicked up spray.

''And you don't object?'' Her tone, and the look she sent him, were challenging.

He smiled. ''No. I don't, and won't object. Your life, and what you do with it, is your business—that is, so long as you do nothing to endanger your pregnancy,'' he qualified in a cautionary tone.

''I won't,'' she was quick to assure him. ''Don't

worry, Ethan, I made a bargain with you and I'll stick to it. You'll have your child."

"Thank you, I'll be forever grateful to you for your agreement," he said in sincere appreciation.

"You're welcome." She shot a curious side-long look at him. "If you don't mind my asking, why were you—are you—so eager for me to have this child?"

"Because it's mine," Ethan answered without hesitation. "He, or she, is a part of me."

"Hmmm." Paula shot him a look that questioned his sanity, and shrugged. "While we're on the subject," she said, absently running a hand over her still flat belly, "I can't help but wonder if you're planning to raise the child by yourself." She paused for another quick glance at him. "Or if you have a prospective new wife and mother in mind?"

Ethan immediately thought of Kate, and just as swiftly dismissed the notion as fantasy. Kate would make a wonderful mother, he knew; hadn't she been mothering her sisters since she was fourteen? And she would make an even more wonderful wife, passionate and loving. But, after his betrayal of her, he felt he'd be lucky to have her friendship; anything beyond that would be wishing for the moon.

"At the moment, there's no prospective wife or mother on the horizon," he finally answered. "Some day, perhaps, but in the meantime, I'll raise the child by myself . . . with some help from a professional nanny."

Paula gave another delicate shudder. "Rather you than me. I have never wanted children of my own," she stated frankly. "All I ever wanted was to trod the boards."

"And you will have your freedom to do so, and the settlement I promised, six months after the child is born."

She heaved a sigh. "I hate the idea of getting big." Her hand again stroked her belly. "So that day can't come soon enough for me."

Me either, Ethan thought, not looking forward to the months ahead. But, until they were both free again, he told himself to make the best of it.

He shot a grin at her to lighten the mood. "And I hope someday to see your name in big letters on a theater marquee on Broadway."

"So do I." Paula laughed. "But, until that someday comes, I'd be happy to land a small part in any production, large or small, in Philadelphia, or any other city."

In a balmy, sun-splashed setting of swaying palms, an abundance of brilliantly colored flowers, and turquoise ocean waters lapping pristine beaches, the days passed by in an atmosphere of relaxed companionship.

So, for all intents and purposes, Ethan and Paula, while not sharing a marriage bed, did manage to share a congenial vacation.

Nevertheless, Ethan was glad to be back home. There was much to be done, and not only in his office.

First off, as his apartment contained only one bedroom, and one bath, he had to move . . . and quickly. Although it was comfortable enough, sleeping on the couch in the living room was not Ethan's idea of the ideal living arrangement.

And Paula was less than thrilled, and not at all averse to voicing her discontent.

So much for relaxed companionship.

Fortunately, Ethan had had the foresight to contact a realtor, one Brad Fielding, before the wedding. Brad's instructions had been to look for a place for Ethan to buy, either a house or condo, it didn't matter to Ethan, so long as it had at the least three bedrooms and two bathrooms.

Brad Fielding presented Ethan with seven listings shortly after he and Paula returned from Bermuda. Ethan bought the second place they viewed, a three bedroom, two bath townhouse nearing completion in a new development, located ten or so miles northwest of the city.

The intervening weeks, while the house was being finished, readied for occupancy, were more than hectic for Ethan. In addition to catching up on the backlog of work in the office, there was shopping for furniture, dishes, cookware, linens, and all the assorted items Paula deemed necessary to make a house into a home.

His back ached from sleeping on the damned sofa. His ears ached from listening to Paula's complaints. His bank balance ached from taking the hit for the purchase of the house and all the things to fill it.

Ethan could only thank his lucky stars that, while still in law school, he had discovered a talent for choosing and making timely investments, and that the bull market was currently running rampant on Wall Street.

On paper, he was worth close to a fortune.

Finally, everything was in place. Moving day arrived. Ethan and Paula settled into the house, and a pattern of dealing with each other with a measure of civility became routine, mainly because they now had enough room to avoid confrontation by not tripping over each other.

In the interim, Ethan managed to consult with all his clients and bring their files up-to-date. All his clients, that is, except one.

He had yet to meet with, or call David, even though there had been a note from David waiting on his desk on his return from Bermuda, requesting he phone him or stop by the house at his convenience.

Stopping by David's house, with the very real probability of seeing Kate, would hardly be at his convenience. He knew as well that even phoning was chancy, with an equal possibility of her answering, especially since school was now out for summer vacation. No, talking to her, seeing her, would never be comfortable for Ethan . . . would never be anything but painful, despite the fact that he longed to see her, talk to her, hold her in his arms as he had . . .

But he had no right, Ethan reminded himself. His longing to look at, talk to, be with her had to be controlled; his wants, needs, desires had to be suppressed.

Ethan put off the call as long as he could. But eventually, he could put it off no longer without running the risk of appearing insultingly indifferent to the other man's concerns, and he couldn't let that happen. David was an old friend of the Winston family, and a valued client to the firm.

Ethan made the call after normal working hours, when he figured David would be home from his office . . . and Kate just might be out for the evening.

Mandy answered the phone.

Ethan swallowed a sigh of relief. "Hello, Mandy, it's Ethan Winston. How are you?"

"Oh, hi, Ethan. How was the honeymoon trip?" the girl asked with eager innocence.

He grimaced. "It was fine. Bermuda's beautiful." Enough said about that, he thought, and changed the subject. "Is your father home?"

"Yeah, he just got in. I think he's in his office. Can you hang on a minute while I check?"

"Of course. Take your time."

"Hello, Ethan." David's voice came on the line a few minutes later, followed by a soft click of the other phone. "Sorry to keep you waiting."

"No apologies necessary," he assured the older man. "Matter of fact, I feel I owe you one for taking so long to get in touch with you."

"Not at all. I'm sure you've had a lot to catch up on," David said. "How was your trip?"

"It was fine," Ethan repeated with a wry smile. "The island and the weather were beautiful."

"And Paula?"

"She's fine." A little bitchy at times, growing more as her pregnancy advances, but healthy, he thought, drawing a silent, deep breath. "She's been busy decorating the new house."

"Yes, your father mentioned that you had bought a house—a little ways outside the city, right?"

"Yes, a townhouse, in one of the newer developments."

"So Mark said. I'd say you've been busy yourself since you returned from Bermuda."

"Well . . . it has been a bit hectic," Ethan allowed. "But, we've settled into the house, and I'm finally getting things under control now, both personally and professionally. So, how can I help you?"

"I suppose I should have just made a regular appointment with your secretary, but . . ."

"Not at all," Ethan interrupted to assure him. Ever since he had agreed to be David's representative, Ethan went to the house whenever the older man desired a consultation. In all fairness, he could not ask the man to come to him, despite his own reluctance to encounter Kate.

"Well, then, I'd like a meeting with you. I want to go over my will and estate plan, update it a bit, and make a few changes," David explained.

"Major changes?" Ethan asked, contemplative, a frown drawing his brows together. Not that it was unusual for a client to make changes in their wills and estate plans; it wasn't. But, in David's case, with the apparent decline in his health, the request was a cause of concern.

"No . . . no, just a few changes," David replied. "But, also, I'd like you to draw up the necessary documents giving Kate my power-of-attorney, plus naming her legal guardian for Mandy and Connie in the event of my death before they have reached the age of consent."

Ethan's concern, and frown, deepened. "Have you discussed any of this with Kate?"

"Well . . . no, not yet. But I will. I want to get this done as soon as possible."

Now Ethan was seriously concerned. "David . . . are you all right?"

"Yes, of course," he answered, quickly and heartily. Too quickly? Too heartily? Ethan wondered.

"I simply want to be certain that my personal business is properly and legally in place," David added.

"I understand," Ethan murmured, afraid that what he understood was the request of a sick man feeling the need to get his affairs in order. Since joining the firm, Ethan had received several similar requests from elderly clients . . . every one of whom was now deceased.

"Also," David went on, changing the subject, "I'd like your advice on some investments I'm considering."

"I'm not a broker, David, as you know," Ethan said, certain David was deliberately steering the conversation in a different direction. But, what could he do about it? Nothing. He had no choice but to go along; David was the client, after all.

"Yes, of course, but, you see, I've been doing a little

trading on-line and . . . I'd simply appreciate your opinion on a few stocks.''

Having dabbled a bit himself, bought a few stocks on-line, Ethan understood the allure. Still, one needed to be careful, and he said as much to David.

''I can tell you now that my personal opinion is to research, check the source, but, of course I'm willing to discuss the subject with you. Did you have a particular day or evening in mind for the meeting?''

''Would you happen to be free this coming Saturday afternoon?'' David's tone held a hopeful note.

''Saturday?'' Ethan murmured uncertainly, thinking Kate would likely be home.

''I know it's an imposition to ask you to come by on the weekend . . . but we would be assured of privacy then,'' David explained. ''You see, Kate and a friend are taking Mandy and Connie to the Camden Aquarium, then on to the Franklin Institute for some sort of hands-on exhibition for youngsters, and from there they'll be going somewhere to have dinner before returning home.''

Ethan was hard put not to sigh aloud in relief. ''As a matter-of-fact, the only thing on my calendar for Saturday is an invitation for Paula and I to have dinner with Mother and Dad. Later in the afternoon would be best, as Paula could visit with my folks alone while we have our meeting.''

''Fine, just name a time, Ethan.''

''How about three-thirty?''

''Three-thirty will be fine,'' David said. ''I'll see you Saturday, then.''

"Yes, sir."

Ethan stared pensively at the phone after he hung up. Should he say something to his father concerning David, he wondered. Or had he jumped to a hasty conclusion about the possibility of David being ill?

Of course, everyone knew the man hadn't been himself ever since Maureen's death. For all that he tried to put up a good front, it was obvious David suffered from depression. But, could there be something even more seriously wrong with him, so serious he felt a pressing need to, in his words, be certain his personal business is legally in place?

Sighing, Ethan decided not to speak to his father, at least not until after he met with David.

All things considered, he thought, Saturday was shaping up to be an eventful day. Fortunately, an encounter with Kate would not be included.

First of those events would be the meeting with David to discuss the changes in his will and estate plan; Ethan made a mental note to review David's file beforehand.

And then dinner with his parents.

Both events should prove interesting.

Intuitively, Ethan felt that, for whatever reason, David believed he was not long for this world. He could only hope the older man was wrong.

As for his parents. Well, sometime before, during, or after dinner, Paula was planning to tell them they were going to be grandparents around Thanksgiving.

Ethan knew his parents would be delighted.

At least, he hoped they would be delighted. Now

that Paula was developing a little belly he certainly was both delighted and fiercely possessive and protective of the child growing inside her.

His parents damn well better be delighted.

CHAPTER EIGHT

They returned to the house earlier than expected.
Still, Kate reasoned, it was understandable. It had
been a long day. Wanting to get an early start, while
the late June morning was fresh and relatively cool,
they arranged for Carol to get to the house by eight-
thirty and have breakfast with the family.

Excited about the outing, Mandy and Connie were
up, and had everybody else up, long before eight. By
the time Carol arrived at the house, the girls were
washed, dressed, and just about finished eating.

Used to Carol around the house since she and Kate
had become good friends, they treated her like one
of the family.

"Hi Carol," Mandy said, grinning as she carried
her cereal bowl and juice glass to the sink. "We're
all finished eating and ready to go."

"Yeah," Connie piped in, clearing her place at the table. "So hurry up and eat . . . please."

"Connie!" Helen and Kate scolded in unison.

Laughing, Carol slipped into a chair at the table. "It's a good thing I'm on a diet," she said, passing with an exaggerated pout on Helen's offer of pancakes. "No thanks, just toast and coffee for me."

Watching your diet and taking the exercise classes are getting results," Kate said, helping herself to two of Helen's light-as-air pancakes. "You've lost what . . . ten, twelve pounds since we began the class?"

"Ten." Carol frowned. "I've been stuck on ten for a couple of days now."

"You've hit a plateau," Helen commiserated. "But hang in there, you'll get past it."

"From your lips to God's ear," Carol said, eyeing the strawberry preserves with longing.

Not wanting to risk being scolded again, or worse, having the outing canceled on account of rude behavior, Mandy and Connie held their tongues throughout the adult conversation, fidgeting in the background.

Making short work of their meals, and sharing a smile, Kate and Carol allowed the impatient girls to hurry them out of the house a few minutes after nine.

After a slow tour of the aquarium, they ate a quick lunch before heading back across the Delaware River to Philly. At the hands-on exhibit at the Franklin Institute, Mandy and Connie eagerly put their hands on everything.

By four, their high energy level lagged, but neither one of them were willing to admit to being tired. The girls then began making noises about feeling starved.

"I'm hungry for ice cream," said Mandy.

"Me, too," Connie parroted.

Tired herself, Kate was more than ready to call it a day, and she felt sure Carol was, too. All she had to do was convince the girls. "It's too late in the afternoon for a sweet snack," she said.

"But I'm starving," Mandy whined.

"Me too," Connie echoed.

"Well . . . ," Kate said, slanting a conspiratorial glance at Carol. "Since you've seen and touched everything here at least twice, I suggest we leave now and have an early dinner before going home."

"Yes." Carol mouthed the word silently.

"Oh, but . . . ," Connie began in protest.

"You can have ice cream for dessert," Kate inserted in a shameless attempt at bribery.

"C'mon, Connie," Mandy grumbled. "I'm hungry."

"Oh . . . okay."

Carol gave Kate a grateful look and a thumbs up as they herded the girls from the institute to the car.

It wasn't quite five-thirty when Kate steered the gleaming silver car past Carol's ancient but still shiny red sporty two-seater parked along the curb in front of the house. Turning into the driveway, she came to a smooth stop.

Their natural exuberance revived by the rest and a substantial meal, and the double dips of ice cream both girls devoured, Mandy and Connie scrambled from the car and took off for the house.

"Do those two ever slow down?" Carol asked, grinning over the car roof at Kate.

"Bedtime." Kate grinned back. "They go out like lights, the two of them. One minute they're bouncing around, and the next they're zonked." She raised her eyebrows when Carol started down the driveway. "Would you like to come in, have a cup of coffee or something cold to drink before you go?"

"No . . . thanks." Carol glanced at her watch. "I told a friend I'd meet him for drinks around seven, if I got back in time. I want to take a shower and change."

"A man?" Kate said, intrigued, falling into step with the other woman. "Someone interesting and special?"

Carol came to a halt next to her car, her expression amused. "I said a friend," she chided, shrugging. "He's an okay guy, interesting to talk to, but not special . . . at least, not in the way I'm sure you mean."

"Too bad," Kate murmured. "I was hoping . . . ," she began, only to be cut off by a soft gasp from Carol.

"Now *that* looks interesting," she said, casting an interested look toward the house.

Naturally, Kate had to look, too—and stopped breathing at the sight of the man exiting the house.

"Who is he?" Carol whispered. "Do you know him?"

"Ye . . . yes." Kate nodded, feeling like a wide-eyed twit for stumbling over the one word. But, his gazed fixed on her, Ethan started down the walkway. She cleared her throat—as if there were something caught there, something substantive besides her stirred emotions. "He's a family friend. His parents live next door."

"God . . . he's gorgeous," Carol murmured.

"And married," Kate muttered, her pulse rate going berserk as he approached them.

"Life just ain't fair," Carol whispered, her lips curving into a bright smile.

Tell me about it, Kate thought, trying to appear nonchalant, while devouring him with her eyes.

Ethan looked tan, and trim, and fit, and . . . absolutely wonderful.

Damn him.

"Hello, Kate, how are you?" He flashed that charming, boyish smile he had given her the first day she met him. It had the same knee-weakening effect.

"I'm fine," she lied, proud of the normal tone of her voice. "And you?"

"I'm fine, too," he drawled, turning to bestow a smile on Carol.

Quivering inside, Kate was forced to quash a spark of jealously. Darn it, would this man always have this shattering effect on her, she thought, her chest tight as she made the introductions.

They shook hands.

Kate's empty palm tingled with pleasure remembering his touch.

Carol, the very same Carol who could be so slashingly sarcastic with Jason, was pure honey-voiced as she exchanged pleasantries with Ethan.

So much for Jason's insinuations about Carol's sexual orientation, Kate mused, amazed to see the other woman actually flush, and flutter her eyelashes at Ethan.

She stood by, her stomach churning, hearing but not registering a word of their chitchat, loving him, hating him, longing for what might have been, for as long as she could bear it. Then, with ruthless intent, she interrupted.

"Have you been visiting David, Ethan?" Lord, what a stupid question, she chided herself. Of course he had stopped by to see her stepfather. What other reason could there be for him to be at the house? Surely not to see her.

"Yes, we had some business to discuss." He shifted his attention back to her, his expression cool, his eyes warm, very warm, making her feel hot, achy, all over.

At that instant, Kate wanted, needed, many things, physical and emotional, but she knew those needs would never be satisfied. So instead, she craved a cigarette after a week and a half of not smoking at all. Carol was right, she mused, disgusted with herself. *Life just ain't fair.*

"Well, gotta go," he said, a strangely sad little smile shadowing his lips. "Family's waiting."

"How is everyone, your parents . . . Paula?" she asked, belatedly remembering her manners.

"All fine." Traces of that sad smile lingered in the corners of his mouth.

Wondering at the cause of that odd smile, she dredged up a smile in return. "Give them my best."

"Will do." Shifting his gaze back to Carol, he gave

her that old, familiar smile, producing a sharp twist of pain inside Kate's chest in the process. "Nice to have met you, Carol," he said, raising his hand in a parting wave before turning to walk away.

"Same here," Carol called after him, a speculative gleam in her eyes as she watched his long-legged gait cover the short distance along the sidewalk to his parents' house. When the door closed behind him, she swung back to Kate, asking, "Is he happily married?"

"Newlywed," Kate answered, surprised and a little shocked by the intent behind the question.

Carol sighed. "Then I suppose he is. Too bad." She shook her head. "It seems all the really interesting looking guys are either married or gay."

Despite herself, Kate had to laugh at the feelings seeing Ethan had churned up inside her. Would she ever figure out Carol's personality, who she really was and where she was coming from?

"Jason's interesting," she felt duty bound to point out. She had gone out with him a couple of times over the previous weeks, and she genuinely did think he was interesting, not particularly exciting, but interesting. "And he's neither married nor gay."

Carol made a face. "Jason's a wimp."

"Carol, really, he is not," she protested. "Why on earth would you say such a thing?"

"Because that's what I think." She shrugged. "Why you bother with him, I can't imagine."

"I like Jason," Kate said truthfully.

"You like him," Carol repeated.

"Yes, I do. He's a likable man."

"Likable, yes, I suppose, if that's what you're looking for." Carol made a face. "But does he excite you, turn you on, make you feel all fluttery inside?"

"Well . . . no," Kate reluctantly admitted, knowing full well only one man had ever aroused those sensations in her.

"I rest my case," Carol said smugly, unlocking and swinging open her car door.

"But that doesn't make him a wimp," Kate objected. "Besides, I really do enjoy his company."

Shaking her head, Carol slid into the car. "Have it your way. Now, I've got to run. See you Monday for exercise class." She raised her eyebrows. "How about staying in town afterward? We could gorge ourselves on shopping and then have a"—she grimaced—"sensible dinner."

"Sounds good, and so far as I can recall there's nothing on the family agenda, but I'll check with David and Helen and give you a call tomorrow. Okay?"

"Sure." Carol nodded. "I'll be around all day. See you." She gunned the motor, waved, and shot away from the curb and down the quiet street.

Wondering how Carol had avoided ever being involved in an auto accident, Kate watched her tear around the corner at the intersection.

As she turned away, her gaze drifted to the house next door. Ethan was in that house. So near, and so far away. Forever, so far away.

She needed a cigarette.

Kate opened her purse, then, with a sharp shake of her head, closed it again.

Get over it, she admonished herself. She did not need a cigarette. She needed to go into the house and find out what had been so important that David had to see Ethan on a Saturday. She felt a sense of unease in her stomach as she started up the walk to the house.

David must have been waiting for her to come inside, because he called to her as she shut the door behind her.

"Kate, is that you?"

"Yes, David," she answered, moving to the open doorway of his office. "Can I get you something?"

"No, thank you." He was seated at his desk, and motioned with one hand. "Come in and sit down, Kate. There's something I want to discuss with you."

Even as the sensation of uneasiness grew stronger, Kate noticed that David looked better than he had for some time, more relaxed and, oddly relieved. Crossing to the leather chair in front of his desk, she settled in and tightly clasped her hands in her lap, somehow certain she wasn't going to like whatever he was about to say to her.

"Ethan was here this afternoon," he said. "You just missed him. He left a little while ago."

"I didn't miss him." She managed a small smile. "I was out front seeing Carol off when he came out. I was surprised to see him." An understatement if she'd ever made one, she thought, but kept her smile in place. "I mean, on a Saturday."

"Yes, well, he said he didn't mind stopping by this

afternoon,'' David explained, ''since he and his wife are having dinner with his parents this evening.''

''I see.'' As slight as it was, it was a strain for her to maintain her smile. ''There was something you wanted to talk to me about?'' she asked, changing the subject.

''Yes.'' He glanced down at the folder on his desk, tapped on it with one finger. ''This contains my will,'' he said looking up at her. ''Ethan advised me to discuss this with you.''

''David . . . ,'' she began, alarm flaring through her.

''Now, it's nothing drastic,'' he said soothingly, reading the concern in her expression. ''It's simply that I've named you guardian to the girls in the event that I should die before they have reached the age of consent. I hope you have no objections to my doing so.''

''No, of course not,'' Kate assured him at once. ''But, David, was that necessary?'' she asked, needing to know, but almost afraid to hear his answer.

''It was prudent,'' he said, not really answering her question. ''Also, I have given you power of attorney.'' He held up a hand, silencing her when she tried to protest. ''To pay bills and so forth if something came up when I wasn't here, or if I should become incapacitated.''

Incapacitated. A chill ran up Kate's spine. The time had come to broach the subject she had been putting off for over a month, ever since the day of Ethan's wedding. She drew a deep breath, and blurted out her fears.

''David, are you ill, seriously ill?''

"No . . . no." He shook his head. "At least, not as far as I know."

His assurance was less than reassuring. "But you told us you were seeing a doctor."

"Yes." He gave her a faint smile. "He's been treating me for depression, which I'm sure you were aware I've been suffering ever since your mother . . ." His voice faded.

"Yes," she said, her heart aching for him.

"Yes." He took a breath, then carried on briskly. "At any rate, I have an appointment with the doctor next month for a full physical workup, blood tests, EKG, stress test—and he's going to start me on a new antidepression medication that has just been approved by the FDA."

"Does the doctor suspect something?" she asked anxiously. "Is that the reason for the workup?"

David sighed at her persistence, but answered frankly. "There are some concerns," he admitted. "But let's not panic," he quickly added. "Let's wait for the test results. Okay?"

What else could Kate do but agree? "Okay."

"And you're certain you have no objections to the responsibility of guardianship for the girls," he pressed. "And the power of attorney?"

Again, what else could Kate do? "No, I have no objections. I just hope I . . . well, you know."

"I understand, and I thank you, Kate." His eyes grew misty and he blinked. "You are as kind and giving as your mother was. You are so young, and you've willingly taken on so much, yet, I know, should the necessity arise, you will take excellent care of Mandy and Connie.''

''They're my sisters, and I love them,'' she said, the sense of alarm expanding. But . . . David . . .''

''Now, calm down,'' he inserted. ''I said *should* the necessity arise.'' He gave her a wobbly smile. ''Either way, I can never thank you enough.'' He blinked again.

Kate also had to blink back a rush of warm tears. ''There are no thanks necessary,'' she said softly. ''You made Mother very happy, and you've always been nothing but kind and generous to me. I couldn't have wished for a better stepfather.''

''I'm happy to hear that.'' David sniffed, swallowed roughly, then smiled. This time his smile was real.

''It's true,'' she murmured.

''The girls made a quick stop in here when you returned,'' he said abruptly in an obvious attempt to steer the conversation in a less emotional direction. ''From their excited chatter, I'd hazard a guess that they enjoyed their day. Did you and Carol enjoy it, too?''

Kate dredged up a shaky smile and went along with him. ''Yes. It was fun. Tiring but fun.''

''I can imagine.'' He chuckled. ''I sometimes think those two are made up of pure energy.''

The rocky emotional moment over, their conversation turned to Mandy and Connie's summer activities, and the gear still needed to outfit them for the two-week summer camp they'd be attending next month.

Discussing the girls jogged Kate's memory concerning Carol's suggestion that they do some shopping and have dinner together after their exercise class on Monday. She told David of her plans.

"Of course you may go, though you might want to mention it to Helen," David said, shaking his head. "Damn it, this is the kind of thing I was referring to concerning the amount of responsibility you have accepted. You're only twenty-five. You should be free to do whatever you like, without having to ask me or Helen if it's all right. It's not fair of . . ."

"David," Kate interrupted him without a qualm, "I promise you I honestly don't mind checking with you and Helen before I commit myself to any plans."

He heaved a sigh. "Okay. Go. Enjoy. But I want to give you some money for your shopping, and to pay for dinner for you and Carol. And I don't want to hear any arguments."

Kate protested.

David remained adamant.

She gave in.

David wrote a check and handed it to her.

At the sight of the amount he'd written on the check, Kate began arguing all over again. How long the standoff might have lasted was anybody's guess, for at that moment, Helen stepped into the doorway and tapped on the door Kate had left open.

"You know, you two sound just like Mandy and Connie when they're squabbling, and I'm sorry, but I couldn't help overhearing the tail end of your discussion. You don't need to check with me about spending a day out. That's what I'm here for," she remarked in a scolding tone.

"I know, Helen, but I don't want to take advantage."

She gave Kate an exasperated look, and an order. "Kate, just shut up . . . and listen to David. Take the money. You've earned it." She switched a much softer look on to her employer. "David, dinner's ready. Come eat." As if fully expecting to be obeyed, not without good reason, she turned and walked away.

"I'd better go eat," David said, lips twitching and eyes brightening a little with amusement as he pushed back his desk chair.

"And I suppose I'd better accept your check," Kate said, sharing a smile with him. "Thank you."

He waved away her gratitude as he strolled to the doorway. "Helen was right, you've earned it." He paused to glance back over his shoulder at her. "I know you've had your dinner, but how about keeping me company while I have mine?"

"Okay," she said, following him from the room. "I'll have a glass of Helen's iced mint tea while you eat."

As it turned out, Mandy and Connie had the same idea about a tall glass of iced tea, and all of them, Helen included, kept David company while he ate.

Distracted by the table conversation, with Mandy and Connie in turn recounting to their father and Helen the highlights of their day, and David's and Helen's questions and comments, Kate was successful at shoving back her worries about David's upcoming physical examination, and his general health.

To her surprise, she even managed to submerge the aching, depressing feelings churned up inside her, the empty and needy sensations aroused in her body by her unexpected encounter with Ethan.

And to her relief, she successfully subjugated her earlier craving for a quick and stealthy cigarette.

CHAPTER NINE

A short distance down the tree-shaded street from David's house, Ethan sat in his parents' living room, paying scant attention to the conversational flow between his parents, his wife, and his sister and brother-in-law.

Having deliberately tuned out, he was gratefully sipping the pre-dinner gin and tonic his father had fixed for him on his return to the house.

He had already felt in need of a thirst-quencher, but on entering the house to the unexpected sight of Sharon and her invisible but decidedly leashed spouse, Charles—never Charlie or Chuck, but Charles—the need had intensified.

Sadly, to Ethan's way of thinking, the only redeeming feature of the drink, light on gin, heavy on tonic and loaded with ice, was that it was wet and cold.

With his nerves jangling from the aftereffects of his unexpected meeting with Kate, plus the haughty tones of Sharon's voice, Ethan would have preferred something stronger . . . much stronger.

Lord, Kate had looked glorious, he reflected, shivering inside his overheated skin. To the torment of his body, Kate's image was crystal clear in his mind.

He took a bigger swallow. It didn't douse the flood of memory flowing through his mind.

The afternoon sunshine, dappled through the leaves of the pear tree next to the curb, played light and shadows over her flushed and glowing face, deepened her eyes to darkened blue, struck glinting sparks of red-gold off her russet hair, disarrayed from her busy day spent in the company of her stepsisters and friend.

Hot, bothered, and semiaroused by the vivid memory, Ethan took another deep swallow of the drink to soothe his parched throat, and hopefully cool the fire within.

"Ethan?" The puzzled note in his mother's soft voice jerked him to attention.

"I'm sorry, Mother." He offered a self-deprecating smile along with the apology. "I'm afraid I was into my own thoughts and not listening. What did you say?"

"I said it's time for dinner." Virginia spoke in a patient, motherly tone, her smile gentle. "Bring your drink." She turned to leave the room. "And come along."

It was only then that Ethan noticed his father and Paula, quietly talking. Charles and Sharon, for once in her life unusually silent, were already making their way out of the living room.

"Yes, of course." Standing, he raised the glass to drain it, realized it was empty except for the remains of too many ice cubes, and set it on the tray, following like a good boy into the dining room.

In keeping with the hot weather, the meal was light but flavorful. At least, he assumed it was flavorful, as everyone else around the table appeared to enjoy it. For Ethan—although he helped himself to a portion of every dish proffered, and ate every morsel—hadn't tasted any of it.

His mind was wandering again, not far, but right next door, to the redheaded resident of the house . . . and of his dreams, and his desires—desires he had ruthlessly suppressed for weeks, desires immediately kindled by the chance meeting with Kate.

Damn he wanted her, yearned to be with her, laugh with her, live with her, love with her. If only . . .

He never noticed Paula rising from her chair.

"I have an announcement to make," she proclaimed in fine dramatic form, effectively bursting his fantasy bubble.

Ethan was alert at once, preparing to play his role in her little performance for his parents.

"A surprise?" Virginia asked, her eyes bright with expectation.

In spite of the low mood seeing Kate had cast him into, Ethan had to smile; his mother did love surprises.

"You've secured a major role in an upcoming production somewhere?" Sharon guessed.

"No." Just for a flickering instant, Paula's smile looked strained. "But a delightful surprise," she continued, her smile easing into one of expectancy as she slowly glanced from Sharon to Virginia, and on to Mark, then Ethan, deliberately drawing out the suspenseful moment. "At least, I hope you will consider it a delightful surprise."

Sharon frowned. Good little mate that he was, Charles mirrored his wife's expression.

Virginia sat forward in her chair in anticipation.

Mark's expression revealed both curiosity and interest.

Allowing Paula the spotlight of center stage, Ethan sat back, calmly waiting for her to drop her baby bomb.

"Virginia . . . Mark . . . everybody . . ." She paused for optimum effect, before rushing into a gush, "I'm"—another pause to glance meaningfully at Ethan—"I mean, we're going to have a baby. I'm pregnant."

Ka-boom, Ethan thought, silently supplying the sound effects, while suppressing a wicked urge to surge to his feet in a standing ovation.

"That's wonderful!" Virginia did not disappoint her daughter-in-law. And she did surge to her feet . . . and actually clapped her hands. "Isn't it wonderful, Mark? We're going to have a grandchild." Sliding back her chair, she skirted the large oval table to give Paula a hug.

"Yes, dear, it is wonderful," Mark agreed, smiling indulgently at his wife's visible excitement. "It's been a long time since there was a baby in the house."

"A baby," Virginia repeated, laughing in delight.

"A baby?" Sharon echoed, in tones of stunned disbelief. "But what about your acting career?"

"I'm putting it on hold for a while," Paula replied, managing a lighthearted laugh.

In fact, she's honing her skills now, on all of you, Ethan thought, slanting a wry look at his sister, the ultimate career woman.

"Rather you than me," Sharon said with a delicate shudder. "Starting a family is the absolute last thing we're considering so early in our marriage Isn't it, Charles?"

"Yes, darling," he answered dutifully.

Ethan beat back a bark of laughter. In his view, Sharon and Charles were made for each other, because they were both so very much in love . . . with her.

"Well, I for one can't wait," Virginia said. "When is the baby due?"

Ah, there's the sticky part, Ethan thought. He and Paula both knew the baby was due in mid-November. And, if she revealed the correct date, his parents would both know that their sudden decision to marry had not been because they were so much in love they couldn't bear to be apart—as they had allowed both sets of parents to believe—but simply because she was already, in polite terms, in the family way.

Paula shot a quick, questioning look at him. Arching a brow, he flicked a hand, as if to say the floor, or stage, was all hers to finish out the scene.

Paula smiled, letting him know she heard his mute

instructions as clearly as a dialogue prompt, whispered from the wings of a theater.

"Well . . . ," she said, her smile conveying shy excitement. "The doctor predicted the due date for the very beginning of the year." She slid a sidelong, demure glance at him and blushed prettily. "We . . . Ethan and I, think I must have conceived on our wedding night."

Bravo, Ethan thought, choking on a burst of cynical laughter as he recalled their wedding night, she dead to the world with exhaustion, while he lay sleepless, sweating and rigid with desire for another woman.

But, damn, Paula was good, he mused, very good in fact. With luck and a few breaks, she'd probably be a success as an actress. In his opinion, she was certainly giving a Tony Award performance here today.

Of course, come November, anyone with fingers to count on would know conception had occurred some six or so weeks before their wedding, he acknowledged.

But then, Ethan quickly discovered, it wasn't over yet, for Paula hadn't quite finished playing out the big announcement scene.

"This will probably sound silly, I know," she said, infusing a youthful uncertainty into her voice, a girlish trill to her burble of laughter. "But . . . for some odd reason, I just feel that this baby"—she hesitated, placing a hand over the slight bulge in her belly for effect—"who is already causing a fluttering inside me, is going to be in such a hurry to be born, he or she will arrive early."

Clever ploy, Ethan conceded, his smile wry as he inclined his head to her in a gesture of respect.

Sharon looked skeptical, but remained silent.

Charles Looked confused . . . but that was nothing new. Ethan had often wondered how the man would have made his way in the business world without his banker-father's influence.

And his dear, innocent mother bought into Paula's artful dodge wholeheartedly.

"Oh, I do hope so, I can hardly wait already," Virginia cried enthusiastically, quickly qualifying, "so long as the baby's all right, of course."

Incredible. This time, Ethan might have laughed out loud, if the entire fiasco hadn't been so damned pitiful, and if he hadn't at that moment been struck by a strong sense of shame for the deception. He hated deceiving anyone, but most especially his trusting mother.

Helluva note, he thought. But he was caught between the equally distasteful choices of breaking his word of honor to Paula, or being her accomplice in the deception . . . which would have to be repeated all over again when Paula reprised her performance for her own parents.

Sticky webs, indeed.

"I'm sure the baby will be fine," Paula hastened to assure the anxious grandmother-in-waiting. "I'm going to be very careful to follow my obstetrician's instructions—take my vitamins, eat well, get plenty of sleep."

You'd better, honey. Though Ethan didn't voice the warning, his flashing glance conveyed the unmistakable message loud and clear. He sure as hell hadn't agreed to this farce only to have his child endangered by her carelessness.

Paula acknowledged his visual warning with a brief nod.

He was fascinated by Paula's ingenious portrayal of the glowing mother-to-be, when in private she was already whining and complaining about gaining weight, losing her svelte figure and—horrors!—possibly getting stretch marks. So caught up in her acting, Ethan hadn't realized that his father had left the dining room, until he strode back in, carrying a bottle of champagne in one hand and a tray of champagne flutes in the other.

"I think the occasion calls for a celebratory toast," he pronounced.

"Yes," Virginia agreed, going to Mark to relieve him of the tray of glasses.

"My, this is an occasion," Sharon drawled. "Dom Perignon, no less."

Ethan sighed, and wished for the evening to be over.

"The doctor said I'm not supposed to drink alcohol." Paula contrived to look damned near angelic and sound oh-so-prim and proper.

"Oh, brother," Sharon muttered.

Don't overplay it, Sarah Bernhardt, Ethan thought, deciding Paula's acting was beginning to reach mammoth proportions. "I doubt a couple sips of wine will cause any ill effects," he said, giving her another warning look.

"Well ... if you think it's okay ... ," Paula said meekly, returning his look with a sweet smile.

Deceitful witch. It was a hard-fought battle, but Ethan kept the denigrating thought to himself.

"I'm sure a sip or two won't hurt," Virginia said soothingly.

"Of course a few sips won't hurt you," Sharon inserted impatiently.

"Why, I remember having an occasional glass of wine with dinner during both my pregnancies," Virginia swept a loving glance between him and his sister, "and both Ethan and Sharon were born healthy and beautiful."

The sense of shame and guilt slashing deeper into his conscience, Ethan was grateful for the excuse to look away from the maternal pride shining from his mother's eyes, to accept the glass of wine his father handed to him.

His father made the toast.

Paula took two dainty sips from the glass before placing it on the table.

Ethan likewise took two small sips after the toast. But, instead of setting the glass aside, he raised it again to his lips and drained the cool liquid like a man on the verge of dying of thirst.

Excitedly chatting away about the expected baby with Paula, his mother didn't notice his crass gulping of the expensive wine.

His father did notice, however, but merely raised his eyebrows.

Thinking, the hell with it, Ethan extended his glass for a refill ... and promptly tossed that back, as well.

He was seriously considering a third glass, when sanity prevailed.

Reminding himself that the results of his one and only bout of overindulgence was at that moment growing in the womb of the woman seated next to him, Ethan switched to coffee.

Two hours later, Ethan was glad he had not given in to his temptation to drown his troubles in champagne, as thirty odd minutes after returning to the townhouse—no way could he think of the place as home—his mental clarity, and moral fiber, were put to the test.

Apparently sailing on what Ethan figured was a perceived superb performance high, Paula, a feline smile curving her lips, sashayed into her bedroom—the master bedroom—without uttering a word, not even a good night.

Shrugging, because he really didn't care, Ethan went to his own less spacious bedroom. He really didn't care about being relegated to the smaller room, either, as it was located next to the central bathroom and directly across the hall from the designated nursery.

He had stripped down to his boxers when his bedroom door opened and Paula appeared in the doorway. Backlit by the hall light, Ethan had a tantalizing look at her nude figure through the filmy material of her loose negligee. The brazen look of her, posing in the doorway, knowing he could see every sleek, lovely inch of her body, her full breasts, the gentle mound of her belly, the triangle of curls at the apex of her satiny thighs, aroused his libido, sent a rush of heat through his veins, and a surge of anger through his heart.

Paula stepped into the room.

Ethan's body and mind went stiff.

It had been months since he had been with a woman . . . with Kate. He was a healthy male. It was only natural that he would respond to the sexy allure of a beautiful and practically naked woman sauntering into his bedroom, as if she owned it, and him.

What in hell was she up to? Ethan railed to himself, willing his sex-hungry body to behave. He stood still and wary as she languidly walked to him.

"You want something?" His voice was cool; his temper was getting hot.

"Ummm," she purred, nodding. "Don't you?"

"No, thanks."

She glanced down, laughing softly at the evidence of his lie pushing against the close-fitting cotton of his boxers.

Damn her. Damn her, Ethan thought, while damning the evidence of his own sexual weakness. Drawing a deep breath, he let his self-disgust color his tone. "Go back to your room, Paula. Sex was not part of our deal."

"But I want it," she said, pouting prettily. "I've been wanting it ever since the morning sickness stopped." She reached out with one hand to draw the tip of a fingernail along the curve of his rigid jaw.

Ethan suppressed a shiver of need. "No, Paula."

"Why not?" Her voice was soft, and sulky. "We're

married. It's legal." Her fingernail traced a line to
the corner of his mouth. "Why shouldn't we take
advantage of the situation, enjoy the pleasure we can
give each other?"

"No, Paula." Ethan's tone was harsh with denial,
of her and his own desire. Fighting to maintain control, he curled his hands into fists at his side.

Her scent teased his senses as she stepped nearer.
Her fingernail probing his sealed lips, her free hand
moving to close around the material sheathing his
erection, she coaxed throatily, "I need that."

"Sorry." Calling on every ounce of willpower he
possessed, Ethan stepped back, away from the wom-
anly scent of her, the enticing, maddening delight
of her caressing fingers. "I'll buy you a vibrator
tomorrow."

"Damn you!" she cried, her pretty pout changing
to an ugly sneer. "What'll I do now, tonight?"

"Improvise."

With a glare she snarled, "Bastard," and spun
around and stormed from the room.

His body rigid, demanding release, Ethan stood
stone still until he heard Paula's bedroom door slam
shut. Cursing a blue streak in muttered tones, he
gingerly made his way to the central bathroom,
securely locking the door before shucking his shorts
and stepping under an icy shower spray.

Victory over base desire proved to be damned
uncomfortable, but he had to admit it was at least
morally satisfying.

CHAPTER TEN

Kate was sweating like a draft horse and panting like a dog chasing a car in August.

"I . . . hate . . . this," she muttered, legs pumping as she pedaled against the tension on the stationary bike.

"Yeah . . . so . . . do . . . I," Carol said, panting as heavily as Kate. "But . . . it's . . . working."

"Yeah." The timer rang on Kate's bike. Heaving a heartfelt sigh, she slumped forward onto the handlebars to rest her head on her forearms. "And it's a good thing I'm seeing results, 'cause if I wasn't, I'd pack in this program in a New York minute . . . whatever the heck that is."

The timer rang on Carol's bike, and she likewise slumped onto the handlebars, her head turned to face Kate, her sigh just as heartfelt. "Well, other than cooling down, at least we're done for today."

Pushing herself upright, Kate nodded. Dismounting, she straightened her spine and drew in a slow, deep breath, then released it as slowly. After completing the breathing exercise several times, she shot a grin at Carol, who was following suit with the breathing routine.

"Now we can get on to the fun stuff."

"Like shopping." Carol laughed. "And lunch."

Kate shook her head. "I'm having lunch at home." She swiped her wrist across her wet forehead and wrinkled her nose. "After I've had a long shower."

"Know what you mean." Fanning her flushed face with her hand, Carol glanced around the large room, a sly smile tugging at her lips. "What do you say we bag the cool down exercise and cut outta here?"

Kate grinned. "Let's make a break for it."

Minutes later, they exited the gym, giggling like two of their young students sneaking out of class.

As they made their way across the parking lot to their cars, Carol's laughter turned into a frown. "I should've thought to tell you to bring a change of clothes with you. You could've showered at my place in town. It would have saved you the run back home."

"Now's a great time to think of it." Laughing, Kate glanced at her wristwatch. "It's just after eleven now. You want to meet somewhere about two?"

"Fine with me." Carol swung open her car door. "How about meeting at Strawbridge's?" She grinned. "I can walk there from my place."

"Okay," Kate agreed, opening her own door. "I know of a parking garage not far from there. And then I can run you home after we've had dinner."

"Deal. See you later." Carol slid into the car and let out a yelp and a few choice curses. "Good grief, it's like a blast furnace in here!"

"So what?" Kate laughed. "You're already hot and sweaty."

"Cute." Slamming the door, Carol fired the motor and took off.

Still laughing, Kate followed in Carol's wake off the lot, but at a more sedate speed.

The house was deliciously cool, and amazingly quiet, considering that it was lunchtime.

"Hello," Kate called, dropping her car keys on to the foyer table. "I'm home."

Her greeting met with silence. Frowning, she strode along the hallway to the kitchen.

Her back to the kitchen doorway, Helen was standing at the sink, rinsing romaine lettuce leaves.

"Hello," Kate called.

Yelping, Helen spun around, spraying droplets of water everywhere. "Oh, Kate," she said, frowning at the water dripping onto the floor. "With the water running, I didn't hear you come in."

"I'm sorry," Kate said, quickly crossing to the sink and turning off the water. "I didn't mean to startle you." A smile tugged at her lips as she pulled a stream of paper towels from the roll next to the sink. "I'll mop up; you finish what you were doing."

"I think I've finished rinsing the lettuce," Helen said wryly, turning to shake the leaves.

After wiping down the front of the cabinet, Kate mopped up the small puddles on the floor. "It's so quiet in here," she said, tossing the sodden towels in the trash. "Where are the kids? Have they had lunch already?"

Helen was shaking her head, and slicing a tomato at the same time. "It'll just be you and me for lunch. Connie was invited for a backyard picnic at her friend Megan's house, and Mandy is having lunch with Mrs. Winston."

Winston.

Ethan.

Kate swallowed a groan of despair. Would the day ever come when she wouldn't automatically ache for him at the mere mention of the Winston name?

"It seems Mandy's over at the Winstons's a lot," she said, ignoring the ache. "I hope she isn't making a pest of herself."

"A pest?" Helen looked surprised. "Not at all. Virginia Winston told me how much she enjoys Mandy's company." She smiled softly. "She said she misses having a young person around the house since Sharon and Ethan have grown up."

Ethan. Ethan. Ethan.

Damn.

"Well, okay, then," Kate said, turning away to conceal her moody expression. "I'm going to grab a shower before I eat. I'm all hot and sweaty from exercising." Not to mention all hot and aggravated by her own weakness.

"Take your time," Helen said, waving her out with a flick of a hand. "I've still got to put together the salad. It's chicken Caesar, okay?"

"Fine," Kate answered, dashing along the hallway and up the stairs to her room.

After a long stinging hot shower to sluice the sweat from the surface of her skin, Kate stood beneath a biting cold spray to freeze the aching needy feeling of her body.

Kate thoroughly enjoyed her salad and iced tea lunch, very likely because it was serenely quiet without the girls at the table chattering away. Kate and Helen were allowed the rare opportunity to talk without being interrupted—and a certain name did not come up again in conversation.

"I've gotta run," she said, glancing at the kitchen clock as she carried her dish, utensils, and glass to the sink.

"So run," Helen ordered, shooing her away.

"You did remember that I won't be home for dinner?" Kate absently asked, rooting in her bag for her car keys. "Where the heck are those darned keys?"

Helen rolled her eyes. "Yes, I did remember . . . and try the foyer table, it's where you usually toss them."

"Right. See you. I won't be home late." Grinning, Kate strolled along the hall, scooped her keys from the small table, and left the house.

"Coffee, coffee, I need a shot of caffeine," Carol wailed, groaning in an exaggerated manner as she lugged the two shopping bags. "Or maybe even something stronger, more potent, with a kick."

"I need to sit down," Kate countered, equally laden with two bulging bags. "And eat."

"That, too," Carol agreed, frowning as she glanced around the parking area. "Where the hell's the car?"

Kate laughed. "About ten feet in front of your nose."

"Goodie." Carol tossed a grin at her. "I was afraid you'd forgotten where you parked it."

"No." With a shake of her head, Kate set down the bags and unlocked the trunk. "I never forget where I park the car." She stashed her bags next to where Carol shoved hers. "It's the keys I usually misplace."

"Great." Carol looked horrified. "Don't even . . ."

Kate silenced her by raising a hand and jangling the keys in front of her face.

The interior of the car was like an oven.

"I'd complain . . . ," Carol began.

"So what else is new?"

"But I'm too grateful to sit down to complain," she calmly went on.

"Good." Smiling, Kate switched on the ignition and then the air conditioner. "It won't take long for the cool air to kick in. Where do you want to go for dinner?"

"I don't know." Carol moved her shoulders in a lazy shrug. "What are you hungry for?"

"Well, I know we've been watching our diets but . . ." Her smile grew into a grin. "I'd love some pizza."

"Now you're talkin'." Carol grinned back. "I know a small shop where they make the best pizza." She raised her eyebrows. "Why don't we go to my place, order one for delivery, and just kick back and relax?"

"You know, Carol," Kate said, sounding and looking solemn and serious, "there are times I think you are absolutely brilliant."

"Yeah, I know, but I can't help it."

"I'm stuffed." Kate sighed and relaxed against the wooden ladder-back kitchen chair.

A couple of pieces of pizza crust and a hint of the lingering aroma were all that was left of the large pie.

"And me." Carol echoed the sigh. "Didn't I tell you they make the best pizza."

"You didn't exaggerate."

"I never exaggerate."

"Of course not." Kate's tone was droll.

Carol moved one eyebrow in a "who cares" manner.

Laughing, Kate pushed back her chair, stood, and began clearing the small table that crowded the small room. She held up a hand when Carol moved to help. "I'll do it . . . if you make a pot of coffee."

"Sure."

Sharing a smile, they got busy, chatting as they worked.

"Did you get back in time to have drinks with your friend Saturday evening?" Kate asked, as she collected and dumped the paper plates and napkins and stiff pizza box in the trash.

"Yeah, he waited for me to get there before ordering," Carol answered, preparing the automatic coffee maker.

"That was thoughtful of him," Kate said, tossing the two empty diet soda cans in the recycle bin. "I know you said he's just a guy you know, a friend, no one special, but is there something stirring between you two, something that you don't want to talk about?''

In the process of rinsing and stashing their glasses in the dishwasher, Carol made a rude noise and tossed a "get-real" look at Kate. "Nothing stirring, not even a mouse," she quipped, moving to wipe the table and countertop. "He's a nice guy—name's Bob, by the way—but he doesn't light my fire . . . or cause any sparks, if you know what I mean.''

Kate knew precisely what Carol meant. Jason didn't light fires or cause sparks in her, either. Only one man had ever managed that sensual feat, and his fire . . .

Forget it.

Pushing away the memories and his image, Kate launched into a rehash of the bargains she had found during their breakneck shopping spree.

Minutes later, steaming cups of coffee in hand, they settled in Carol's living room, which wasn't much bigger than the kitchen. Carol dropped into a big, deeply cushioned chair, which though worn, looked as comfortable as an old friend.

Kate curled up into the corner of a loveseat that actually looked newer but was every bit as cushiony and comfortable.

It was the first time Kate had been to her friend's apartment, and she looked around with curious interest. Though clean, the place was cluttered. The furniture bordered on shabby. Still, she liked it, and said as much.

"This is nice, homey."

"Thanks." Carol skimmed a glance around. "It's cramped, but it's home." She didn't make excuses for the shabby furniture or the clutter of books and magazines stacked in piles on the coffee table and the floor. "I came into town and went apartment hunting after I got hired by the school," she said.

Kate looked at her in surprise. "You came to town? I thought you were from Philadelphia."

"No." Carol shook her head. "I was born in Hamburg, a small town north of here. I earned my teaching certificate at Kutztown State."

"I've heard of Kutztown State," Kate said, but went on to confess, "but I've never heard of Hamburg . . ." She grinned. "Except, of course, for the one in Germany."

"That's okay, I'm sure a lot of people never heard of it." She shrugged. "Doesn't matter . . . but it's a nice little town . . . if you like little towns."

"And you don't?"

"Don't misunderstand me, I like it. All my family and old friends are there." She sighed. "Maybe I saw too many movies or something when I was a kid, but . . . it's just that, for years I've thought it'd be cool to live in a big city. I didn't even bother looking for a place closer to the school."

"And you like it . . . living in the city, I mean?"

"Like it? I love it!" Carol exclaimed. "It's everything I dreamed it would be." She made a dismissive hand gesture. "Oh, sure, it's got its mean streets, looking like war zones with broken buildings and abandoned cars. And it's got crime, drugs, and other

junk all big cities have. But it also has great restau-
rants, museums, theaters, not to mention the Avenue
of the Arts, the zoo, the sports and entertainment
stadiums and venues.''

"I know, I live here, too, remember?" Kate said.

Carol made a face at her. "It's not the same, there
in the high rent district where you live . . . and we
work. It's more suburban than city, and you know
it."

"Well, yes," Kate conceded. "But I didn't always
live there. I lived here in the city until my mother
married David, when I was eleven."

"And you don't miss it, the energy, the rhythm that
flows through the city?"

"No." Kate shook her head. "Although I do
appreciate and take advantage of everything the city
has to offer, I prefer living right where I do."

"Well, David's house is beautiful, set in the middle
of that big yard, with all the flowers and trees," Carol
allowed. "But it's so quiet, pretty much like the area
where I grew up," she said, shrugging. "And that's
too quiet for me." She arched her eyebrows. "Don't
you ever yearn for a little action and excitement in
your life?"

"Not at all. I like my life quiet and peaceful." Kate
sighed, recalling those weeks with Ethan, the action,
the excitement . . . the spirit crushing aftermath. "I'll
stay right where I am, thank you."

"You're too young to bury yourself in quiet and
peaceful." Carol grimaced. "All you ever find there
are the dull and boring Jasons of this world."

"That's not true," Kate protested.

"You're right," Carol admitted, her expression thoughtful, a spark of interest flaring in her eyes. "Your former neighbor, that delicious looking Ethan Winston, comes from that world, doesn't he?"

Ethan. Kate swallowed a groan. Always Ethan.

"That's not what I meant," she said, a little too sharply. "I wasn't referring to Ethan."

"I know." Carol shook her head. "I was. Now, he's exciting. How could you have lived right next door to him all this time and not have made a play for him?"

"I don't make plays for men," Kate said. "Besides, since the day I arrived there, Ethan has been the boy next door, my friend, my best friend."

"I hate to be the one to tell you this, but your best friend Ethan is no longer a boy, far from it, in fact. He's a man, a man, moreover, who exudes sexuality."

As if she didn't know that better than most, Kate thought, quivering inside from the vivid memory of his sexuality.

"We were discussing Jason," she reminded the other woman, desperate to steer Carol away from the subject of Ethan. "And what I meant was that it's not true that Jason is dull and boring."

Carol rolled her eyes. "Boy, if you honestly believe that, you have been stuck in the fringe-boonies too long."

"Really, Carol, I don't understand your contempt of Jason," Kate said impatiently. "He's attractive, pleasant and a genuinely nice man."

"He's a wimp," she said sarcastically, sneering. "Matter-of-fact, I've often wondered if he was gay."

"Gay?" Kate stared at her, partly in amazement, partly in amusement at the remark, comparable in both manner and tone to Jason's recent insinuation about Carol. "I think I can assure you that he is not gay."

"You've had sex with him?"

"Of course not." Though Kate didn't know why, she was shocked by the blunt question. Carol had never before asked her anything of an intimate, personal nature.

Carol gave her a superior look. "Why not?"

"Why?" she repeated, unable to believe Carol was persisting in this vein. "Because Jason and I do not share that kind of relationship," she answered defensively.

"How thrilling," Carol drawled. "May I ask what kind of relationship you do share?"

Kate was tempted not to answer, but then, she figured, what difference did it make? "Jason and I are friends. We have a lot in common, and enjoy many of the same things."

"Friends," Carol muttered, shaking her head. "I don't get it. You're also just friends, albeit best friends, with the boy next door—the boy I might add who grew into one sexy and great-looking man."

"Looks aren't everything," Kate inserted, silently acknowledging the truth of Carol's statement.

"Maybe so," Carol laughed, then shrugged. "But the fact is, physical attractiveness is the first thing noticed between the sexes."

"I know that," Kate said impatiently, asking herself

why she had allowed herself to be drawn into this discussion. "And Jason is an attractive man."

"And a wimp."

"I don't understand you at all, Carol," Kate exclaimed. "You say Jason's a wimp, and Bob, the man you had drinks with Saturday evening is okay, but doesn't cause sparks or light fires. What are you looking for in a man?" she asked in exasperation.

Carol went stone still, a faraway look in her eyes.

Appalled at herself for prying into her friend's personal life, Kate was on the point of apologizing when Carol focused on her and smiled.

"Growing up in a small town, there's really not an awful lot to do," she said in a musing tone. "So my friends and I watched a lot of TV and rented a lot of videos, new and old. I liked the Western and action adventure movies. My favorites were John Wayne and Clint Eastwood in the older films, and Harrison Ford and Mel Gibson in the later ones." She paused a moment, frowned. "There were a few others, but not many, and I can't think of their names offhand."

Feeling as though she had missed something in Carol's rambling statement, yet positive she had heard and comprehended every word, Kate stared at her, perplexed, waiting for Carol to continue, explain.

She didn't. All she said was, "Sean Connery was pretty good, too. Wasn't he?"

Kate threw up her hands. "Wasn't he what? Carol, I haven't a clue what you're talking about."

"A hero." Carol's tone and expression suggested the answer was obvious. "You asked me what I was looking for in a man. Didn't you? Well, I'm looking for more than any man, any lover. I'm looking for a hero."

A hero. Incredible.

Kate was still marveling over Carol's startling pronouncement an hour or so later as she drove home in the summer dusk.

Imagine, the sarcastic, cynical, sometimes profane Carol, a romantic at heart.

It boggled the mind.

It tugged at the heart.

For Kate, the tug was painful, because it was so reminiscent of her own feelings and longings, when she was young, several months ago.

Of course, at the time, she had believed she had found her hero, right next door. Ethan had never been just any man. And she could testify that he was more, much more than just any lover. Problem was, her next door hero had turned out to be as insubstantial as any fictional screen hero.

Kate honestly hoped that Carol would eventually find her hero, but just as honestly, and more realistically, feared she would not. In her newly pessimistic opinion—other than knights of war and self-sacrificing heroes—the type Carol had set her hopes on were rare, if they existed at all.

It was a bitter reality to face, Kate thought. But one had to grow up sometime.

But, damn, it hurts, she admitted, soon distracted as she steered her new compact around David's much larger car parked in the driveway at home.

Young, carefree laughter greeted Kate as she entered the house. The sound lifted her low spirits. Smiling, she set her shopping bags to one side out of the way, then followed the sound to its source in the kitchen.

Jabbering away between bouts of the giggles, Mandy and Connie were busily engaged in creating banana splits from an array of ingredients cluttering the table.

Helen stood by the sink, a silent observer, an indulgent smile on her lips.

"I don't want pineapple sauce," Mandy yelped, catching her sister just in time from dropping a blob of the stuff onto a dip of vanilla ice cream in her dish.

"How can you make a real banana split without pineapple sauce?" Connie asked, dumping the sauce onto the ice cream in her own dish.

"Is there some rule that says you must have pineapple sauce on a banana split?" Mandy demanded, pausing in the act of shaking a whipped cream container.

Spying Kate standing in the doorway, Helen grinned and rolled her eyes.

Kate laughed, drawing the girls' attention.

"Hi, Kate," Mandy said. "Want a banana split?"

"With pineapple sauce?" Connie chimed in.

"No, thank you," Kate said, eyeing the gooey concoctions the girls were preparing, and the mess on the table. "I'm still full from dinner."

"This is our dinner," Mandy said, proceeding to squirt a mound of whipped cream all over the three dips of ice cream in her dish.

"Really?" Kate raised her eyebrows at Helen.

She shrugged. "Neither one of them wanted dinner. I thought the banana splits would be all right, as they both said they'd been eating all day."

"Something nourishing, I hope."

At the tinge of sternness in her sister's voice, Connie grabbed hold of her dish, as if afraid Kate would whisk it away from her. "I did," she said. "I had all kinds of good stuff at Megan's house. Her dad cooked hamburgers and shrimp on the grill, and her mother baked potatoes and made a big salad with a whole bunch of vegetables in it."

"And Mrs. Winston cooked a huge lunch for us," Mandy piped in. "We had salad, too, and roasted potatoes, and broiled chicken breasts in lemon sauce. It was yummy. I ate so much I wasn't hungry for dinner."

"Me neither," Connie agreed.

"Well, in that case," Kate said, "I guess the banana splits are okay."

"Yes!" the girls chorused in unison.

"But you will clean up this mess after you've finished eating," she command.

"Sure," Mandy said.

"Of course," Connie mumbled around the glob of ice cream she had spooned into her mouth.

Sharing an amused look with Helen, Kate asked, "Is there any iced tea?"

"Yes." Helen nodded. "Sit down, I'll get it."

"No, you sit down," Kate ordered, crossing to the refrigerator. "I'll get it. Do you want some?"

"Yes, thank you." Helen pulled out a chair and sat down. "How was the shopping trip?"

"Exhausting." She laughed, pouring out two glasses of tea. She added ice and sat down next to Helen. "And I spent way too much money."

"You did cash the check David gave you, didn't you?" Helen asked sharply.

"Yes." She flashed an impish smile. "And I spent every dollar of it." Her smile faded. "Where is David? Has he had dinner?"

"Yes." Helen took a quick sip of tea. "He and I ate dinner about an hour ago. I think he's in his office. He said he brought some paperwork home with him."

"How is he?" Kate murmured, too softly for the girls to hear over their banter.

"He seems fine," Helen answered in a similar tone. "And for once he ate well, didn't just pick at his food. Kept up a conversation through dinner, too."

Somewhat relieved, Kate took a deep, thirst-quenching swallow. It felt good, right, sitting with her family. This was real, she thought, taking another swallow of the cold tea. This was life, the day-to-day ups and downs, the give and take of reality. No legendary heroes and heroines here, just everyday people, doing the best they can.

"That was sooo good."

Drawn from introspection, Kate glanced at Connie, smiling at the smear of chocolate rimming her lips. "Everything you eat looks good on you, honey, even the chocolate around your mouth," she observed dryly.

Grinning, Connie reached for her napkin.

"Mrs. Winston is really excited," Mandy confided, rising to begin clearing the table. "She was smiling and humming to herself off and on all day." She paused for effect before adding, "And I'm excited, too."

"What about?" Kate asked, exchanging a puzzled look with Helen.

"Yeah, what about?" Connie echoed with eager curiosity.

"They're gonna have a baby."

"The Winstons are going to have a baby?" Kate blurted out in shocked disbelief.

"Hey, neat," Connie chirped, clapping her hands. "When?"

"In January."

"I don't believe it," Helen exclaimed. "Virginia Winston!"

"No. No." Mandy shook her head. "She's not having the baby; she's going to be a grandmother."

Sharon? Kate thought. The idea of Sharon being pregnant was almost as shocking as Virginia Winston being pregnant. Sharon had made it clear to everyone that she wanted a career first, and children at some distant date in the future.

"That's wonderful," Helen said. "But who is having the baby. Sharon?"

"No, not Sharon." Mandy shook her head again. "Paula and Ethan."

CHAPTER ELEVEN

A chill permeated Kate's being, and she felt hollow, as if the bottom had dropped out from beneath her.

Standing at the far corner of the patio, arms wrapped around her midriff, Kate stared into the darkness and listened to the night noises of the summer insects.

Ethan.

Eyes hot from unshed tears, Kate blinked and raised one arm, bringing the hand holding a cigarette to her lips. She drew deeply, grimacing at the acrid taste.

Kate really didn't want the smoke; she needed it, needed its soothing effects to calm the riot of emotions churning sickeningly inside her.

Hours had passed since Mandy had made her neighborhood news delivery. Hours that to Kate seemed endless with the ongoing discussion about the anticipated birth of Paula and Ethan's baby.

For awhile, after the banana split ice cream, sauces, and dishes had been cleared away and the kitchen set in order, Kate had distracted the girls by producing the surprise packages she had bought for them while shopping.

But once the excitement of new, wildly patterned tank tops, shorts, and flower decorated flip-flops had worn off, they trooped en masse to the patio. Thinking the subject of the prospective baby had finally been exhausted, Kate breathed a sigh of relief.

It was short-lived, as David joined them on the patio and, naturally, the girls eagerly launched into a full repeat of the exciting news. But, thankfully, they eventually ran out of words and energy.

"Time for bed," Helen at last decided, noting the telltale signs of their lagging energy. "And time for one of my favorite TV programs."

Good nights were exchanged, and Helen herded the girls into the house and up the stairs.

"I'm for bed, too." Chuckling, David got to his feet. "You know, from the girls' excitement, you'd think this baby was due to arrive any minute, rather than months from now. And I'm sure we haven't heard the last of it."

"Yes." Somehow, Kate managed to smile, cringing inside at the certainty that Mandy would dutifully relay every tidbit of information she received from Virginia Winston concerning the progress of Paula's pregnancy.

Fighting tears, and despising herself for still caring so much for Ethan that she actually felt devastated by Mandy's news, Kate remained on the darkening patio, waiting until all was quiet inside. When she felt certain the others were asleep, she crept into the foyer to retrieve the mangled package of cigarettes from the bottom of her purse. Then she went into the patio.

The cigarettes were bent and stale. Making a face, Kate nevertheless straightened one, lit it, and took a deep drag. The smoke burned her tongue and her throat and made her cough. So she took another drag.

And now she was on her second cigarette.

A record for her, Kate thought with dark, cynical humor. Never before had she chain-smoked two cigarettes.

Damn Ethan.

No. Kate shook her head and crushed the half-smoked butt beneath her sandal.

Damn her weakness, her longing and desire for a man who had so ardently made love to her, gave her a taste of ecstasy, only to snatch it away, rejecting her and the unconditional love she yearned to offer him.

Of course, she knew they were having sex, but ever since the night of his wedding, when she had so vividly visualized Ethan and Paula entwined in a passionate lovers' embrace, Kate had closed her mind to any and all thoughts of them together in an intimate way.

But, while she managed to maintain rigid control over her conscious thoughts, her unconscious took wild and erotic flights of fantasy during sleep. There were nights when Kate dreamed he was there, making sweet and hot love to her, filling the hollow spaces in her body and her heart.

She'd wake, her face wet with tears, her body trembling and unfulfilled, her womb empty.

She had wanted his baby.

He had conceived a child with another woman.

Served her right for making a hero out of a mere man, Kate chastised herself.

Drawing a deep breath, she pulled a tissue from her skirt pocket, wet it with her tongue, and crouching, picked up the two flattened butts. With the damp tissue she wiped away any evidence of her cigarettes.

Standing, she wrapped the butts in the still damp tissue and tossed it into the trash. Drawing the crumpled cigarette pack from her other pocket, she hesitated an instant, then tossed that into the trash, too.

Straightening her shoulders, Kate decided it time to give up her dependence on the cigarettes, no matter how seldom she indulged, and it was long past time for her to stop obsessing over Ethan Winston.

Kate was well aware that her biological clock was running, ticking away the minutes of her reproductive life. She longed for children of her own, a family of her own.

Perhaps with Jason? The thought popped into her head unbidden.

Jason?

Kate considered the possibility as she slowly entered the house and secured the locks for the night.

Jason, she mused, mounting the stairs to her room.

As Kate had repeatedly assured Carol, she genuinely liked Jason. He was interesting and she enjoyed his company, his sense of humor, his thoughtfulness.

Yes, perhaps with Jason, Kate mused on. It was an idea worth serious but prudent consideration.

The long days of summer wore on.

Kate accepted more frequent dates with Jason, laughing off Carol's predictable ridicule.

Then the Fourth of July holiday loomed large in Kate's mind. Traditionally, her family had shared a backyard celebration of the holiday with the Winstons. This year was to be no exception. Even though David told her Jason was welcome to join the gathering, Kate did not want to attend.

Unknowingly, Carol came to her rescue by inviting Kate to spend the holiday with her and her family at the house they had rented in Ocean City, New Jersey.

Kate accepted at once, grateful for the excuse to avoid the misery of spending the day in Ethan's company.

She had a great time with Carol at the shore. It was hot, and they lazed away the days on the beach, laughing as they judged the attractiveness—or the lack thereof—of the males in their immediate vicinity.

"Check it out," Carol murmured their first day at the beach, indicating a bronzed lifeguard. "He can save me any day of the week."

"Not bad," Kate agreed, shading her eyes against the glare of sunlight on the sand bouncing off the ocean as she aimed for a better look at the man. "But, boy, does he know it."

"Yeah." Nodding, Carol dismissed the guard and glanced around for other likely candidates, many of whom were casting speculative glances at her and Kate.

By their third and last day on the beach, they gave up on the males.

"Why does it seem that the best-looking guys are either married, gay or, like our Adonis lifeguard, so taken with themselves that they hardly notice anyone else?" Carol grumbled.

"You're asking me?" Kate replied, laughing at Carol's disgruntled expression.

"Are you the one sitting next to me here?" Carol replied. "And what's so funny?"

"You." Kate composed herself, except for an errant smile teasing her lips. "What were you expecting? To meet Prince Charming in swim trunks, be swept off your feet and fall madly in love, swept into a whirlwind courtship, all in a three-day stay at the shore?"

"Could happen," Carol said.

"Oh, sure," Kate agreed. "In the movies, on a television sitcom or," she picked up and flourished the historical romance paperback Carol had brought to the beach with her, "in a romance novel."

"Hey, I like romance novels," Carol protested, snatching the book from Kate's fingers.

"So do I." Kate displayed her own contemporary romance paperback. "They're terrific, a great way to escape and relax. But I'm certainly not going to go through life expecting to live the fantasy of suddenly tripping over a dynamic and handsome Mr. Right who'll make all my wildest dreams come true."

"Yeah, well," Carol drawled, obviously unimpressed by her friend's speech. "But you know me, the woman waiting for her hero."

"Yeah, well," Kate drawled back at her, blaming the anchovies in her lunch salad for the sudden burning sensation in her stomach. "Lots'a luck, friend . . . but I'm afraid the only heroes you're ever going to trip over are the ones you read about in these books."

"Boy, and I thought *I* was cynical," Carol chided, settling comfortably on the beach blanket and opening her book.

Kate shook her head in denial. "I'm not cynical, just realistic," she said, opening her own book and wishing she had kept her mouth shut, and her memories of a certain former hero shut away in the back of her mind. Darn it, why couldn't it be thoughts of Jason teasing her?

In the evenings they strolled the boardwalk. Agreeing to forget their diets until after the holiday, they gleefully feasted on pizza, cheese steak sandwiches, boardwalk fries, and double scoops of swirled vanilla frozen custard and orange sherbert. They balanced it all out by having salads and fresh fruit cups at lunchtime.

On their last evening, Kate, who was already showered, dressed, and ready to leave for their final stroll on the boardwalk entered the bedroom she shared with Carol to see what was taking the other woman so long to get ready. She found her standing in front of the dresser mirror, brush in hand, trying to smooth her hair and cursing the heat and high humidity.

"What's the problem?" Kate asked, noticing the ends of Carol's silky ear-length bob flipping up.

"I'm having a bad hair day," Carol muttered.

"Only one day?" Kate shifted her gaze to the mirror, to her own unruly mass of long curls cascading in a ponytail from the crown of her head. "I've had a bad hair life."

Carol laughed. "That red mop of yours does tend to frizz, doesn't it?"

"It's always been fuzzy." Kate laughed with her, hiding a pang of sadness, and swallowing a groan as a certain image rose to fill her mind; it had been a long time since she'd heard the word fuzzy, recalling how she had been called Miss Fuzzywig.

She spun away from the mirror.

Other than having those occasional disturbing memories, it was a wonderful three-day getaway.

Kate returned home relaxed, sunburned, and feeling at least five pounds heavier than when she left. She didn't even have to listen to Mandy and Connie regale her with an update on Paula's condition when they rehashed the holiday gathering for her, as Paula and Ethan had not been there. According to Mandy, via Virginia Winston, Paula was not feeling up to tolerating the heat and humidity, so they had decided to stay home.

"That's too bad," Kate murmured, thinking that if she had any luck at all, it would remain hot and humid for the rest of the summer, immediately feeling guilty for the unkind thought.

Time to get really serious about serious considerations regarding a possible future with Jason, Kate told herself, especially as she had a dinner and movie date with him next Saturday.

CHAPTER TWELVE

"Well, see you later," Carol said Saturday morning after exercise class. She wiped the sweat beading her brow with the corner of the towel draped around her neck. "And have a good time tonight with the wimp . . . if you can."

"Thanks . . . I guess." Kate shook her head, not even bothering to chide her for her derogatory crack about Jason.

Carol shrugged, unlocked her car door, and taunted, "Then you're a lot more tolerant of bores than I am."

"Goodbye, Carol," Kate said, gasping as she slid onto the hot leather seat behind the wheel in the stifling hot car. "Wow, it's like an oven in here. I should have folded my towel onto this seat."

"Thanks for the heads-up," Carol called. "Talk to you later. Ciao."

Feeling overheated, in need of a shower, and a little annoyed by Carol's continuing ridicule of her association with Jason, Kate fired the engine and took off like the proverbial bat. It was the first time since they had started working out together at the gym that she beat Carol off the lot.

Kate cleaned up, cooled off and calmed down by the time Jason arrived to pick her up.

To lift her spirits, she pulled three outfits from her closet before selecting an underskirt in a silky flowing fabric of sea-mist green with a sheer overskirt in aquamarine, and a sleeveless, loose overblouse the same sea-mist shade as the underskirt. She took extra care in applying her makeup, bemoaning the fact that it required a lot of work to look natural and glowing. Last, but never least, she smoothed her hair enough to work the mass into a reasonably tamed twist at the back of her head.

But the extra time and effort paid off.

"You look terrific . . . even with the touch of sunburn." Jason's tone held a note of teasing, but his gleaming eyes were bright as he took note of her careful, attractive appearance.

"Thank you, kind sir," Kate teased back, her spirits further buoyed by his compliment.

"So, how was it down at the shore?" Jason arched his brows questioningly as they strolled to his car, a sensible, mid-sized, mid-priced, two-year-old sedan.

"Hot, sticky, sandy, noisy, and a lot of fun," she

said, laughing as he gallantly opened the car door for her.

"It's supposed to be hot, sticky, sandy, and noisy," he said, laughing with her as he circled the car and slid into the driver's seat. "On second thought, I could do without sticky," he amended. "I can do without the high humidity and hot breezes from inland instead of off the ocean." Starting the car, he slowly backed out of the driveway.

"And me." Grimacing, Kate touched her hair. "Sticky humidity freaks out my hair."

"Hey, I like your hair." He grinned. "Even when it is freaky."

Miss Fuzzywig.

No. *Stop it. Forget it.*

Forget him.

Kate gritted her teeth and did her best to grin back. "Trust me, if this mop was on your head, you'd hate it."

"No . . . I'd have it cut." He slanted a sparkling look at her, quickly returning his gaze to the road. "Or shaved."

Kate burst out laughing. "Now, there's a thought. Maybe I should consider it."

"Make a fashion statement," he urged.

"Start a trend," she said.

"Do your own thing."

"Set a militant example," she cried, nearly choking on her laughter.

It was pure silliness, but it was great fun, and it set the mood for the evening.

They kept up the nonsensical banter all the way to

the restaurant, and through dinner, but on a more subdued level. At one point, midway through the meal, Kate was startled by the sudden realization of how similar their bantering was to the conversations she and Carol often shared.

Jason was revealing a new and pleasantly surprising facet of his personality, a quirky sense of humor not unlike Carol's—when she wasn't being bitchy and cynical.

So why, she couldn't help but wonder, couldn't her two friends get along with each other?

Dismissing the thought, Kate concentrated on Jason, and on having an enjoyable evening.

She certainly enjoyed the movie, a romantic comedy with an improbable plot but a lot of funny lines. And if his laughter was a true measure, so did Jason.

"How about something to drink?" Jason suggested as they exited the suburban multiplex located some five or so miles from the restaurant.

"Fine," Kate agreed, almost gasping at the sudden humid heat after the coolness of the air conditioned theater. "Where would you like to go?"

"We could drive into town to one of the jazz clubs."

Kate thought about it for a moment, then shook her head. "I'm really not in the mood for a noisy club tonight. Why don't we just go to that neighborhood tavern not too far from home?" She smiled. "It's quiet there, we can relax, have a drink and talk."

"Suits me." He started the car, hesitated, and gave her a curious look. "Is that the place that serves those great potato skins and hot peppers?"

"Jason, after the big dinner you ate," she said chid-

ingly, "not to mention the enormous bucket of pop-
corn you wolfed down during the movie. You can't
possibly be hungry."

"Sure I can." He grinned. "I'm a growing boy."

Hmm, some boy near thirty, Kate thought. Wondering how he managed to consume so much food and
still stay so slim, she said, "If you continue to pack
the food away like this evening, you'll be growing
around the middle."

"No I won't," he replied with supreme confidence,
driving into the tavern parking lot. Killing the engine,
he turned to smile at her. "You see, I run every morning, and work out in a gym three days a week."

"Do you?" Kate said, opening the door and getting
out of the car before he could circle to play the gallant
gentleman. They headed for the tavern. "So do I."

"So do you what . . . run every morning or work
out in a gym?" he asked, opening the entrance door
for her.

"Work out in a gym," she answered, smiling her
thanks as he held a chair for her at a corner table.
She gave him the name of the gym. "I meet Carol
there three times a week, and we work out together."

He grimaced. "How exciting for you." He smiled
for the waitress who came to a stop at their table.

Kate ordered a diet cola.

Jason ordered a draft beer, potato skins and hot
peppers. He grimaced again as soon as the waitress
turned away. "It must be real fun working out with
old acid mouth."

"Jason, really, I don't understand this antagonism
between you and . . . ," Kate began in exasperation.

"Look, forget it," he interrupted her. "Carol just rubs me the wrong way, so let's leave it at that. We were having a good time, and I don't want to ruin it now. Okay?"

"Okay," Kate agreed, conceding his point. They had had a fun time, so why spoil it?

They chatted for a while, Jason asking her what kind of exercises she was doing, Kate asking him how many miles he ran a day. General stuff. The waitress then set a large plate piled full of potatoes and peppers and she went back to chiding him about the amount of food he was packing away.

But the food did smell good, so she helped herself to a fair sized portion of it, in an act of pure altruism, of course, to keep him from getting fat.

It was late when Jason brought Kate home. The house was dark, everyone obviously in bed.

While she dug her key from her purse, Kate considered inviting him in . . . and immediately reconsidered. She trusted Jason, he was a decent guy. But he was a guy, nevertheless, and she didn't relish the possibility, no matter how remote, of having to fight him off in defense of her honor . . . tarnished as it might be.

Kate said good night at the patio doors, as she always did.

Bending his head, Jason took her in his arms and kissed her, as he always did.

And, as always, it was a nice kiss, gentle, undemanding, and not in the least exciting.

Too bad, Kate thought, smothering a sigh as he lifted his head, released her, and stepped back.

"It was fun." He smiled.

"Yes, for me, too." She smiled back.

"I'll call you." He raised his eyebrows. "One night next week?"

"Any night. I have nothing planned."

He hesitated, as if unsure whether to stay or go. "Okay. Good night, Kate. Go on in, I'll wait until you're safely inside."

Whispering another good night, Kate unlocked the door and slipped inside. Too bad, she thought once more, watching him cross the patio, and wishing his kisses stirred her, aroused her, if only a little bit.

Through the following weeks, Kate went out with Jason whenever he called. He called a lot.

The days of July dwindled.

David began taking the new antidepressant, and started the series of tests his doctor prescribed.

Mandy and Connie prepared to go off to summer camp for two weeks. Excited, their shrill voices ringing through the house, they ran around, practically in circles, gathering the stuff they needed to take with them.

David dealt with the upheaval with equanimity . . . a clear indication that the new drug was effective.

By the time they finally left, Kate, David, and Helen all felt as if they had been running around in circles. Looking frazzled, Helen poured out glasses of iced tea, dropped into a kitchen chair, heaved a deep sigh, and shifted a glance from David to Kate.

"I thought they'd never get out of here."

Both Kate and David laughed in perfect understanding, and agreement.

Two days later, Helen complained, "It's too darned quiet in here."

They made a small dinner party the day David learned the results of his tests.

"Other than a few minor problems, Doc Jenkins said everything looks good," he announced.

"I'm so relieved," Kate said, not until that moment fully realizing how very concerned she had been.

"That's wonderful, David." Helen pulled her head out of the fridge to frown at him and demanded, "What problems?"

David rolled his eyes at Kate. "My cholesterol and triglyceride numbers are a little high and, it appears, there's a small blockage in one of my arteries."

"That's minor?" Kate interjected.

"I don't think so!" Helen exclaimed.

David held up his hands. "Calm down. Everything's under control. The doctor prescribed medication to treat both conditions. In fact, he said he already called the prescriptions in to the pharmacy. I'll pick them up tomorrow right after work."

Kate shook her head before he'd finished speaking. "No, I'll run to the pharmacy right after dinner."

By the time Labor Day rolled around, Kate was seeing so much of Jason he was becoming a regular fixture around the house. David liked him. The girls liked him. Helen liked him.

Kate liked him, too, a lot. But, though fond of him, she was not falling in love with him, as she was beginning to suspect he was with her.

The new school year began. Though it wasn't yet officially autumn, for all intents and purposes, after the kids were back in school, summertime was over.

Football took precedence over baseball. And, even though the roses were still in gorgeous bloom, the flowers of choice were chrysanthemums in shades of rust and gold.

There was a definite improvement in David. Kate gave silent thanks for the medication that had finally lifted his spirits from the depth of depression he had slipped into after the death of his wife, her mother.

Kate worried about David as the anniversary of Connie's birth, and Maureen's death approached, afraid the memory of that heartbreaking day might have an adverse effect on him.

She felt somewhat reassured when David gave his enthusiastic approval when Connie asked to have a birthday party exactly like Mandy's, with all her friends and classmates present. As her birthday fell on a Saturday, the party was planned for that day.

They awoke to a chilly rain the day of Connie's birthday celebration.

Soon after breakfast, each family member and Helen, wearing raincoats and carrying an umbrella in one hand and a single rose in the other, somberly got into David's car for the drive to the cemetery. They didn't linger long, just long enough to place their roses near Maureen's name marker and say their own silent individual prayer.

In the way Maureen had kept Colin's memory alive for Kate, she had kept Maureen's memory alive for her sisters. And so, even never having known their mother, Connie and Mandy shared David's and Kate's abiding loss.

The rain continued throughout the day. It didn't matter to Connie, since the arrangements had been made for an indoor party, anyway, just in case the mild autumn weather suddenly did turn rainy and cool.

Kate, Helen, David, and Mandy were kept busy handing out prizes for the party games, serving the food and collecting the wrappings from the mound of gifts Connie received from her friends and classmates, as well as those she received from David, Kate, Mandy, and Helen.

When everyone's voice was raised in the birthday song, Kate and David exchanged bittersweet smiles of remembrance of the pain of losing Maureen, and the joy of gaining Connie.

The laughter of the afternoon celebration balanced the sorrow of the morning ritual. And, after eleven years, the pain was not quite as sharp.

As in the previous school year, Kate again found herself playing buffer between Jason and Carol. Somehow, over the summer months, the amusement of the situation had faded. There were instances when, feeling yanked in different directions by her friend and her . . . male friend, Kate increasingly felt sorely tempted to tell them both to grow up and behave like adults.

Kate did no such thing, of course. But there were times when she willfully ignored the two of them.

Then, Kate got what she hoped and prayed was a brilliant idea. Maybe, just maybe, if she brought the antagonists together in a social situation where they would be forced to conduct themselves with cordiality, they might each discover that the other wasn't so offensive, after all.

With David's permission, Kate invited both Jason and Carol to the house for Thanksgiving dinner.

"I'd love to. Thank you." Jason accepted at once, adding with a laugh, "It'll be a zoo at my folks' house. Besides my brother, his wife and their two kids, I believe my mother has invited a half-dozen other assorted relatives for the big holiday meal."

"Sorry, but thanks anyway," Carol declined. "I'm driving home right after school lets out on Wednesday." She laughed. "My two brothers and my sister and their families will be there. Six kids altogether. It'll be fun . . . a real zoo."

Oh well, so much for that brilliant idea, Kate reflected, thinking it funny that both Jason and Carol referred to their family gatherings as a zoo.

Perhaps she could get them together sometime during the Christmas holidays, Kate mused, deciding to ask Jason and Carol about their plans.

As always, and with Kate's assistance, Helen produced a spectacular Thanksgiving feast. On the large dining room table the turkey took pride of place, surrounded by all the traditional trimmings.

"That was so good." Connie heaved a contented sigh after everyone finished eating.

"And I'm so full." Mandy fell back in her chair.

"Everything was delicious, Helen," Jason complimented. "I'm afraid I ate too much."

"Thank you," Helen said. "But I didn't do it alone. Kate did her share."

"So, you know what that means, don't you, troops?" David said, shifting a pointed look between Mandy and Connie as he pushed back his chair. "Helen and Kate prepared the meal; now we'll clear it away while they go rest."

His decree set off real groaning.

"Oh, Dad."

"Must we?"

"I ate, so I guess that means I have to help, too," Jason grumbled . . . flashing a grin at Kate.

Dismissing the women with a wave of his hand, David ordered his "troops" into action.

Knowing full well what to expect, Kate followed Helen into the living room. Hiding a smile, she strolled to the window to stare out, listening to Helen surf through the TV channels, wondering how long it would take before Helen gave up and ended the resting farce. Kate's smile grew into a grin when she heard an exasperated sigh.

"There's nothing on the tube worth watching," she grumbled. "So I might as well just go help clean up."

Laughing to herself, Kate trailed after the older woman into the kitchen.

When the cleaning was completed, Mandy and Connie took off for the living room, and the TV. David went to his office, and his lounge chair for a nap. Declaring that a nap sounded good, Helen went to the tiny sitting room in her own small suite of rooms

David had added to the house when she had agreed to make her home with them.

Kate and Jason took a long, hand-in-hand walk in the chilly late afternoon air. It was dark by the time they returned to the house.

"I'll bet Helen is already getting things out for a cold supper. And, impossible as it would seem, I am hungry. How about you?" Kate asked, reaching for the doorknob.

Jason stopped her with a tug on her other hand. "I can't stay, Kate. I promised my mother I'd put in an appearance for supper. Thank you for inviting me to spend the day with you and your family, and please convey my thanks to your father and Helen. It's been a wonderful holiday."

He kissed her good night. It was a nice kiss, friendly, warm, and pleasant.

Shivering, not from his kiss, but in the chill night air, Kate watched him walk to his car.

"Supper's on the table, Kate," Mandy called on hearing her close the front door.

"Coming." Smiling, Kate hung her coat in the foyer closet and started for the kitchen.

It was then that she realized that she and Jason had passed the Winston house, and she had caught herself only briefly wondering if Ethan and Paula were inside, spending the holiday with his parents. Kate hadn't thought much about Ethan, or wanted a cigarette, all day.

Jason was right, it had been a wonderful holiday.

CHAPTER THIRTEEN

Paula didn't look like a woman who was about to give birth, let alone a woman who was nearly a week past her due date. By carefully watching her diet, eating nourishing but low calorie foods, and taking long walks in addition to faithfully following a regimen of exercises prescribed by her gynecologist, Paula looked more like a woman in her seventh rather than her ninth month of pregnancy.

"Didn't I tell you I'd probably be late?" She gave him a smug look. "My mother was three weeks late with my brother and two-and-a-half weeks late with me."

"Yes, you did tell me," Ethan acknowledged. You told me at least ten times, he added to himself.

"Well, then," she snapped. "Why are you so edgy and uptight about my being a measly week late?"

She snapped at him a lot, always in private, of

course. When in the company of others, primarily his parents or sister, she was sweet as sugar, and to his mind, twice as sickening. But the sugar melted when they were at home alone.

She had been snappish with him from the first month of their marriage, when Ethan had refused to service her in bed. But her snappishness wasn't what had him edgy and uptight. So far as he was concerned, she could snap, snarl, pout, rant and rave and bitch at him every minute they were together. As he generally ignored her outbursts, they didn't bother him.

What did bother Ethan was a suspicion beginning to scratch at his mind and claw at his insides, the ugly suspicion that he may have allowed himself to be had, big time.

"I'm getting a little anxious, that's all," he replied with what he thought was commendable equanimity, considering that he was sorely tempted to indulge in a spate of ranting and raving himself.

Paula rolled her eyes and threw up her hands. "Oh, you're as bad as your mother, fussing over the damned date." She spat the accusation at him. "She nearly drove me to drink while she and your dad were here on Thanksgiving. Only with Virginia it's just the opposite, she's hoping I'll be early."

"It's your own fault. You're the one who said you felt sure you'd be early. And Mother's anxious to be a grandmother," he pointed out in Virginia's defense.

"I know, I know." She heaved a long-suffering sigh. "But now you've started, just because I'm almost a week late. I want to be late, and a week is no big deal." Getting up out of the deeply cushioned chair with an agility unfamiliar to most women at the end of their third trimester, she pronounced impatiently, "I'm going to bed." She started to walk away, but paused to glare at him over her stiffened shoulder. "This baby will come when it's damn good and ready."

Yeah, Ethan thought, his eyes narrowing as he watched her storm up the stairs to go to her room. She slammed the door—a little performance she played out for his benefit on a boringly regular basis.

This baby will come when it's ready, he reflected in silent agreement. But, will this baby's eventual arrival be one, two or even more weeks late?

Unable to sit still, Ethan got up and began pacing, from the living room, through the dining room, into the kitchen and back again into the living room, only to turn and repeat the course, all the while chewing on the same unpalatable thought.

Did the baby growing in Paula's womb belong to him . . . or had he bought into the oldest female con job around?

Ethan knew that it was not unusual for babies to be late. He should know . . . hadn't he read every piece of literature on pregnancy Paula had brought home from her gynecologist? He had read every word, plus some additional books on parenting and the joys of fatherhood he had picked up in a bookstore.

And yet, Ethan's suspicions weren't allayed by all his acquired knowledge, because Paula didn't look like a woman past her due date. She looked much more like a woman with a month or so to go before her due date.

Ethan felt sick at the mere thought of the possibility that Paula had lied to him about not having been with any other man for weeks before—and after—they had slept together. Still, he could barely think of anything else.

Had Paula been with another man? Yet another man to soothe her ego over the man who had rejected her? Not two months after they had slept together, of course, but possibly three or even four weeks after that night?

The only consideration that kept Ethan from confronting Paula, if not actually accusing her of deceiving him, was the fact that, originally, she had wanted to have an abortion, had insisted on having one.

He was the one who had argued against that option. And he was the one who had bargained with her for the child, proposing a limited marriage with a date certain for a divorce, and promising to take full custody of the infant.

Paula wanted a career, not motherhood.

Or so she claimed.

His mental wheels stripping gears, Ethan came to an abrupt stop midway in his third round of walking through the house, brought up short by the connotations within the thought.

He had also promised to settle a sizable sum of money on Paula to compensate for the inconvenience of carrying and giving birth to his child, and the time lost in the pursuit of her career.

And Paula wanted to pursue a career in the theater, an occupation legendary for young, hopeful thespians, usually broke, picking up work as food servers, store clerks, et cetera to keep body and soul together between acting jobs.

With a substantial financial settlement from him to tide her over, Paula wouldn't need to scrounge around for living expenses in between tryouts for parts.

Damn. Ethan grimaced. Had he allowed himself to be used, a sucker as well as a meal ticket?

Ethan didn't want to believe that Paula had so coldly and ruthlessly deceived him. And his feelings ran much deeper than the indignity of being suckered.

Rage on a short fuse flickered deep in his consciousness. He had betrayed Kate by walking away from her without so much as a hint of a reason or explanation. Because he had given Paula his vow of silence, all he could offer Kate was a mealy-mouthed excuse. If he had lost Kate, along with his bright hopes of a future with her, because of Paula's deceitful and devious machinations . . .

Ethan felt ready to explode just thinking about it.

But time would tell, he told himself, controlling his anger with the assurance. Time, and perhaps the physical appearance of the child when it finally did arrive.

Time passed, leaving November behind. They were into December. Paula went about preparing for the fast approaching holiday season without revealing a twinge of pain indicating the beginning of labor.

The first full week of December came to a close, and they were into the second week. Though he worked hard at concealing his feelings, Ethan's suspicions escalated into near certainty.

He no longer felt edgy; he felt downright nasty.

Maintaining a civil manner and tone of voice required every ounce of control he possessed.

And then one morning, less than a week and a half before Christmas, Ethan was having a quick cup of coffee and skimming the newspaper when Paula entered the kitchen.

Alerted, every cell, molecule, and nerve in Ethan's body began to quiver in expectation. Paula never got up in the morning before he left for work.

"Is it time?" he asked, cringing inside at the anxious note in his voice that he couldn't hide.

"I don't think so." She shrugged. "At least, not yet. It's just a little backache. But I couldn't lie in bed any longer. I had to get up, move around a bit."

"Labor often begins with backache, doesn't it?" Ethan said, recalling reading that somewhere.

"Yes." Paula sighed. "But I'm not in labor yet. So just go on to work. I'll call your office if this develops into the real thing."

"No." Ethan gave a sharp, decisive shake of his head. "I'll stay home, just in case."

"Oh, really, Ethan, that's not necessary," she said. "You'd probably drive me batty prowling around the house, watching me like a hawk."

"I'd still prefer to stay home," he persisted.

She rolled her eyes. "You've read all those books. You know that, even if this backache is the beginning, the average labor with the first baby is around nineteen hours."

"Nevertheless," he said, his tone adamant. "I'm staying right here."

"Honestly," she snapped with clear exasperation.

"I don't believe you. You'd think you were the first man ever to become a father."

If in fact I really am the father. Ethan clenched his teeth to keep from voicing his suspicion. Instead, he retorted, "It will be the first time for me."

"For me, too," she reminded him.

"Then I'd think you'd want me to stay here with you," he pointed out as reasonably as possible.

"So, stay home, then, for heaven's sake," she cried, beginning to pace back and forth in front of the table. "But don't blame me if your day's wasted."

Ethan's day was not wasted.

Paula's labor began midmorning, and rapidly proceeded from one stage to the next. Her water began leaking shortly before noon. Ethan immediately went to the phone and placed a call to the doctor. The doctor advised him to take Paula to the hospital to safeguard the baby against any infection.

To Ethan's surprise, Paula didn't argue; she admitted that the contractions were getting stronger; she even confessed to being glad he had not gone into the office. He suspected she was scared.

So was he . . . on several emotional levels.

At the hospital, Paula was put to bed.

Ethan went into coach mode.

Paula's fear became obvious as her labor swiftly progressed. Using language he had never heard from her, she swore she would never again allow herself to be pregnant cursing all men in general, and Ethan in particular.

The doctor arrived an hour later, a scant fifteen

minutes before Paula delivered a seven pound, two ounce son.

Ethan got a good look at the baby after he had been cleaned up a bit. He was stunned by a sense of awe, a surge of elation energizing him. Ethan stared at the dark-haired infant, his tiny, still slightly mottled face, and saw a mirror image of his own in miniature.

There wasn't a shred of doubt that the baby was his.

His son.

In that instant, Ethan fell in love.

CHAPTER FOURTEEN

Less than two weeks remained until Christmas. The rush was on to get everything done in time for the big day.

Kate dropped Mandy and Connie off at home after school before driving to the malls at King of Prussia for her prearranged meeting with Carol.

The girls, even the now teenage and supposedly more mature Mandy, growing more hyper with each passing day, chattered away excitedly about helping Helen bake their favorite holiday cookies, the cut-out shapes of Santa and stars and reindeer that they iced and decorated with red and green sprinkles.

Although Kate had always enjoyed baking and decorating the cookies too, she still had some heavy duty shopping to do, as she not only had her own shopping to do, but most of David's as well.

She and Carol had made the shopping date during

exercise class the previous Saturday when Carol had groaned about still having mounds of gifts to buy for her extended family.

The deal was that they would shop till they dropped, with a brief rest period midway to grab something to eat.

And by the time she got home around nine, Kate did feel about ready to drop. But she was lugging three brightly decorated holiday shopping bags, and had crossed off every name on David's list and all but a couple of the names off her own much longer list.

One of those names was Carol's, because of course, Kate couldn't shop for a gift for her friend while Carol was right there with her. Another name still on the list was Jason's, because, with the other woman's continued antagonism for the man, Kate wasn't about to shop for a gift for Jason while Carol was with her. Kate didn't need that kind of aggravation.

"Hey, Kate," Mandy yelled, bursting into the hall from the kitchen as Kate shut the front door behind her. "Wait'll you hear the . . ."

"Hold it right there," Kate ordered, moving to the stairway as quickly as she could while toting the shopping bags.

"But, Kate, listen . . ." Mandy tried again.

"Mandy, I need to go to the bathroom," Kate interrupted again, continuing on up the stairs, and cursing under her breath as she banged the knuckles of her hand against the railing posts. "I'll be down right after I lock these bags inside my closet. It'll keep till then."

Some ten or so minutes later, feeling much relieved, with the presents safely locked away from the snooping young girls, Kate walked into the kitchen.

"Okay, what's all the . . ." That's as far as Kate got before Mandy delivered a blow to her equilibrium with the news she blurted out.

"Paula had a baby boy!" Mandy beamed at her. "Mrs. Winston called me up this afternoon to tell me. Isn't it neat? I can't wait to see him."

"Me, neither," Connie chimed in.

"She had the baby?" Kate frowned, and tried to ignore the awful feeling inside her. "So early? I thought the baby wasn't due until sometime in January."

"That's right." Mandy nodded vigorously. "But Mrs. Winston told me Paula said from the first that she thought she would be early. And she was right."

"And now it's time for you two to go to bed," Helen said in a no-nonsense tone.

"Aw, can't we stay up for just a little while longer?" Mandy coaxed.

"Yeah, for just a little while," Connie echoed.

Both girls turned their pleading faces toward Kate.

"It's nine-thirty," Kate said, glancing at the clock. "And already half an hour past your bedtime."

"I told them they could stay up until you got home," Helen explained. "They promised they'd go straight to bed as soon as Mandy told you the news."

The girls began a wheedle-and-whine chorus. The mild headache that had begun nagging Kate while she was shopping blossomed into a painful thumping. She raised a hand to massage her temple.

"That's enough, girls." The voice of authority came

from David as he walked into the kitchen. "Your sister's tired, and I suspect she has a headache. So, say good night now and march up those stairs."

Without another protest, and after bestowing good night hugs and kisses, the girls marched off to bed.

Fighting what she told herself was an inexplicable and stupid urge to cry, Kate dredged up a smile for David. "I finished your shopping."

"Thank you." David's smile was warm and caring. "I don't know what I'd do without you, Kate."

The urge to cry grew stronger. "You'd manage." Her smile wobbled. "You and Helen."

"Me?" Helen contrived to look shocked. "Are you kidding? There are times I don't know what *I'd* do without you."

Even as close to tears as she felt, Kate had to laugh. "You'd do as you always do . . . just fine."

"Definitely," David seconded. "Now, how about a cup of decaf coffee and a taste of those cookies you and the girls baked this afternoon?"

"That I can handle," Helen drawled. "I'll even join you. How about you, Kate?"

"Yes, thank you," she answered, deciding the distraction of eating cookies was better than moping around and allowing the news about Ethan's baby to eat at her.

Helen served Kate two painkillers with her decaf and cookies. The cookies were delicious, as they were every year, Christmastime being the only time Helen baked them. Kate had always liked the cut-out cookies best.

But what she really hungered for was a cigarette,

and as she hadn't had one of those for weeks, she felt sure the ones left in the pack she'd buried at the back of a dresser drawer were by now stale and acrid.

At that moment, however, acrid held a certain appeal.

Minutes after finishing his snack, David said good night, pushed back his chair and started for the hallway. "Oh, by the way," he said, pausing in the kitchen doorway. "I spoke to Mark Winston earlier. He said that although the baby arrived early, both Paula and the baby are fine." He stepped into the hall, then stuck his head back inside the kitchen. "I almost forgot. Mark also said the baby weighed seven pounds, something or other; I don't remember the ounces. Thought you'd like to know. Now I really am off to bed."

Except for the carpet-muffled sound of David's footsteps moving along the hall to the stairs, there was complete silence for a couple of seconds.

Seven pounds? A faint frown creasing her brow, Kate turned a puzzled look on Helen.

The older woman arched a skeptical eyebrow. "To quote my mother, 'Well, well, ain't it amazing, another seven month, seven pound premie.' "

"You're not buying it?"

Helen laughed. "Hardly. Six pounds . . . maybe. But seven and odd ounces? No way. The Winstons can believe what they will, but I'd say this baby was full term, which means, of course, that the lovely Paula was pregnant when she walked down the aisle in white."

"Yes." It wasn't easy for Kate to smile, feeling as

though a fist was squeezing her heart, but she pulled it off. She had to smile, or cry out against the pain. Helen had no way of knowing the depths of hurt she felt on hearing her own suspicions confirmed.

Ethan had not only been seeing Paula, but making love with her, the whole time he had been making love . . . having sex, with Kate.

"Their business, not ours," she murmured, suppressing a shudder, forcing herself to move, clear the table, act normal. "And not at all unusual in today's society."

"Or any other period of society, come to that," Helen drawled. "Young women have been having seven pound premies, I suspect, even during the repressed Victorian age."

She, too, might have joined their numbers, as well, Kate reminded herself, absently rinsing the coffee cups while Helen wiped the table. If Ethan hadn't used protection. Hadn't he used that same protection with Paula? Or had it failed?

Of course, if the latter was the case, Kate reflected, it would explain the jarring suddenness of Ethan's unexpected and crushing phone call of rejection to her.

Reliving the shock and pain of that call set what felt to be the hammers of hell pounding in her head.

"You look pale, Kate," Helen observed sympathetically. "Didn't the painkillers work?"

"Not yet." Kate managed a wry smile. "Maybe I should have regular coffee."

"You're right, the caffeine might help. I'll make a cup for you," Helen offered, moving to the cabinets.

"No." Kate started to shake her head, but immediately stilled at the vicious stab of pain. "No, thank you. I think I'll just say good night and go on up to bed. By the way, the cookies were delicious, as usual."

"Thank you." Helen flushed with pleasure at the praise. "Good night, Kate."

While Kate stood under a warm, soothing shower, the painkillers caught up with the intense pain in her head, reducing the pounding to a dull, tolerable ache.

Relieved, she pulled on a knee-length flannel nightshirt and returned to her room. Walking to the side of the bed, she turned back the thick down comforter and top sheet. Sitting on the edge of the bed, she reached for the clock on the nightstand. As she pulled out the alarm plunger, she glanced at the nightstand drawer, the drawer in which her notebook journals were kept. The drawer she hadn't opened since . . .

Don't do it.

Even as she cautioned herself, her hand grasped the brass handle, slid open the drawer and withdrew the last of her journals, the one with the shiny bright green cover, the one with writing on only a quarter of the pages, the one she hadn't opened since the night of her last date with Ethan.

Beginning to shiver, Kate stroked the smooth cover with trembling fingers. Telling herself she was a fool, and a weak one at that, she flipped the pages to the last one with markings on it.

Her vision blurring, she looked away, blinking against the hot sting of tears in her eyes, swallowing against the burning sting of bitterness in her throat.

Suddenly impatient with herself, she raised a hand

and swiped the moisture from her eyes. Glancing back at the notebook, she read the words she had so happily written that night in early spring.

Ethan. Ethan. Ethan. How I adore him!

We were together again tonight. I can't believe there was ever a lover as gentle, as caring, as passionate as Ethan. His touch, his kisses, his lovemaking sets my mind whirling, sets my heart racing, sets my body on fire with desire for him, to be part of him, one with him.

I almost told him tonight, while he was inside me, while we were one. So incredible were the heights we reached as one, so ecstatic my ultimate pleasure, so strong the shudders that shook his body in release, I almost cried out my love for him.

But I bit back the words, waiting to hear them first from Ethan's lips. He groaned, and with his spent body pressing me deep into the mattress, he whispered words of praise, words of his delight in me . . . but no words of his love.

Maybe next time.

Kate couldn't see the words anymore through the tears filling her eyes, running down her face. But she didn't need to see the words; they were seared into her memory.

Slamming the book shut, she shoved it into the drawer, and then slammed it shut.

Idiot, Kate berated herself. Why hadn't she let well enough alone . . . left the journal in the drawer? Better yet, why hadn't she thrown the notebooks into the recycle crate, or put them through a shredder, or burned them?

Jumping up, she slid her cold feet into fuzzy winter slippers, pulled on an ankle-length velour robe, dug the crumpled pack of cigarettes from the back of a dresser drawer, and strode from her room.

The clear night sky was like black velvet, the stars like glittering shards of ice. Quivering inside from emotional upheaval, and shivering from the cold air, Kate lit up a bent cigarette and took a long, deep drag.

It tasted awful, and made her cough. So she took another drag, and coughed again. By the end of the cigarette she was no longer coughing. She lit another.

By the end of the second cigarette, Kate felt slightly light-headed, a little nauseated, and dumber than the flagstones beneath her feet.

But, unlike the flagstones, she was hurting, badly, suffering once again the staggering feelings of betrayal and rejection, of being used and tossed aside.

Damn it. What had happened to all her firm decisions of months ago, she chided herself. When had she lost sight of her determination to get on with her life? Had she, on a subconscious level, been harboring a glimmer of hope that some day, some way, Ethan would . . .

Forget it. Kate cut off the thought with ruthless intent. Forget him . . . or, at least any misguided dream of the possibility of a future with him.

Ethan was married. He was now a father. Beyond her childish hopes and dreams. End of story.

It was time to fashion new hopes, new dreams, a

new life story, Kate told herself, absently lighting yet another stale cigarette.

Frowning, she stared at the dull red glow at the tip of the crooked cigarette, thinking that it was long past time to ditch the tobacco crutch. Dropping the smoke to the flagstone, she crushed it out and scooped up all three of the butts. Going inside, she dropped the smelly things into the sink, turned on the water and washed them down the garbage disposal. Now, if only she could dispose of other pointless habits as easily, she thought, watching as the water whirled the evidence away.

Sighing, Kate turned off the kitchen light and went back to her room, certain she wouldn't be able to sleep.

Whether from physical tiredness from shopping, or the mental weariness caused by circling thoughts going nowhere, or possibly from standing so long like a dimwit in the cold night air, Kate would never know, but she fell asleep within minutes after crawling into bed and burrowing beneath the comforter.

CHAPTER FIFTEEN

Christmas was only a few days away. The heavy work was done. The entire house was resplendent with garland and holly tied with dark red bows. Pillar candles of various heights and widths were grouped on a corner of the slate fireplace around and on top of the mantelpiece.

A seven-foot blue spruce tree, decorated with delicate ornaments, glittering with tiny white lights and silver tinsel, towered over the tall living room windows at the front of the house.

The only things missing were the presents. By family tradition, the gifts would not be arranged beneath the tree until Christmas Eve, after church services.

At six o'clock it was dark outside, dark and cold. A light snow flurried in the breeze. Inside, the aroma of Yankee pot roast permeated the air.

Other than the rustle of movement and the murmur of voices in the kitchen, the house was quiet. Mandy and Connie were in their rooms, wrapping presents. David was in his home office, probably having a snooze before dinner. Helen and Kate were busy in the kitchen, Helen washing vegetables for a salad, Kate setting the table.

The doorbell rang.

"Now, who could that be at dinner time?" Helen wondered aloud, raising her voice above the sound of running water. "Were you expecting someone?"

"No." Kate shook her head as she turned away from a cabinet, a stack of plates in her hands. "I'll get it." She set the plates on the table as she made her way to the hall.

On reaching the door, Kate flicked on the outside light and peered through the peep hole in the door. The figure of a tall man filled her vision, and a mixture of excitement and despair filled her when she recognized the caller. Disgusted by the tremor in her fingers, she opened the door.

"Ethan?"

"Hello, Kate." He stood silent for a moment, just looking at her. "May I came in?"

"Oh, yes, yes of course." Embarrassed, feeling as awkward as a smitten teenager, Kate swung the door wide and backed up, putting some distance between them.

A faint, wry smile shadowed his lips. "David is expecting me," he said.

"Is something wrong?" she asked anxiously, alarm flaring; David had seemed so relaxed and well lately.

"No, no," Ethan quickly assured her. "I told him

I'd stop by with some stock options I thought he might want to add to his portfolio," he explained.

"Oh, I see." Kate exhaled a sigh of relief.

"How are you?"

"I'm fine." She frowned as she saw him glance up, amusement shimmering in his dark eyes. "And you?"

"Fine." He laughed.

Puzzled, she looked up, too, and felt her face grow warm at the realization that she was standing directly beneath the ball of mistletoe fastened to the foyer light hanging on a chain from the ceiling.

"I haven't seen one of those in years," he murmured, slowly moving toward her.

Kate froze, knowing she should step away, run away, yet was incapable of moving from her spot. "Connie saw one for the first time while watching an old, sappy romantic holiday movie," she said, knowing she was babbling but unable to stop. "She insisted we had to have one."

"Then it would be a shame to waste it," he said, closing in on her.

She stirred and began to turn away. He lightly grasped her waist, holding her still. He lowered his head.

"Ethan." Kate's voice quivered. She raised her trembling hands to his chest, drawing in a quick breath.

"Merry Christmas, Kate," he murmured, his breath filling her mouth as his lips brushed hers.

Though his lips still held a chill from the outside, the kiss was warm, warm but without heat, amounting to nothing more than one mouth lightly pressed against another. There was no sense of urgency, no demand, but it was sweet, gentle, almost familial, and yet . . .

Kate felt a jarring charge of sexual electricity sizzle her entire body. She wanted more, so much more, but she was afraid, afraid to move, afraid to respond, afraid to breathe, afraid he would pull away, deny her the mouth she craved more than breath.

He groaned.

She whimpered.

"Kate." Her whispered name had the effect of his tongue thrusting into her mouth.

A spasm rocking her, Kate curled her fingers into his chest, and mindlessly arched her body against his.

"God." Ethan's hands tightened around her waist, and for one rapturous moment his mouth crushed hers. Then a shudder ripped through him and he tore his mouth from hers and stepped back, as if out of harm's way.

Raising fingertips to her tingling lips, Kate stared at him, feeling shocked, bereft, lost and empty.

"Kate, I . . . ," he began in a strained tone, breaking off when David's voice called out.

"Is that Ethan I hear?"

"Yes. I was . . . just taking his coat."

Watching her, his eyes darker than dark, Ethan shrugged out of his coat and handed it to her.

Shaking under the pressure of his probing gaze, grateful for the excuse to break eye contact, Kate abruptly turned and walked to the foyer.

"Kate, I . . . ," he began again.

She silenced him with a quick shake of her head.

"Don't say anything," she muttered, desperate to avoid hearing him apologize. "Nothing happened . . . really." She spun around to face him, her tone, eyes, and expression flat, guarded. "Nothing important. Just a silly Christmas kiss between neighbors under the mistletoe."

"Silly?" His voice sounded odd, rough. "Yes, of course. I understand." He smiled—at least it was almost a smile. "If you'll excuse me? David's waiting." He didn't pause for a response, but turned and strode away.

He understood? Kate gnawed her lower lip. What had he understood? That she was a fool, quick to surrender to the most innocuous of kisses? Or, in light of her involuntary response to his kiss, did Ethan now believe that she had tried to make a fool of him, or a play for him?

The very thought was mortifying.

But Ethan had kissed her, not the other way around, Kate reminded herself.

And he was a married man, a new father.

He shouldn't have . . .

Oh, God. Why did it still hurt so much?

And why had she trashed the last couple of cigarettes that were still in the pack the night Ethan's baby was born?

Silly. Just a silly Christmas kiss.

The echo of Kate's flatly unconcerned voice continued to torment Ethan hours after he left David's house.

Sitting in the rocking chair next to the crib he had set up in his own bedroom, his sleeping son lay cradled securely in his right arm. An empty nursing bottle hung limply from his left hand as Ethan rocked the chair slowly back and forth, staring into space, seeing nothing of his surroundings, only hearing Kate's voice.

He should never have touched her, Ethan reflected, not even to bestow a "friendly" Christmas kiss . . . not to bestow a kiss . . . of any kind.

Touching his mouth to Kate's, as brief and cool as he had intended, that kiss had nevertheless heated his blood, hardened his body, fired his imagination.

He should have known better. He had been celibate, without a woman for close to eight months, Ethan rationalized. And Kate had responded, if only for an instant—probably instinctively—igniting the spark. His physical reaction had been that of a normal, healthy male starved for sensual pleasure.

But the rationalization only partially explained his behavior, and Ethan knew it. Throughout those seven plus months, he had been around numerous women in the office, had inadvertently and innocently brushed against several in passing, and had not been affected in a sexual way.

No, his celibacy had played only a small part in his reaction. He hadn't wanted a woman, he had wanted Kate. No surprise. No matter how hard he tried to deny it, he had been wanting Kate, only Kate, every day since the last time they had been together.

No, that wasn't the complete truth either, Ethan

admitted to himself. The complete truth was that he had wanted Kate since the first time he kissed her.

The hell of it was, nothing had changed since his wedding night; his feelings had not changed. He was afraid he would go on wanting her for the rest of his life. Ethan could only continue to hope and pray that his fears would eventually prove wrong.

Sighing, Ethan shook his head to clear away his thoughts. Carefully getting to his feet, he carried the baby to the crib, to gently settle him on his back. Gazing on the child with pure unadulterated love, he covered his small body. Raising his right hand, he touched his fingertips to the baby's lips, then to his downy soft cheek.

His love for his son unconditional, Ethan couldn't for the life of him understand how Paula could remain indifferent to the beautiful child. Yet, from the day he had brought Paula and his son home from the hospital, she had paid scant attention to her baby. She never fed him, bathed him, or changed a diaper, leaving those "messy chores" to the nanny he had hired to care for the infant during the day. Ethan himself cared for the baby in the evening and throughout the night.

After less than a month of the routine, Ethan, tired and physically exhausted, acquired a whole new perspective, respect, and appreciation for the role of mothers, especially mothers who worked outside the home.

Even so, he had made the right choice, Ethan decided, trailing his fingertips to the tiny rosebud mouth. As much as giving up Kate for his son had hurt, still hurt, he had made the right choice. For even after having the baby in his life for such a short period of time, Ethan could not imagine life without his son being a part of it.

Ethan consoled himself with the thought that perhaps, someday, there would be someone, some woman he could love, or care for enough to marry, who would be a wife to him, a mother to his son, maybe even give him more children.

Someday.

"Until then, it's just you and me, kid," he whispered, drawing his hand away when the baby made a whimpering sound and moved restlessly.

Someday, perhaps, Ethan repeated to himself. But, in the meantime, it was almost Christmas, and there wasn't even a tree set up in the living room for his son.

The morning of Christmas Eve dawned bright and sunny, seasonably cold but without a snowflake in sight.

"Darn, there's not a cloud in the sky," Connie complained from her position at the kitchen window. "I was hoping for a white Christmas."

"You've been watching too many repeats of old holiday movies that have been running so frequently on TV for the past month," Kate said, exchanging a smile with Helen. "Forget the weather and come eat your waffles before they get cold."

"Actually, I can't remember the last time we had a white Christmas," Mandy observed, her attempt to sound mature overshadowed by having to mumble around the forkful of waffle in her mouth. "Other than a couple of flurries." She swallowed, clearing her voice. "And that doesn't count."

"I can only remember snow at Christmas a few times," Kate concurred. "We don't often get snow, a lot of snow, so early in the winter in this part of Pennsylvania."

Crestfallen, Connie shuffled to the table and plopped into a chair. "There was a lot of snow in this part of Pennsylvania the Christmas George Washington's army wintered at Valley Forge," she muttered, relaying the information she had recently gleaned from her social science studies.

"Yeah, but that was way over two hundred years ago," Mandy pointed out in superior tones, as if the number of years between had any bearing on the subject at hand.

Connie glowered at her sister. "What does that have to do with anything, anyways?"

"Now, girls," Kate said in mild warning, sensing an argument in the making between the two, hyper in expectation of the "big day" and the gifts to come.

"You know, I can recall one Christmas in particular when I was thirty or so," Helen mused aloud, obviously trying to defuse the situation. "By midafternoon the temperature was in the sixties and there was a dandy thunderstorm."

"I hope it doesn't do that tomorrow!" Connie cried, horrified. "I asked for new rollerblades," she reminded them, as if they needed reminding after weeks of hearing her broadly dropped hints, while conveniently forgetting that just minutes before she had bemoaned the lack of snow.

Kate hid a smile behind the coffee cup she raised to her lips, and arched a brow at Helen.

"I'd say the chances of that happening are slim to none," Helen responded. "The weather report is for clear but cold weather, with a high temp of thirty-four degrees."

"Oh, good." Connie heaved a noisy sigh of relief.

Mandy rolled her eyes, murmuring, "What a ditz," beneath her breath.

Though the topics changed, the atmosphere at the holidays was always the same, charged with nervous excitement, Kate thought, smiling at the girls with indulgent affection. She hated to even think of what it would be like after the girls both reached the age where they outgrew the magic of the holiday. There would be no one to plead for mistletoe balls or snow or to hold on to the magic. In Mandy's case, even at the advanced age of thirteen, she teased her sister with tantalizing dares to find the ever new and secret places where her presents were hidden.

Before that dreaded day arrived, Kate decided, she would just have to have a child of her own, to continue the magic after the girls outgrew it.

But a child needed a father.

The thought conjured an image. Kate rejected the vision. Ethan already was a father . . . and a husband. Yet, against her will, the image of his face returned and along with it the vivid memory of the taste of him just two nights ago during that brief but devastating kiss.

Damned if she would allow thoughts of him, the memory of his kiss, to ruin her holiday, Kate decided, getting up to refill her cup.

"Carol's late, isn't she?" Helen asked, diverting her attention.

Grateful for the distraction, Kate glanced at Helen, then at the clock. "Only a couple of minutes. I expect she'll be here"—the doorbell rang—"any minute now," she finished, grinning as she headed for the door.

"Merry Christmas," Carol greeted Kate when she swung open the door, carrying two bulging shopping bags, one of which she thrust at Kate before stepping inside.

"Merry Christmas to you, too." Laughing, she relieved her friend of the other bag.

"Geez, it's cold out," Carol said, shrugging out of her coat. "But not a snow cloud in sight, thank goodness. I'd hate to drive home in the snow."

When Carol had told Kate about her plan to drive home the day before Christmas, and not return until New Year's Day, Kate had invited her to the house to have breakfast before making the long drive north. She had then in turn invited Jason.

To Kate's disappointment, Jason declined, as his mother was entertaining relatives for breakfast and expected him to be there, since he had already accepted Kate's invitation to spend Christmas Eve, and attend church services, with her and her family.

And so, once again Kate had been thwarted in her attempt to get Carol and Jason together in a social situation, hoping they might discover that they actually could tolerate each other.

Perhaps after the holidays, or in the spring, Kate thought, resigned to playing buffer between her two friends for at least awhile longer.

"I'm starving," Carol announced, "And something smells divine."

"Waffles with strawberry sauce topping, and sausages," Kate said, turning from the foyer closet to lead the way to the kitchen. "Or bacon, if you prefer."

"I love breakfast sausages. Merry Christmas, everybody," Carol called as she walked into the kitchen.

The girls and Helen returned the greeting, along with an invitation to sit down and dig in to the steaming waffle Helen had just removed from the waffle iron.

"Where's David?" Carol asked, glancing around as she drew her chair up to the table.

"He went into the office till noon," Kate explained. "Then he's taking his secretary to lunch."

"What's this?" Carol raised her eyebrows. "Do I detect a possible romance?"

"Naw." Mandy shook her head.

Connie giggled.

Helen rolled her eyes.

"Hardly," Kate drawled. "David's secretary, Stella Myers, will be sixty-two on the twenty-ninth. She's retiring, and as David's business is closed for the holiday week, this is her last working day."

"Bummer," Carol said, winking at the girls.

The room rang with laughter during breakfast, and afterward, while they all exchanged Christmas gifts.

The shopping bags Carol had brought with her were quickly emptied, replaced by the presents that Kate, Helen, Mandy and Connie had placed under the tree earlier that morning for Carol.

She left shortly before noon. All in all, Kate reflected, the morning had been a great kickoff for the holiday.

The trend continued through the rest of the day and evening. David came home at midafternoon in fine holiday spirit, and proceeded to tease the girls about the abundance of presents that would be piled around the tree after church that night.

"Little presents and big presents," he confided to the giggling duo. "All wrapped in colorful paper with big and little bows."

"Can't we have one now, Daddy?" Connie coaxed, practically dancing in expectation.

"Just one?" Mandy took up the plea.

"Presents? What presents?" Helen contrived to look confused. "I never saw any presents."

"You know, I remember seeing one or two sloppily wrapped things, but that was weeks ago." Kate managed to look concerned. "Do you think maybe they were stolen?"

"Oh . . ." Connie stamped her foot. "They're just teasing us, Mandy."

"Well, of course they are." Mandy made a face at her sister. "Don't they every year?"

As arranged, Jason arrived at the house for Christmas Eve supper at six o'clock on the dot.

"Merry Christmas, Kate."

"Merry Christmas, Jason. You're right on time.

Helen and the girls are putting the food on the table now." Kate took his coat and turned to hang it in the closet.

"Good, I'm hungry."

When she turned back, she felt a catch in her throat, and a jolt to her nervous system. Jason was standing directly under the mistletoe ball, his arms held out in invitation, grinning at her.

For one instant, everything inside Kate seemed to freeze. She couldn't, she just couldn't go to Jason, walk into his embrace, touch her lips to his, not after the other night, after the taste of . . .

Pride came to her rescue, saving her from making a fool of herself, and hurting his feelings.

Grow up, for God's sake, Kate upbraided herself, curving her lips into what felt like a half-decent smile. Damned if she would allow memories to ruin her holiday. It was only an old tradition beneath a silly ball, anyway. He was asking for a kiss, that was all.

They had kissed before, many times. Although Jason's kisses lacked the rousing power she had always felt from Ethan's, she had not been repulsed by them. Quite the opposite, she had found them pleasant and comforting.

Dismissing that other disturbing kiss from her mind, Kate walked into Jason's embrace.

She kissed him again, late that night after they returned from midnight church services.

Kate enjoyed both kisses, as well as she enjoyed the entire holiday season.

CHAPTER SIXTEEN

The holidays were over. The house seemed bare and dull without all the colorful decorations. The tree, looking naked and forlorn, was propped against the garage for the recycling truck to collect.

School was back in session. Kate was back to playing referee between Carol and Jason.

January dragged on, bleak and gray, with the occasional fits and starts of snow, leaving an inch or so on the ground. But none developed into a substantial, school-closing snowfall, much to the disappointment of the students and more than a few of the teachers.

But, though the weather was cold, Jason's ardor was growing warmer with each successive date. His kisses, gentle and pleasant before, grew firmer, more demanding.

"Kate, you don't know how much I want you." After the first time he groaned the words into her ear, on New Year's Eve, Jason said the same thing every time he kissed her. "How much I want to make love with you."

Well, yes, Kate thought each and every time, she knew quite well how much he wanted her. She could hardly not know when she felt the hardness of his erection pressing against her when he pulled her close to him.

And, in truth, it was getting increasingly more difficult to deny him, because in denying Jason, Kate was denying herself, her own natural inclinations.

Ethan had expertly schooled her body, her senses, in the art of erotic pleasures, the exquisite exhilaration to be attained by scaling the heights to shattering satisfaction.

But could she reach those same incredible heights with Jason?

Kate seriously doubted it.

After Ethan, could she settle for mere release?

Kate wasn't sure . . . and so she held Jason at bay with excuses.

"We've only been seeing each other on a steady basis for a couple of months. It's too soon," she told him near the end of January, the first night he came right out and asked her to go to bed with him.

"I'm not ready yet," she said in late February, lifting his hand from her breast before he became aware of the involuntary response of her nipple to his touch.

"I'm not sure," she admitted in mid-March, which was the absolute truth.

The only thing Kate was sure about was that a year had elapsed since she had placed her love, her faith,

her trust in a man, only to have them thrown in her
face after she had given herself unconditionally to
him.

She had felt sure of Ethan's sincerity then, and she
had been wrong. How could she feel sure about any
man? Uncertain, wary, she remained undecided.

Kate wouldn't have been surprised if Jason had
given up on her, but he didn't. He didn't tell her he
was in love with her, either. Maybe he wasn't in love
with her, she reflected, with the sharp, painful recol-
lection of another man who had wanted to make love
with her. Maybe, like that other man, Jason was simply
in lust with her.

But, by the same token, weren't the demands of
her own body the same thing?

Late in March, with a hint of spring in the milder
air, Kate, along with her family and Helen, reluctantly
and against her better judgment, attended the christening ceremony of Ethan's son.

Paula looked as beautiful as ever. The baby, chris-
tened Robert Paul for his two great-grandfathers, was
adorable, a smaller version of his father. Ethan looked
tired, strained . . . but still wonderful.

Kate hated herself for noticing.

Throughout the proceedings, and at the gathering
at the elder Winstons home afterward, Ethan barely
spoke to her, and yet, Kate imagined that his hooded
gaze followed her every move, his eyes shadowed,
dark with an expression she couldn't, and wasn't sure
she wanted to read.

Her heart raced the entire time she was in his company, but she came down to earth with a crash as soon as she returned home, confronting her image in the mirror.

Ethan belonged to another woman. He was the proud father of a beautiful child, Kate chastised herself. Even worse, he had used her, then dumped her. Dreaming about him, secretly longing for him, hoping against hope, when there was no reason for hope, was self-destructive, if not downright sick.

For the third or fourth or tenth time, Kate was determined to get over it, get over him. But, she would need some help.

Grabbing up her handbag, Kate left the house, got into her car, drove to the nearest convenience store and plunked down way too much money for a pack of cigarettes. Taking deep drags, and coughing with every one, she nevertheless smoked three of the cigarettes before going back into the house.

She soothed her smarting conscience with the rationalization that at least the cigarettes were extra lights.

The next week, the first in April, David left to attend a four-day technology conference in California.

That night, Jason proposed to her.

For long seconds, stunned by the unexpected suddenness of his proposal, Kate just stared at him, not knowing quite what to say, how to respond.

"Jason ... I ... I ...," she began, groping for some sort of intelligent reply.

"Don't say no, Kate." He grasped her hands and held on tight. "We could make a go of it, I know we could. We get along so well, have great conversations, laugh together a lot." He paused for breath.

She jumped in. "I know all that is true. And I do love you . . . but, Jason, I'm sorry, but I'm not . . ."
He silenced her with a sharp shake of his head.

"I'm not unconscious, Kate. I know you're not *in* love with me. The kind of love you're referring to is the caring love of friendship."

Kate heaved a sigh, beginning to relax, relieved that he understood.

"But I'm still asking you to marry me."

She blinked in confusion.

He released her hands to draw her into his arms. "Kate, we could make a good marriage together, have a good life together. I know we could." He brushed his lips over hers, following up with the glide of his tongue.

Kate was unable to hide a quiver of response.

"You see?" he murmured, close to her ear, intensifying the quiver. "We could, would be good together." Drawing back, he grinned. "And look at it this way. We're both pretty darned good-looking. We'll produce great looking kids."

Kate's lips twitched before she gave way to the laughter bubbling up inside her.

Jason laughed with her. "What do you say? I believe that, historically, there have been some very successful marriages between men and women based on friendship love."

Kate drew a quick breath. "May I have time to think it over before answering?"

"Of course," he said grandly, flicking his left hand.

"You may have ten minutes," he added, glancing at his watch.

"Jason!" Kate tried to sound insulted, in spite of the laughter she couldn't contain.

His teasing expression settled into one of tender caring. "You may have as long as you need," he assured her. "But, I really don't see why you need it, Kate."

In all honesty, Kate supposed he was right. But it was such a big decision, a life decision. Gazing into his dear face, she felt affection for him well up inside her.

And just a week ago she had vowed to get over her fantasy, get on with her life.

She had always longed for a man of her own, children of her own, a family of her own. And here was Jason, offering to fulfill every one of her longings. Well, not every one, but enough, or what should be enough, and what, in reality, would have to be enough.

Kate was genuinely fond of Jason. She enjoyed his company, his sense of humor, his thoughtfulness.

Looking deep into Jason's soft eyes, Kate pondered his proposal. Could fondness for someone grow into love over time? Should she grab at the chance for a home, husband, and family of her own before Jason grew impatient with her indecisiveness and changed his mind?

"Wake up, Kate." Jason's quietly teasing voice caught her attention.

"I'm sorry," she apologized. "I was thinking."

"Get anywhere with it?"

"Yes." The decision made, her voice was firm, steady. "I'll marry you, Jason."

"Kate!" He tightened his arms around her, nearly crushing the breath out of her. "That's wonderful!"

"On ... two ... con ... ditions." Kate got the words out between gasps for air.

"Conditions?" Frowning, Jason loosened his hold on her to lean back and stare into her face. "What conditions?"

Kate drew a deep breath before attempting to answer. "One, we wait until David gets home to announce our engagement."

"Okay." He gave an airy wave of one hand.

Kate drew another deeper breath, certain he wouldn't be as blithe about the second condition. "Two, we wait until our wedding night to become lovers."

Instead of an airy wave, Jason raised his hand to rake it through his hair. Though obviously frustrated by her request, he reluctantly agreed.

Three days later, on the evening David was scheduled to return home from a conference, Kate answered the ringing phone, expecting it to be Jason.

"Is this the residence of David Gardner?"

"Yes." Kate frowned at the unfamiliar male voice.

"May I speak to a Ms. Kate Quinn, please?"

For some inexplicable reason, a chill of foreboding trickled up Kate's spine. "Speaking," she responded, suddenly dry-mouthed and shaky.

"Ms. Quinn, this is Patrolman Caleb Straub from the Pennsylvania State Police. I'm sorry to have to tell you that Mr. Gardner suffered what appears to have been a heart attack on I 95 near the airport.''

Kate went cold, all over. "Was there an accident?"

"No, ma'am. He managed to pull the car off onto the shoulder. A passing motorist stopped, called 911 from a cell phone."

"Is he . . ." She gulped. "Is David . . ."

"He's alive," the patrolman inserted. "Or at least he was when the ambulance left for the hospital."

"What hospital?" she cried. "Where did they take him?"

At the panicky sound of her raised voice, Helen ran from the kitchen.

"What is it, Kate? What's wrong?"

Kate held up a hand for quiet, straining to hear the patrolman's answer.

"Thank you. Yes. Thank you."

"Kate?" Helen grasped her arm. "What is it?"

"David," Kate said, moving to the foyer closet for her coat. "That was a state policeman on the phone. He said David apparently had a heart attack while driving home from the airport. He's been taken to the hospital." She named one of the most prestigious hospitals in the country as she put on her coat. "I've got to go to him, Helen." With a frantic look around, she spied her purse exactly where she had dropped it when she came in, on the table just inside the door. "You'll look after the girls?"

"Of course," Helen said. "Do you want me to tell them, or wait till you know if . . ." Her stark voice faded.

If. Oh, God. Kate felt her stomach roll. "I guess

you'd better tell them." She walked to the door, glanced back. "I'll call as soon as I know anything definite."

Helen nodded, and bit her lip.

Kate left the house and ran to her car. . . . The car David had bought her for her twenty-fifth birthday.

CHAPTER SEVENTEEN

Kate stood in the dimly lit room, listening to the bleeps and gurgles of life support machines, staring down at the unconscious figure lying in the narrow hospital bed.

David looked so diminished, so vulnerable. She swallowed to ease the tightness in her throat, blinked to clear the mist clouding her vision. He was so still, so pale, almost as white as the regulation hospital sheets and blankets.

On her arrival at the hospital, Kate had been directed to the intensive care unit waiting room. Within minutes, a white-haired man in a white jacket strode into the room. He introduced himself as Dr. Something-or-other. Upset, rattled by apprehension, Kate caught his name, then immediately lost it from memory.

He was all business, and did not pull his punches.

"You're Mr. Gardner's daughter?"

"No." Kate shook her head. She took his extended hand. "His stepdaughter, Kate Quinn."

"Well, Ms. Quinn, I'm afraid the prognosis is not good." He squeezed her hand, as if to infuse his strength into her. "Your stepfather suffered a coronary thrombosis, followed by a massive heart attack."

"Wi . . . will he survive?"

"Doubtful. Right now, the only thing keeping him alive is the life support system." He sighed and shrugged. "But who knows? I've seen patients who were written off make amazing recoveries. But at this point, in my professional opinion, I'd have to say no."

A shudder quaked through her body.

"Are you all right?" he asked sharply.

"Yes." Kate drew a breath. "May I see him, please?"

The doctor led her to a glass-walled room. She had been there ever since touching David's fragile-looking hand lying on top of the blanket.

Staring at him. Staring at him.

Through her eyes, Kate saw the man, the shell of the man on the bed, his lifeline: the machines he was connected to.

In her mind, Kate saw flashes of another man; the younger, smiling David, sweeping her laughing mother up into his arms to carry her over the threshold of his home the day they were married; the proud, thrilled David the day he had become a father for the first time; the ever kind, gentle-voiced David who had not only accepted his wife's fatherless child, but had always treated her as one of his own.

"Oh, David." Kate didn't realize she had whispered

his name aloud, didn't hear her choked voice, didn't feel the tears streaming down her face.

Nor was Kate aware that someone had entered the room, come up behind her. She felt his touch on her shoulder at the same moment she heard his quiet voice.

"Kate."

"Oh, Ethan." Without thought or hesitation, she turned into his embrace. "He's dying. David's dying."

"I know. Come. There are only two visitors allowed in the room at one time." He started to turn away, taking her with him. It was then she noticed his father standing at the foot of the bed, his expression stark with sadness.

"But, Ethan," Kate protested, resisting his move toward the door. "I can't leave him alone."

"He won't be alone." He exchanged meaningful glances with his father; she was beyond discerning any meaning. "Dad will be here."

"But . . ."

"Come, Kate." He moved her to the door. "I need to talk to you."

Still reluctant, glancing back at the still figure on the bed, unable to fight Ethan's gentle determination, Kate found herself being led into the waiting room.

"Ethan."

"Would you like some coffee?"

She frowned at him, shook her head, and shrugged off the arm he had clamped around her shoulder. "No. I want to go back and be with David."

He grasped her hand. "Kate, I brought you out

here because"—he paused an instant before saying bluntly—"because they are disconnecting the machines."

"What?" Stunned, Kate stared at him in horrified disbelief. "But, they can't do that," she cried, unsuccessfully trying to shake off his hand. "The machines are keeping him alive."

"Kate, listen to me." Ethan's voice was both patient and firm. "They have no choice. David had me draw up a living will. In the event of a situation such as this, his specific instructions were that no heroic measures were to be taken to maintain his life."

"No," Kate moaned in anguish, and shivered as if she were freezing. "No . . . no." A sick sensation invaded her stomach. Moaning softly, she felt the room closing in on her, darkness creeping in on her, and felt her knees buckle. Feeling herself begin to sway, she shut her eyes.

Ethan caught her, drew her close, held her steady until the darkness receded.

"I'm sorry, I . . . I . . ." Breaking off, Kate drew a deep breath and opened her eyes, to stare into the compassionate, caring eyes of her best friend. "Oh, Ethan," she wailed, feeling like a young girl again, lost and alone. "I can't believe this is happening. What am I going to do?" She shuddered against the deepening chill inside her.

"I'm here for you, Kate." Releasing her, Ethan took off his suit jacket and draped it over her shoulders. "I'm here," he repeated, enclosing her trembling body into the protective comfort of his arms when she broke down and began to cry. "I'm here," he crooned, gently rocking her back and forth. "Cry it out."

Cradled against the solid strength of Ethan's chest, warmed by his body heat, soothed by the crooning tone of his voice, Kate gave way to the sobs of grief tearing at her throat.

A sense of familiarity stirred a memory in her consciousness, an almost sixteen-year-old memory of the day her mother died, of a warming windbreaker being wrapped around her, of being held protectively, comforted by the same voice, while she then, as now, wet Ethan's shirt with her tears.

The worst of the weeping storm had passed. Still enclosed within Ethan's embrace, Kate dried her face with some tissues when the doctor and Mark Winston entered the waiting room.

Loosening his embrace, but keeping one supportive arm around her, Ethan and Kate turned to face them.

"Is he . . . ?" Kate didn't need to continue; she knew the answer from the doctor's somber expression, the misty-eyed, grief-stricken look on Mark Winston's face.

Stepping up to her, the doctor took her hand. "Yes, Ms. Quinn. I'm sorry to say, he is gone."

Not trusting her voice, Kate nodded and blinked against a fresh rush of tears. But she had herself pretty much under control, thanks in part, a big part, to Ethan, his comfort, his support, his very presence.

Drawing a breath, she extended her hand. "Thank you, Doctor." Her voice cracked, then steadied. "I know there was nothing more you could do."

"Will you be all right?" he asked, peering into her face. "I can prescribe something to . . ." He broke off at her quick, definite head shake.

"I'll be fine . . . really."

"She is stronger than she looks," Ethan inserted. "And she has weathered other similar storms."

"Very well." The doctor smiled. "Now, if you'll excuse me, I'm needed." He didn't say any more.

"Yes, of course." Kate managed to return his smile. It was wobbly, but it was there.

As though her smile, meager as it was, had been what he was waiting for, the doctor gave a brief nod to Ethan and Mark, then turned and left the room.

"Now what?" Kate looked to Mark Winston. "Is there anything I must do? Sign anything?"

"Ethan and I can take care of the details," he said, his voice rough with emotion.

"Thank you." She gave them a puzzled look. "How did you know about David?"

"Helen called me," Mark answered. "And I called Ethan."

Kate nodded. "Helen, yes, of course. I should have . . . Oh, God, I have to tell them. Helen and the girls."

"Would you like me to tell them?" Ethan offered.

Kate was tempted, sorely tempted, to allow him to relieve her of the responsibility, but she didn't give in to his enticing offer. "No. Thank you. I must do it, and not over the phone. I must tell them in person." She shivered. "Is it all right for me to leave now?"

"Yes." Mark's voice was soft with compassion. "Ethan and I will take care of everything here."

"Thank you." Vaguely aware of how often she had said thank you in a brief amount of time, Kate started for the door and halted, remembering Ethan's jacket draped around her shoulders. She didn't want to remove the garment. Having it around her not only warmed her, it lent a feeling of comfort, made her feel as safe as she had felt in his arms. It also retained the scent of his body, his cologne, and strangely that was comforting, too.

Reluctantly taking it off, she walked back to hand it to him. "I'm sorry." She gave him a sincere, faint apologetic smile. "I forgot I was wearing it."

Ethan scanned the waiting room. "You left the house without a jacket, didn't you?" he said.

"Yes, but . . ."

"It's chilly out," he cut in, trying to hand it back to her. "Keep it. I'll get it later."

Kate was shaking her head before he had finished speaking. She couldn't hide inside his coat anymore than she could hide from reality inside his embrace. "I don't need it. Really, I'll be fine. I'll turn the heater on in the car."

Once again she started for the door, and stopped with the sudden realization of a dreadful but necessary duty she had to perform.

"Kate?" Ethan frowned at the expression on her face as she turned to face him. "What is it?"

"A funeral director must be notified, arrangements made. When . . . who . . . ?" She broke off when he shook his head.

"You look about ready to collapse," he said gently. "You go on home. I'll call the mortician. As to the funeral, it's all taken care of. David prearranged and prepaid everything over a year ago." Stepping around her, he opened the door. "Now, go. If you need anything, anytime, call me."

Holding herself together by sheer force of will, Kate walked into the hallway.

"And, Kate." Ethan called after her.

"Yes?" She glanced back at him.

"Drive carefully, please."

She sighed, nodded. "I will."

CHAPTER EIGHTEEN

The house was full, with still more people arriving by the minute.

Kate stood in the foyer, greeting the callers, accepting their condolences, numbed by the events of the previous days, from the time of David's death, through the heart-wrenching moments of telling Mandy, Connie, and Helen. She was numb from trying to comfort the inconsolable girls, and from the ordeal of the funeral less than an hour before.

Other than an emotional need for moral support, Kate had no practical reason to call on Ethan. But, even if she had a reason, she wouldn't have had to call, for he called her up several times each day.

The mere sound of his encouraging voice on the phone was comforting, bolstering her flagging spirit, helping her deal with the reality of David's death.

She was tired. Her legs ached from standing so

long, first while greeting mourners at the funeral home, now in the foyer of David's home. Her head ached from not enough hours of sleep and too many tears of grief. Her heart ached, for David, for her sisters, and for herself.

But her eyes were dry. After hours and hours of crying, Kate had cried herself out. She could even smile, as she continued to greet and chat with the seemingly endless stream of callers.

Kate had had no idea David knew so many people, had so many friends and acquaintances. He had been so quiet, had kept to himself, especially after her mother died. He rarely went out, and yet, all these people had attended the funeral service, and come back to the house to extend their sympathies.

The elder Winstons were there to lend their support. Kate caught sight of Mark, his face somber as he moved from group to group. With a quick glance around, Kate found Virginia, seated on a settee, speaking to Mandy and Connie situated on either side of her. Sharon and her husband, Charles, were there, aloof and reserved, but there. And Sharon's coolly delivered words of sympathy sounded genuine, sincere.

Carol and Jason were there, actually being civil with each other as they, like Mark, moved about the room, introducing themselves, engaging the callers in casual conversation. They had both been there for Kate, offering their support ever since she had notified them of David's death. It was then, when they had arrived simultaneously at the house the morning after, that hostilities between them ceased.

Kate didn't hold out much hope for the cease-fire to last much longer. But, for the moment, the peace was lovely, and she greatly appreciated having Carol and Jason close by so often, lending a hand, or holding her hand.

Ethan and Paula were not there. They had both attended the funeral services at the funeral home and at the cemetery, but as yet had not put in an appearance at the house.

Irrational as she knew it to be, Kate felt wounded by his failure to come to the house to pay his respects. Ethan had done so much already, showing up at the hospital, taking care of the paperwork, and contacting the funeral director. And, as David had made Ethan his executor, there was a lot more for him to do before the estate was settled.

The stream of people slowed to a trickle, and finally came to an end. Leaving her post in the foyer, longing to sit down, if only for a few minutes, yet mindful of her duty as hostess to circulate, Kate went first to the kitchen to check on how Helen and the caterers were getting on.

The services at the funeral home had been scheduled for ten-thirty, and it was now past noon. Their guests had to be hungry, as very likely Mandy and Connie were as well, even if Kate wasn't. They deserved to be fed.

As usual, Helen had everything under control, even herself, although her eyes were still red-rimmed, her face drawn and pale, her normally crisp voice subdued.

"Can I do anything to help?" Kate asked, skimming

a glance into the dining room and at the containers of food being unpacked by the two servers sent by the caterer.

"No." Helen shook her head. "Go mingle until the food has been set out on the dining room table." She heaved a sigh. "I'm so glad we listened to the caterer about ordering more food than we thought we'd need. I never dreamed there would be this many people."

"Neither did I," Kate said, gazing with longing at the coffee pot, and secretly yearning for a cigarette, a vice she had indulged in too often the previous three days. "May I have just half a cup of coffee before I mingle?"

"You'll have a full cup. You look like you need it," Helen said, moving to the restaurant-sized coffee urn the servers had brought with them.

"You may have a gallon of coffee if you want."

Kate had to suppress a shiver at the sound of the dear voice, the featherlight touch of a familiar hand at her back, the distinct and tantalizing scent of Ethan.

"I'll have one, too, Helen, please," he added. "A cup, not a gallon."

"Oh . . . Ethan . . . I didn't know you had arrived." Flustered, she felt guilty for her immediate response to his voice, his touch, his scent. She reminded herself that even though there had been no formal announcement, and she wore no ring, she had accepted Jason's proposal. Kate frowned and glanced around. "Isn't Paula with you?"

He shook his head. "No. She decided to stay home with the baby," he explained rather tersely, smiling his thanks to Helen as he accepted the two cups of steaming coffee she handed him. "I suggest we sit down with this." Without waiting for her agreement, he walked to the kitchen table.

"Oh, but, I have to . . . ," she began, only to have her attempt at protest overridden.

"Come sit down for a few minutes, Kate, before you fall down," he ordered gently.

She complied. But not because he had told her to sit down, Kate assured herself, perching on the chair opposite him. But because she wanted to do so. She had never taken orders from him; suggestions, yes, orders, no. And she wasn't about to start at this late date.

He smiled, as if he read her thoughts clearly in her expression, and set one of the cups in front of her. "Go on, Ms. Fuzzywig, drink your coffee. I think you need the caffeine jolt."

Talk about jolts. It had been so long since she had heard him call her Ms. Fuzzywig, Kate felt the jolt of surprise shoot through her entire system. For one mad instant, she felt a compelling impulse to jump up, circle the table, and crawl onto his lap and into his arms.

Of course, she did no such thing. Quashing the impulse, she reached for the cup in front of her. Noting the tremor in her fingers, she cradled the cup in both hands before daring to raise it to her lips.

"It's been a rough three days," Ethan said quietly, obviously also noting the tremor in her fingers. "And today is the worst."

Kate started to nod in agreement, but paused and

shook her head instead. "Today was—is—hard, but the worst was the night David died." She broke off, shuddering with the memory, and took a steadying sip of coffee. "And then afterward, telling Mandy, Connie, and Helen. It was awful."

"I'm sure it was." His voice and dark eyes were soft with sympathy. "I spoke to the girls before coming to the kitchen to find you. They seem to be all right, or at least over the worst of the shock."

"Yes." She nodded and took another, deeper swallow of coffee. "Your mother has been wonderful with them."

"I know." He smiled. "She's fond of both of them, and has a special soft spot for Mandy, as you know."

"Yes." Kate smiled back. "Mandy adores her."

"Mother is aching for them," he said. "Much the same way as she used to ache for you."

"Me?" Kate blinked. "Why me?"

Ethan took a swallow of his own coffee before answering. "Oh, because she thought you looked so lost and alone when you first came here to live." He smiled in remembrance. "For awhile, aware of how very much in love Maureen and David were, Mother worried about you being left out of their magic circle, so to speak. She told me, years later, when you were in college, that she was glad I had allowed you to trail after me while you were growing up, being a brother figure to you." He chuckled, and it had a hollow, almost sad note.

Kate wanted to question him about the melancholy sound of his voice, but he continued on, his tone lighter.

"You know, Mother would have liked a third child of her own, but couldn't have any more after I was born. I believe she fell in love with Mandy the first time she held her in her arms. I suspect that after David's mother died, my mother happily became her surrogate grandmother."

The girls never knew David's father, who had succumbed to a massive heart attack when he was in his mid-fifties. David's mother had passed away when the girls were three and five respectively, and as Maureen had been an orphan, the girls, like Kate, had no grandparents at all.

"As Helen became Connie's," Kate inserted, knowing that while Helen loved both girls, she had a special soft spot for Connie, quite like Virginia had for Mandy. For herself, Kate was grateful to the two loving and caring women, and happy for her sisters.

"I try to treat both girls the same," Helen said in a concerned tone, obviously having overheard Kate's remark. "I always have."

"And you've succeeded," Kate assured her, draining her cup. "But, right now, I'm failing as a hostess." She stood, pausing when Ethan touched her hand.

"Take time for another cup of coffee," he urged. "There's something I need to discuss with you."

"Can't right now." She shook her head. "I've got to mingle, thank people, for David's sake."

He grasped her hand. "Before you run off, will it be convenient for me to stop by tomorrow afternoon for the reading of the will?"

Kate stiffened; she hadn't given a thought to David's

will; she didn't want to think about it. Having a reading of the will made everything so . . . so final.

"Kate?"

"Yes, all right." She pulled her hand from the warmth of his and started for the doorway.

"Kate." This time it was Helen who stopped her. "The servers have everything ready. You can tell everyone to help themselves to the food in the dining room, coffee and soft drinks in the kitchen."

Having been given an actual task, rather than simply to mingle, Kate left the kitchen.

Ethan was right behind her. "Okay, here's the game plan," he murmured as they approached the wide entrance into the spacious living room.

Game plan? Kate paused to give him a puzzled look.

"You take the left side of the room to invite people to help themselves to the food and drinks, and I'll take the right." He slanted a quick grin at her. "Then stand out of the way to avoid being trampled by the mad dash to the dining room and kitchen."

Kate fought a return grin, thinking a display of humor unseemly under the circumstances. But she couldn't control the twitch of a smile at the corners of her mouth.

"There's my Kate," he said, his slight grin sliding into a soft smile. "Resilient and strong." Raising his hand behind her back, he caught a spiral curl with his fingers, gave a light tug, and turning right, strolled into the room.

There's my Kate. My Kate.

Kate stood immobilized for a few moments, her heart tingling from the quick, painless tug, the echo of Ethan's voice reverberating inside her head, a great sadness welling up inside her.

If only she were his Kate.

If only . . .

God she needed a cigarette.

One of the guests moved past her, from the right side of the room.

Kate came to her senses. What she needed was to get her head out of the clouds, and her rear end in gear. Giving herself a mental shake, she walked into the room and turned left.

Minutes later, she was alone. Kate had never seen a room empty out so fast. Even Ethan had gone into the dining room, escorting his mother, Mandy, and Connie. Kate felt certain his intention was to coax the girls into eating something.

Kate wasn't hungry. All she wanted was for this seemingly endless day to be over.

She was standing by one of the long front windows, staring out at the sun-splashed but cool spring midday when Carol, her expression determined, strode into the room. She was wearing her own jacket and carrying Kate's blazer.

"Let's go," she said, thrusting the blazer into Kate's hands.

"Go?" Kate frowned, absently putting on the classic black wool blazer. "Go where?"

"For a walk." Pulling on her jacket, Carol grasped Kate's arm and headed for the doorway, tugging Kate along with her. "You need some fresh air."

"But, I can't leave now," Kate protested, stumbling

along in the other woman's wake, while pulling back her arm in a fruitless bid to break Carol's grip.

"Sure you can," Carol replied, charging ahead down the front walk. "I told Helen and that gorgeous hunk Ethan that I was taking you for a short walk." She flashed a grin of triumph as, reaching the sidewalk, Kate fell into step beside her. "They both said it was a good idea, and for you not to worry, they'd hold the fort."

"Okay, okay, I'll walk," Kate surrendered, beginning to gasp for breath. "But will you please slow down?"

Carol glanced back over her shoulder before nodding and slowing her forward rush. "Okay, we're out of sight of the house now." She reached into her pocket, grasped something, and held it out. "Here. I thought you might need this."

Kate stared at the mangled pack of cigarettes she had last seen at the bottom of her purse, the package she had bought the day of Ethan's baby's christening. "You're right, I do need one," she admitted, taking the pack. Shaking one of the cigarettes from the pack, she smoothed out the bends in the cylinder before asking, "How did you know?"

Carol smiled. "I caught sight of a pack one day months ago, while you were rooting in your purse for your car keys after exercise class."

"Yet you didn't say anything." Kate lit the cigarette, took a drag and coughed. The cigarette was stale and tasted as awful as every other one she'd smoked since the night David died. She took another drag, and coughed again.

Carol rolled her eyes. "What's to say? If you want to ruin your lungs, that's your business."

"I don't want to ruin my lungs." Kate heaved a sigh. "I don't smoke often, never did, only when I'm tense and anxious." The tension showed in the jerky movement of the hand she raised to her mouth. She took a deeper drag. This time she didn't cough.

"Matter of fact," she continued, turning her head to exhale the smoke away from Carol, "I had quit." Her hand tightened around the pack, mangling it even more. "I bought this package . . ." Not about to confess to when and why she purchased the cigarettes, she broke off, allowing Carol to draw her own conclusions.

"You don't owe me any explanations, Kate." Carol grasped her free hand and gave it a quick, reassuring squeeze. "We're friends. You can smoke like a chimney, and although I would be concerned for your health, it wouldn't change anything. We'd still be friends. And with the tensions of today, I could see you needed one. That's why I dragged you out here."

A film of tears misted Kate's eyes. "Thanks, friend." Her voice was tight with emotion. Tossing away the butt, she immediately lit another. "I appreciate your concern, but I really did need this."

"You're welcome." Carol shot a grin at her. "Smoke away, we'll walk awhile."

They walked to the intersection. Stopping, Kate squashed the butt and stashed it and the first one in her pocket.

"Feeling better, less tense?" Carol asked, falling into step with Kate as she started back to the house.

"Yes." Kate smiled. "Thanks again."

Shrugging, Carol said casually, "By the way, I learned something today."

"Something other than the fact that your friend has absolutely no willpower?" Kate asked, dryly.

"Oh, knock it off," Carol said impatiently. "So you need a smoke now and then. So what? Christ, it's not like you're blowing your mind with hard drugs or alcohol. And it's not true anyway. You're one of the strongest-willed people I know—and I'm no slouch in the will department, myself." Her voice softened. "Besides, you're even tempered and tolerant—and I'm cynical and impatient."

"I know." Kate smiled, really smiled for the first time in days. "But it's an act."

Carol laughed. "Don't you believe it, friend. But that's beside the point. Do you want to hear what I learned today, or not?"

"Sure," Kate said, feeling better, breathing easier.

"I learned that Jason isn't such a bad guy after all." Carol frowned. "Weird, huh?"

Not knowing whether to laugh or cry, Kate just shook her head. After all her failed efforts to get Carol and Jason together in a social situation, she would never have imagined that David's funeral would be the venue.

CHAPTER NINETEEN

It was finally over.

Kate resumed her post in the foyer, once again thanking their guests as she saw them out. She felt exhausted. It had been a long, trying day. It was now late afternoon. She never dreamed the people, or at least some of them, would linger so long at the house. But now only a few remained.

Carol and Jason were in the kitchen, helping Helen, Mandy, and Connie put away the surprising amount of food that was left over.

The elder Winstons and Ethan were the last to approach her; Sharon and Charles had left immediately after lunch.

"My dear," Virginia said, taking Kate's hands. "If there is anything more I can do, don't hesitate to call me."

Kate squeezed the woman's hands, and blinked

against a surge of moisture to her eyes. Lord, she had believed her tear well had run dry, Kate thought, smiling mistily at the older woman. "Thank you, but you've done so much already, I . . ."

"Nonsense," Virginia interrupted.

"She's right," Mark inserted, drawing her hands from his wife's and into his own. "And we will have the girls over to the house tomorrow while Ethan explains the details of David's will to you."

"Thank you . . . again," Kate murmured, controlling a shudder at the mention of David's will. "I don't know what else to say."

"Nothing else is necessary." He released her hands to take his wife's arm. "You need to rest, Katelyn. You look like you're on the verge of collapsing."

Her throat closed up at the concern in his voice, yet Kate had to smile, if faintly: Mark Winston was the only person who persisted in calling her Katelyn.

"I'll be fine, really," she managed to choke out.

"We know you will, dear. It'll take some time." Virginia opened the front door. "Coming, Ethan?"

"In a few minutes, Mother." He stepped forward to shut the door after his parents. "You really do look beat, Kate," he said, frowning as he turned back to peer into her pale face, her grief-dulled eyes. "Would you rather wait a day or so for me to go over the will with you?"

"No." Kate shook her head. "I appreciate your concern, but I'd prefer to get it over with."

"Okay." Unlike his parents, Ethan did not take her hands, he took her into his arms. Holding her in a loose embrace, he gazed into her up-turned face. "I had my secretary clear my appointment schedule after two." He raised his eyebrows. "Will two-thirty be all right?"

"Yes." Her unsteady voice betraying the quiver of response inside, Kate held herself still, thrilling, too much, to his touch, afraid he'd pull her closer, hold her tighter, afraid he wouldn't.

For a moment, a long, breathless moment, Ethan just stared at her. Then his arms grew taut and . . .

"Kate?" Carol called, her voice preceding her footsteps along the hallway.

Kate suppressed a groan of despair.

Letting his arms fall to his side, Ethan stepped back, turned, and opened the door. "I'll see you tomorrow. Get some rest." He repeated his father's advice and smiled, again almost sadly. Then he was gone.

"Was Ethan the last?" Carol asked, coming up beside her, purse and jacket in hand.

"Yes." Kate turned to smile at her friend.

"Are you okay?" Carol peered at her in much the same manner as Ethan had. "I saw him holding you."

"Yes, just tired," Kate answered. "Ethan's a good, caring neighbor and friend."

"Lucky you." Carol grinned.

"He's also a husband and father." Kate wasn't sure if she was reminding Carol or herself.

Carol sighed. "Yeah, I know. Oh, well." She shrugged. "Need a quick smoke?" she asked in a conspiratorial murmur. "I'll cover for you if you do."

Kate laughed. It felt good. "No, thanks anyway. I guess I'd better go lend a hand in the kitchen."

Carol shook her head. "Not necessary. The food's

away, and the kitchen and dining room have been restored to order. Jason's talking to the kids, Helen's making a fresh pot of coffee for you, and I'm outta here." She started for the door.

Kate caught her by the arm. "Carol . . . I . . ." She smiled. "I don't know how to thank you."

"Don't even try," Carol warned, grinning. "How does that old song go? 'That's What Friends Are For.' Or something like that?" Reaching for the doorknob, she turned it and pulled the door open. "I'll call you after school tomorrow."

"Okay," Kate agreed, then exclaimed, "no, wait a minute. There was so much food left, as you know. If you don't have other plans, why not come here after school and have supper with us?"

"Well . . ." Carol hesitated. "Today was pretty stressful for all of you. Are you sure you wouldn't rather have a day of peace and quiet tomorrow?"

"What . . . you're gonna bring a brass band with you?" Kate asked wryly.

Carol gave her a get-serious look.

Kate nodded and explained, "To tell the truth, I'm not sure how any of us are going to handle the quiet tomorrow."

"Too much time to think?"

"Yes," Kate admitted.

"Gotcha. I'll be here."

"Thanks again, Carol."

"Shut up." She grinned, waved and stepped outside. "See you, then." Not waiting for a response, Carol pulled the door closed.

Her smile soft, thinking how lucky she was to have

a friend like Carol, Kate turned around and nearly bumped into Jason who had come up behind her.

"Oh, Jason, you startled me!"

His hands shot out to grasp her shoulders, steadying her. "Sorry."

Kate gave a shaky laugh. "I didn't hear you."

"Obviously." Smiling, he slid his hands over her shoulders and down her back, drawing her into his arms. "Maybe I should have whistled or something."

"Or something," she agreed, smiling back at him because, even though his embrace did not give her thrilling shivers, he really was a nice guy. "Carol told me Helen was making coffee. Did she send you to get me?"

"No. But, since I was on my way out, I told her I'd tell you the coffee was ready."

"You're leaving, too?"

He nodded. "I . . . ," he began, only to be interrupted by a quick knock on the door.

"Now, who . . . ?" Frowning, Kate slipped out of his arms and moved to open the door.

Carol stood there disgruntled. "My car won't start," she explained, stepping inside. "I guess the battery's dead." Spying Jason, she brightened. "You wouldn't happen to have jumper cables, would you?"

"No, sorry." Jason moved his shoulders in a helpless shrug, and looked to Kate. "Do you?"

She shook her head. "No."

Carol sighed. "Then I'll have to call the three A's to send a tow truck." She started for the phone on the foyer table. "It'll probably take hours for someone to get here."

"I can give you a lift into town," Jason offered.

"But how will I . . ."

"Then pick you up on my way to school tomorrow," he continued, cutting her off. "And drop you here after school to pick up your car."

Carol looked skeptical. "I don't know."

"Why not?" This time it was Kate who cut her off. "I can have the battery charged while you're at school, and you were coming here afterward anyway."

"She was?" Jason asked. "Why?"

"Do I need a reason?" Carol bristled. "I mean other than friendship?"

"Well . . . no, but . . ."

"Jason, I invited Carol to come after school and stay for supper," Kate said impatiently. "I was going to invite you, too, before you left."

"Oh." His smile was sheepish. "I accept."

"And I accept your offer of a ride," Carol said, with more annoyance than gratefulness. "Were you planning to leave anytime soon?"

The look Jason shot at Carol should have turned her to cinders, Kate thought, repressing a laugh. But, unsinged, Carol returned his glare with a serene smile.

Jason's eyes narrowed.

Carol's eyebrows arched.

Kate coughed to smother the persistent urge to laugh tickling her throat.

After a moment, Jason surrendered with a noisy sigh. "Okay, let's get going."

Kate managed to contain her amusement until a

few moments after the door closed behind the two antagonists.

Hours later, her amusement long gone, Kate stood wrapped in her winter coat on the still and cold night-darkened patio, smoking the second to last stale cigarette she had shaken from the crumpled pack.

Her eyes burned from tiredness and tears, fresh tears shed with Mandy and Connie. She had held them in her room, crooning words of comfort as they wept for their father, their own losses, until they had finally cried themselves to sleep in her bed.

Her heart aching for them, and herself, Kate had tenderly covered them, then tiptoed from the room, to seek the quiet of the night, and her own meager comfort in the cigarette.

Alone, her guard down, her shoulders slumped from weariness. After three harrowing days, and three nights of only snatches of sleep, she was tired, so very tired.

And it wasn't over yet.

Ethan was coming to the house tomorrow to read and explain to her the contents of David's last will and testament.

The stamp of finality on a life.

Kate shivered, blinked, sniffed, and raised a hand to swipe a finger under her nose.

She felt so alone, so terribly alone. Even with her sisters and Helen close by she felt the chill of being alone, alone and scared of the cold weight of responsibility for them that now rested upon her shoulders.

The scared feeling would pass in time, Kate knew, as would the shock of David's death. She could and would handle the responsibility of her sisters, and even Helen.

But this chilling sense of being alone, brought so forcibly home to her by David's death—would that ever pass?

Maybe with Jason, after they married . . .

Kate took a shaky drag on the awful tasting cigarette in a fruitless attempt to mentally dodge the obvious, that being: if she still felt so very alone after all these months with Jason, why would the symbolic act of him slipping a ring on her finger make any difference?

With a sigh of defeat, Kate faced the cold, hard facts. In spite of Jason's optimistic outlook for a future for them together, she knew, deep down inside, that she would never feel anything other than caring, respect, and friendship for him. And Jason deserved better. He deserved to be loved, deeply loved, by some special woman.

Kate knew she wasn't and could never be that woman. Her heart wasn't free, hadn't been since her seventeenth year, the year she had unconditionally, without full adult realization, given her heart, her undying love to the man who, hours ago, for a few precious seconds in a loose, almost casual embrace, had banished the chilling sense of being alone.

Ethan. Kate's heart cried out for him.

He belongs to another, her conscience chastised.

For a moment rebellion flared. Her imagination took flight. So what if Ethan belonged to another? He had been seeing, making love with that "other" woman all the while he had been seeing, making love to her, Kate reflected.

He had held her in his arms at the hospital, and again just that afternoon. He had brushed her waist, touched her hand with his fingertips, tugged on her hair . . . as if compelled to touch her.

Rebellion extended the moment as excitement ran wild within her. If she were to encourage Ethan tomorrow when he came to the house to read the will . . .

How might he react?

Might he chase the chill inside her by taking her into his arms, warm her with the crushing pressure of his hard, heated body, set her on fire with his hot mouth and tongue, as he had before when they were together?

"Oh damn!" Kate jumped in pain; forgotten, the cigarette had burned down to the filter, singeing her fingers.

Calling herself the biggest of fools, she cast the butt to the flagstone. Crushing the butt beneath the toe of her shoe, she raised her stinging fingers to her lips. But Kate was smarting more in her conscience than the tender flesh on the inside of her fingers.

The startling shock of the burn had brought her to her senses, ending her erotic flight of fancy. Her rebellious moment had vanished with the smoke.

She loved Ethan and was beginning to fear she would always love him. But he could not be hers— not even if he were willing to indulge in an extra-marital affair.

Imaginary flights of fancy were one thing, acting

them out was something else altogether. No matter how much she loved him, yearned for him, physically ached for him, Kate knew that with the values instilled by her upbringing, she could never be part of such a liaison.

She knew as well that, whether or not he was willing to take a chance on her, those very values demanded she tell Jason she could not in clear conscience marry him.

Rather than lightening the load, Kate's decision weighed more heavily on her shoulders.

Sighing, she turned to slowly walk back into the house, for the first time forgetting to pick up and discard the cigarette butt.

Kate had a sinking feeling Jason was not going to be happy with her decision.

Perhaps she'd put it off for a couple of days, at least until she had her own emotions more firmly under control.

Having opted for the path of least resistance for the time being, Kate hung her coat in the foyer closet, climbed the stairs to her room, slipped out of her robe and crawled into her bed between her sleeping sisters.

Popping the tab, Ethan took a deep swallow of beer from the cold can, and let out a deep sigh.

Bobby was asleep at last.

Resting his head back against the sofa, he contemplated the lateness of the hour and the vagaries of babies. For over a month now, Bobby had been settling in early, usually before eight, and sleeping through the night.

But tonight, of all nights, with Ethan feeling beat, mentally, physically, and emotionally strung out, Bobby demanded Daddy's undivided attention until nearly midnight, just a few minutes ago.

Ethan knew he should go to bed, and he had every intention of doing so, just as soon as he finished his beer.

Raising the can high, he rubbed the cold metal surface over his aching forehead before slowly lowering it to his lips. As the can passed his nose, Ethan caught the distinct scent of wild strawberries on his fingertips. His hand stilled and he drew in a deep breath.

Wild strawberries. The scent of Kate's shampoo. In that instant, Ethan could feel the silky texture of her hair, the satiny skin of her hand, the trimness of her waist against his fingers, the fingers with which he had touched her.

An act of self-torture, for certain, Ethan chided himself, drawing in another deep breath to capture the scent of her, before lowering the can to his lips, gulping the cold liquid in hopes of dousing the heat building inside him.

Would he want her forever?

Ethan gave a soft laugh; it had a ragged sound.

On this chilly spring night, he realized he had been celibate for over a year. Not that he hadn't had opportunities. He had. In fact, he had been presented with several blatant propositions from some very attractive, professional women, no strings attached.

He had turned down every one of them.

Out of a sense of loyalty to Paula?

Hell no, Ethan thought, letting out another ragged laugh. Paula had quite frankly admitted to him that, as he had continued to decline her offer of mutual sexual satisfaction, she had been to bed with two different men since recovering from the "messiness" of pregnancy and childbirth.

So, had he remained celibate out of a sense of his own honor and integrity? Yes, and besides, feeling rightly or wrongly, as if he had betrayed her, he believed he owed that honor and integrity to Kate.

So, yeah, Ethan figured he would want her forever, and he feared his desire would be forever frustrated. But that was before he had held her in his arms to comfort her the night David died, comfort her, and again this afternoon at the house, when he had felt the quivery response of her body to his touch.

A spark of expectation flickered inside Ethan. Could it be possible that Kate still had feelings for him? If she did, she had hid them well over the past year, for all he had seen in her attitude had been casual friendship.

And then there was that guy, Jason . . . whoever. He seemed to be around a lot. He had begun to suspect that Kate and Jason were involved in a relationship.

Yet, Ethan was certain he had not mistaken her response to him on both occasions. He took a swallow of beer, pondering the seeming contradiction. Come to think of it, he mused, taking another deep swallow, Kate had responded, if briefly, to his kiss under the mistletoe at Christmastime, too. His memory had imprinted the feel of her pliant lips, the quick upward surge of her body against his, the quickening of his own body before he had stepped back, away from temptation, to stare down at her, wanting, wanting . . .

Could it be possible that she wanted him, too?

Ethan gulped down the last of the beer to quench the sudden thirst created by a flash of excitement.

In two months or so, as prenuptially arranged, he and Paula would be parting ways, seeking divorce. Though he would have full custody of his son, he would be a free man again, free to explore possibilities with Kate, maybe even . . .

But suppose it was only a physical thing with Kate, a persistent itch that, for whatever reason, wasn't being scratched by Jason?

Ethan reminded himself that he knew, probably better than anyone else, the depths of Kate's sensuality. He had been the first to plumb those intoxicating depths.

The first. Was Jason slated to be the last?

It was a good thing the can was empty, because Ethan's clenching hand squashed it.

Frowning, he stared at the crumpled can. Damn it, he wanted more than a physical relationship with Kate—he had always wanted more. He wanted everything, the whole romantic scenario. Love. Marriage. The works.

A daughter. Ethan heaved a sigh. He adored his son but, he would love to make a baby girl with Kate.

He wanted another beer. Standing, Ethan started for the kitchen, then paused, shaking his head. His mind was already rambling, waxing sentimental. Another beer and he'd likely be downright incoherent. Time for bed.

Changing direction, he went to his bedroom, and straight to the crib along one wall. His son was finally out for the count. A soft smile curving his lips, Ethan drew the blanket up over Bobby's chest.

Turning away, he stripped out of his clothes and slid naked between the sheets, saying a silent prayer for his son to sleep through the night, at least until the nanny he had hired arrived at seven-thirty.

Ethan sighed and settled in. He had a full schedule in the morning, an appointment for lunch with an important client, and in the afternoon the meeting with Kate at the house, to go over David's will with her.

Kate was in for a surprise.

Kate.

His body stirred.

Damn it, Ethan told himself impatiently, knock it off and go to sleep.

CHAPTER TWENTY

Kate was more than surprised; she was stunned. Speechless, she simply sat there, staring at Ethan.

He frowned. "Are there any questions?"

Questions? Kate thought. Of course there were questions. Questions she probably should have asked David, but never thought about asking, and wouldn't have, in any case, believing it not her place to ask.

Of course, she had known David had given her power of attorney, and she had had occasion to use it, too: once when David was out of the country on a business trip, and several times to write checks to cover household expenses, as well as personal expenses, for her and the girls. And she had known, as well, had agreed—almost a year ago now—to David naming her legal guardian of the girls, in the event that . . .

The event had occurred, and now Kate stared at

Ethan in shock and surprise at what she had not known.

"Kate?" Ethan's voice scattered her thoughts.

She blinked. "Yes?"

"Is there some confusion? Would you like me to go over some of the details? Something you don't fully understand?"

"No." She shook her head. What wasn't to understand in the details? Kate ticked them off in her mind.

One. The house and the majority of David's estate, including the lion's share of the stock he held in the technology, company he co-owned, and other investments as well, went to Mandy and Connie—with the stipulation that both Kate and Helen, if they so chose, be allowed to make their home with the girls for as long as they wished.

No surprises there; Kate had expected no less.

Two. David had bequeathed a generous sum of money to Helen, in addition to a retirement fund he had set up for her when she had moved into the house. The fund was now worth a very generous amount of money.

Other than the accumulated amount of the fund, there were no surprises there, either. Kate would have been surprised if David had failed to provide something for Helen.

Three. David had made provisions for a number of shares of company stock, shares of other stocks, plus a more than adequate separate income for Kate herself.

That had surprised her. But the biggest surprise of all was the extent of David's estate.

"Kate?"

"What?" She gave a half-laugh, half-exhalation of disbelief. "I had no idea David was so . . . so rich."

"Didn't you really?" Ethan asked, his expression both surprised and curious.

"No." Kate shook her head. "I mean, I presumed his income was substantial. We've always lived comfortably—" She paused when he smiled. "Okay, maybe a little more than comfortably," she allowed, "but certainly not extravagantly or lavishly. There was nothing pretentious or ostentatious about David or his lifestyle."

"While all that is true," Ethan allowed, "it is also true that you had to know how well the technology market has been doing for some time now?"

"Well . . . yes, even though I don't pay much attention to the Dow or Nasdaq." She moved her shoulders in a slight shrug. "I guess I'm basically ignorant when it comes to the stock market. Besides, I thought David's company was fairly small."

"In comparison to some of the giants, it is," he granted. "But it has been growing at a steady pace. Also, in addition to his own business, David had invested in other unrelated companies, as you now know, and had a diverse portfolio." He smiled. "The bottom line is, Kate, that David's estate is quite extensive."

The word extensive brought a frown line to her brow. "Is it going to entail a lot of work?"

"Not for you, if that's what's worrying you." He held the will aloft. "As executor, I will take care of everything."

"That's a relief," she admitted. "Because . . . right now I'm feeling pretty stupid."

He gave her a chiding look. "You're not stupid, and you know it. You're very bright. You're just stock market illiterate, as you said." He grinned. "But, stick with me, kid, and I'll educate you."

He was teasing her. Kate knew he was only teasing, and yet she experienced a jolt of excitement, felt an impulse to say she would stick with him straight through hell.

Naturally, she said no such thing. Hadn't she resolved that issue on the patio last night? Instead, she produced a wry smile and a taunting tone. "If you'll recall, I'm the teacher here. But I suppose even teachers can be educated, if they're interested in the subject."

"And you're not interested in learning?"

Why did she suddenly feel positive he was no longer talking about the stock market? The jolt of excitement expanded in Kate. Dare she continue along this line of discussion, find out exactly what the line of discussion might be, despite her lofty determination to stick to her high moral ground?

Temptation lured. She decided to chance it.

"I'm interested in learning lots of things," she replied, starting to quiver inside.

"I'm a good tutor." His voice had the texture of velvet, and his eyes darkened to a shade of rich chocolate.

Dear heavens. Kate felt her breath catch. She was living proof of how very good he was as a tutor of one particular, sensuous art form. But surely he wasn't referring to, suggesting . . . or was he?

Tantalizing thought. Tempting thought. Terrifying thought. Kate wished she could come up with a clever or witty response to relieve the sudden sensual tension hovering between them.

But intellectual thought deserted her, superseded by physical urges.

Ethan remained silent, intent, watching her, as if waiting, expecting a sign or something from her.

Kate's breathing grew slow and shallow, while her heart rate increased to a racing thud. Instinctively, she knew the sign he was waiting for.

He wanted her. In that instant, Kate knew he wanted her with the same depth of desire, the same fiery passion he had wanted her before.

And she wanted him . . . had always wanted him, just him. Not Jason or any other man . . . just Ethan.

If only . . . If only she could forget her principles, blank out her conscience.

Barely breathing, teetering on the edge of surrender, Kate stared into his passion-darkened eyes.

If only . . .

The tension stretched out, crackling between them—only to snap when a timid knock sounded against the office door. Mandy, home already from the Winstons's, poked her head into the room.

"Jason's here, Kate," she said, slanting an apologetic smile at Ethan. "Will you be much longer?"

"No." Returning her smile, Ethan stood and began sliding documents into his attaché case. "We're finished here for now." He shifted a wry, telling glance at Kate and arched his brows. "Unless you have questions?"

Double meaning? Kate didn't know, and didn't want to know. What she did know, understand, was the relief pouring through her at having been saved from committing the unthinkable by Mandy's interruption. She had been on the verge of confessing to Ethan that she needed him.

Shaking her head—in silent denial of him, or despair of her weak self?—Kate stood to face him across David's desk. "No." She infused firm conviction into her voice.

He gave her a sharp, probing look of comprehension. "If you think of any, just give me a call." His voice was brisk, professional. He started to the door.

"I will." Mandy had disappeared. Reminded of her duty as hostess, she followed, intending to see him out.

At the door, he stepped back for her to precede him. "I'll be in touch to keep you up to speed on the legal process."

"Fine." So polite. So proper. So banal, Kate thought, passing him to lead the way to the front door.

Just as she reached the foyer, Jason walked out of the living room, Mandy right behind him.

"Ahh . . . there you are." His smile tender, he walked to her and took her into his arms. "Are you all right?" His gentle eyes searched her face. "You look tired. Rough day?"

Fully aware of Ethan standing behind her, imagining she could actually feel his gaze drilling into her back, Kate worked up a smile for Jason, while suppressing an urge to tear herself out of his arms.

"I am still a little tired," she admitted. "But, fine, really." She frowned. "But where is Carol?"

"She's putting her briefcase in her car, and probably trying the ignition to make sure it turns over," Jason replied in odd, carefully modulated tones. "She'll be here any minute."

As if on cue in a well-rehearsed play, there was a light rap on the door.

Kate felt Ethan move, but he wasn't quick enough. Mandy shot to the door and swung it open.

"Hi, Carol."

Carol grinned. "Hi, kid, Kate." She swept a strangely guarded look over Kate, still held loosely in Jason's embrace, before moving on to the silent man standing to the rear of Kate. "Hello, Ethan. You coming or going?"

"Hello, Carol," he responded, moving away from Kate. "And I'm going."

Feeling embarrassed for not doing so sooner, while fully aware she had not done so deliberately, so that he'd draw his own conclusions about the seriousness of the relationship between her and Jason, Kate stepped out of the circle of Jason's arms. "I'll get your coat."

"I wasn't wearing one." The glance he sent her was cool, his tone remote.

Oh, yes, Kate thought, Ethan had definitely drawn his own conclusions. Contrarily, she wanted to cry out that it wasn't so, that his conclusions were wrong.

She didn't, of course. Instead, she inanely murmured, "Oh . . . er . . . That's right. I forgot."

"Not important." He shrugged, his tonal inflection seeming to indicate that nothing she had to say could possibly be of any importance to him.

Wounded, cut to the quick, Kate stifled a gasp. Suddenly desperate for a cigarette, she regretted creeping from her bed, through the house and into the patio early that morning. She had intended on collecting the butt she had left on the flagstone last night, but had stayed to smoke the last cigarette in the crumpled pack, swearing to herself that it would absolutely be the last one she would ever smoke.

Then again . . .

Mere seconds elapsed, and yet she had the weird sensation that they were all standing there in the foyer, she and Ethan, as well as Carol and Jason, frozen in some bizarre tableau riddled with undercurrents she couldn't fathom.

"Why don't you stay for supper, Ethan?" The young, innocent sound of Mandy's voice broke Kate's momentary thrall. "There was plenty of food left over."

Kate was torn, wanting him near, needing him to go.

Ethan's cool gaze warmed as he shifted it to Mandy. "No, thank you. I'm expected home."

Paula. Of course, Kate thought with bitter acceptance. Though he had insinuated a willingness to indulge in a little, or perhaps even a lot, of extramarital play, his wife and child took precedence.

"See you, Mandy," Ethan said to the disappointed

girl. "Kate, Carol." His hooded gaze moved to Jason, and he nodded. "Larson." There was more than a hint of insult in his use of Jason's surname.

Jason returned the nod and the backhand. "Winston."

Finally, he was gone, the door closing quietly after him, leaving Kate relieved and bereft.

And yet, throughout what was left of the afternoon, and through supper, despite the seeming normality, the sensation of strange undercurrents persisted, baffling Kate.

Although there had existed between Carol and Jason an undeclared truce since David's death, they again now seemed uncomfortable in each other's company, edgy, as if ready to fly at each other on the slightest pretext.

Kate was almost as relieved to see them leave as she had been when Ethan left. Then, to compound her puzzlement, instead of kissing her lips, Jason placed a chaste kiss on her cheek when he wished her good night. It was almost as though he didn't want to display emotion in front of Carol.

Was it possible Jason and Carol were enemies again? Kate wondered, waving them off as the two cars pulled away. Or was Jason simply hesitant to kiss her in front of Carol? Kate shook her head, perplexed. She'd have thought, if they were on the verge of resuming hostilities, Jason would have derived a measure of devilish satisfaction from kissing her in Carol's face, so to speak.

Sighing, Kate locked the door, said good night to Helen, who was in her room watching TV, then headed up the stairs to spend some time with Mandy and Connie before they settled in for the night.

It was the first night since their father's death that the girls didn't cry themselves to sleep. Encouraged, Kate decided that the three of them, she and her sisters, would return to their classrooms that coming Monday.

Only two more months remained of the current school year. As a teacher as well as their caring older sister and legal guardian, Kate knew it was important that neither of the girls miss more school than was absolutely necessary.

As for the situation between Jason and Carol . . . well, she would have to wait to see what developed.

And . . . oh hell, Kate thought, she couldn't put off telling Jason that she could not, in good conscience, marry him.

Brushing her teeth, Kate grimaced at herself in the vanity mirror above the sink.

Right or wrong, like it or not, whether or not she believed him capable, if not eager, to be unfaithful, she was still in love with Ethan.

Kate spent half that night composing, recomposing and rehearsing the least hurtful words of explanation for Jason that she could come up with, which she had to admit to herself weren't all that great, considering the emotional strain she was under.

Damn, Kate thought somewhere around three A.M., after rejecting yet another arrangement of inadequate words. How she wished she had a cigarette.

To Kate's surprise, and relief, she was granted more composing time the following two days, Friday and

Saturday. Though Jason called her up to ask how she was feeling, he didn't offer to stop by, or invite her out.

Kate decided that he was being considerate, giving her time to spend with Mandy and Connie, allowing them, as a family, to come to grips with their grief.

While she appreciated Jason's thoughtfulness, the extra time didn't really help much; Kate Lay awake long into the nights, agonizing over how to break off with him in the gentlest possible way.

In the end, all of Kate's late night agonizing proved unnecessary. On Sunday evening, Jason came to the house and asked to talk to her privately.

Her curiosity aroused, not only by his odd request, but by his strange, almost nervous demeanor, Kate took him into David's office.

"Kate, I'm here to ask you to release me from the commitment we made to each other before David died," he blurted out the minute she shut the door.

Stunned, relieved, while simultaneously feeling ridiculously insulted, Kate could only stare at him for a few seconds until she gathered her wits and found her voice.

"You want to break our engagement?" she asked, just to make sure he had actually said what she thought she had heard him say.

"Yes." His expression and voice were apologetic. A dark flush of color stained his cheeks. "You see . . . er, I . . . we . . . that is . . . Carol and I . . ."

"Carol?" Kate interjected into his stumbling attempt at explanation. "What does she have to do with this?"

"We . . . umm . . . you see," he began again, looking very uncomfortable, "Kind of thrown together, as we were, out of concern for you when David died, Carol and I . . ."

"Discovered that all along, the antagonism between us was caused by a strong physical attraction." This time it was Carol who interjected. "We're in love."

Startled, both Kate and Jason jerked around to find Carol standing in the doorway.

"May I come all the way in?" she asked, her voice more quiet and subdued than Kate had ever heard.

"Yes, of course," Kate said, glancing from Carol to Jason and back again to Carol.

"You don't hate me?" she asked, taking a tentative step into the room.

"No, I don't hate you," Kate assured her. "How could I? You're my friend." She glanced at Jason. "You are both dear friends. But, all this time, I thought you could barely tolerate him."

"So did I." Carol shrugged.

"Thanks a lot," Jason muttered.

The two women looked at him, then back at each other, and had to share a smile. "Men." Heaving a sigh of exasperation, Carol crossed the room to him, kissed him on the cheek, and summarily ordered him from the room. "Go away, Jason. Up till now, you've done a lousy job of explaining."

"But . . . ," he said in protest.

"I'll do it," Carol interrupted him, taking his hand and leading him to the open doorway.

"But . . . ," he tried again.

"Go, darling."

As if she had uttered the magic word that pushed all the right buttons, Jason's expression softened, he smiled, and walked out of the room, closing the door after him.

Carol shot Kate a wry look. "Aren't men wonderful?"

Kate had to laugh; same old Carol, apparently not even love would change her, if indeed, she was in love.

"I thought you were waiting for a hero?" she said, moving to two leather chairs and motioning for her friend to take one while she seated herself in the other.

"I found him." Carol smiled.

"Jason?" Kate couldn't hide the note of disbelief in her voice; she liked Jason, very much, but a hero?

"Yes." Carol nodded. "At least, the hero for me. I watched him, Kate," she went on to explain. "During those awful days following David's death, but most especially the day of the funeral. Jason was so thoughtful of all the guests, and so caring, so considerate, not only of you, but of the girls and Helen. He was wonderful."

He was? Kate decided she would have to take Carol's word for Jason's wonderful behavior, for she had no memory of it. All she recalled was Ethan, seemingly everywhere, the hospital, the house, the cemetery, offering his help, his kindness and consideration . . . the featherlight, encouraging brush of his fingers whenever he drew near to her.

Ethan.

Suppressing a sigh, Kate smiled at her friend. "Yes,

Jason was very supportive," she politely agreed. "And that's when you realized you were in love with him?" she asked, finding it hard to believe in light of Carol's previous and very vocal antagonism toward Jason.

Carol shook her head. "No, that's when I realized I had been wrong in my assessment of him."

"As a wimp?"

"Yes."

Kate frowned. "But, then, when did you realize that you were in love with him, and he with you?"

"The day of the funeral when my car wouldn't start and Jason offered to drive me home."

Kate nodded.

"He kissed me."

Kate was taken aback. "Jason did?" Incredible. Mild-mannered Jason? "Just out of the blue?"

"No. I provoked him," Carol admitted. "I taunted him about not knowing anything about cars. I'm not even sure why, since I don't know diddly about cars myself." She paused, as if to reflect. "No, I do know why. I deliberately taunted him to get his attention." She drew a breath. "Anyway, I kept it up, from one dumb thing to another until . . . well, I guess he reached a point where it was either kiss me or slug me."

Jason? Kate marveled. Unbelievable. "Wait a minute," she protested, thoroughly confused now. "How did you get from you taunting him to falling in love?"

"The kiss." Carol visibly shivered. "Oh, Lord, that kiss." She wrapped her arms around herself in a shiver containing hug. "It was . . . it was . . . an explosion . . . inside . . . my body and my head. It was the whole of everything wonderful, mystical, magical, sensual, and exciting, the most earth-shattering experience I've ever known. And all from that one kiss." She sighed. "Kate, you can't imagine how I felt."

Yes, she could, and did, Kate thought, her imagination too vivid of just such thrilling emotions.

"I know it sounds trite and hackneyed, maybe even a little nuts, but"—Carol laughed self-consciously—"suddenly, out-of-the-blue, I am so very much in love with Jason and, most wonderful of all, he is in love with me, too."

"Then be happy with him."

Carol gnawed her Lower lip. "You're sure you're all right with this? You should at least be angry."

"I'm not angry. Not at you or Jason," Kate said with firm conviction. "Jason is a wonderful man, and I do love him." She held up her hand when Carol tried to speak. "But I love him as a friend, nothing even remotely close to the emotional roller coaster you just described."

"Jason and I were both worried."

Kate smiled. "Don't be."

"We're still friends then?" Carol looked and sounded like she needed reassurance.

Kate didn't hesitate in giving it. "Still friends."

"Oh, Kate." Her eyes suspiciously misty, Carol jumped out of her chair and crossed to take Kate by the hands and pull her up into a bear hug. "Thank you."

Her own eyes moist, Kate hugged her back. Laughing around the sniffles, they didn't hear the door opening.

"May I join this hug-fest," Jason asked plaintively. "Or am I now persona non grata?"

Laughing easily, and turning as one, Kate and Carol each held out an arm to him in silent invitation.

Yet, even while they laughed together and hugged one another, and with her sisters and Helen close by, Kate was aware of an empty sensation.

She was alone again.

Groaning softly so as not to wake the baby, Ethan levered himself up on one arm to glance at the clock. Both hands stood straight up, as if in prayer.

Midnight. Exhaling, he flopped back onto the mattress. He froze as Bobby shifted, made a muffled sound. Straining to hear the slightest noise, Ethan slid out of bed and padded to the crib to reassure himself that the baby hadn't somehow wriggled beneath the cover and was smothering himself.

His heart pounding, he peered into the crib; his son lay peaceful, blowing bubbles in his sleep.

Damn fool, Ethan ridiculed himself, yawning and stretching his arms over his head, raking his hands through his hair as he padded back to bed.

Damn fool in more ways than being overanxious about his son, he thought in self-disgust, sprawling in abandon across the king-size mattress.

He had come so close, too close, to making an ass of himself with Kate that afternoon, and he was still smarting over the near disaster.

Using the language of double-talk, and thinking himself so clever for doing so, Ethan had told her, without putting it into explicit words, that he was willing . . . no, eager, to engage in an affair with her.

And for a couple of minutes, a few exciting minutes, he had actually thought, believed, she might agree.

Ethan could again feel the surge of hope, expectation, and desire he had experienced during those brief moments. On reflection, he knew the shimmering hope had been to simply be with Kate again in a sensual way, and even more importantly, in all the other ways of togetherness, in conversation, in laughter, in sorrow.

For a couple of minutes he had held, nourished, that nugget of shining hope . . . until Mandy had interrupted them to tell Kate that Jason had arrived.

So it was Jason who would know, share the togetherness, in all the ways, if he wasn't already. From the familiar way Jason had embraced Kate, it appeared he was already sharing all those special things with her.

Sighing, Ethan flung an arm over his eyes.

All he had was the sorrow.

CHAPTER
TWENTY-ONE

Kate, Mandy, and Connie went back to school the next day. It wasn't easy for any of them, most particularly the girls, but Kate decided the sooner they resumed a normal schedule, the better. Nothing would change the harsh reality of David's death. As Helen, the fount of old sayings, reminded them, life indeed did go on, and they had to go on with it.

The only difference in her relationship with Carol and Jason was that, as the two were now together, at times romantically Kate no longer had to act as a buffer between them.

The first week back was the hardest. Though well-meaning, the solicitousness of the administrative staff and her coworkers began to wear on Kate, and she could tell the same applied to the girls in regard to their friends.

Kate didn't want to be treated as though she were

fragile and made of glass, and neither did her sisters. They wanted their daily lives to be as normal as possible.

By the end of the second week that goal had been reached, at least in respect to the hours they spent in school. At home, although the subject was never voiced, Kate felt certain she wasn't the only one who occasionally caught herself halfway expecting David to arrive home just in time for dinner.

By the third week they were over the worst.

Helen rolled up her sleeves figuratively, declaring her intention to start spring housecleaning. Privately, she asked Kate if she should begin with David's room, but not only with the biannual cleaning, but the folding and packing away of his clothing and other personal items.

Relieved by being spared some of the bittersweet chore, Kate gave her the go-ahead on the cleaning.

"Pack the clothes up in cartons and I'll drop them off at the Goodwill store when you're finished," Kate said. "But set the personal items aside, please," she added, knowing they all would want to keep a memento or two. "The girls and I will help you sort through those things later."

After all the years Helen had been with them, and keenly aware of her preference to work alone, Kate, Mandy, and Connie resumed their former activities.

Connie and a few other girls spent a lot of time at their friend Megan's house, making exciting plans for the fast-approaching summer.

Mandy also spent some of her free time with her

friends, including her most treasured older friend, their next-door neighbor, Mrs. Winston.

Kate took up her previous pursuits of attending exercise classes, and going shopping or to a movie or dinner with Carol. Other than Carol checking schedules with Jason before making definite plans with Kate, everything remained just about as it had been before.

Ethan called two or three times a week on average, to keep Kate apprised of the progress being made in the settling of David's estate.

For all intents and purposes, Ethan sounded as he always had, his voice friendly, his manner neighborly. Still, Kate sensed a detachment, a distance between them.

It was chilling . . . and it hurt.

So, naturally, she did her best to project carefree manner she really did not feel, a happy facade to disguise the sharp, seemingly never ending pain of loving him, and his rejection of her love.

She politely asked about his family, despising the shameful jealously she felt for his wife, the searing envy she suffered for the child that was not hers.

Other than to say she was fine, Ethan never discussed Paula, but he eagerly talked about his son. While he rattled on and on about Bobby, what a delightful child he was, how fast he was growing, relating the sound of his laughter, the warmth of his smiles, Ethan's voice took on a warmth that was absent during their conversations.

Kate wished she could see his precious child, but where once she wouldn't have hesitated to invite him to bring the baby over for a visit, she now wouldn't dream of doing so, simply because she felt certain he'd refuse.

When his calls began to taper off, Kate was both sorry and relieved. She missed the sound of his voice almost as much as she missed the sound of David's. In a way, she felt she was grieving for Ethan, their former closeness, in much the same way she grieved for her stepfather.

Could it really be over a month since that awful night, the night Ethan had held her in his arms, as if to absorb some of the pain of loss she suffered?

Ethan. Kate sighed. Would she ever completely get over loving him?

She was gone.

Ethan stared at the note in his hand, rereading the flourished script Paula had scrawled across the lavender note paper she had left propped against his pillow.

Ethan, Although I know it's over a month earlier than I had promised, I am leaving now, today, for California. I received a telephone call from, of all people, my former male friend. . . . You know, the one who left me to go to Hollywood to take a part in the nighttime drama series, and sleep with the lead actress? Anyway, he said there was a part opening in the series that he felt certain he could get for me . . . if I could get out there within two days. So, I'm off. Do whatever

you like about a divorce and Bobby. I won't contest.
Wish me luck.

Her scribbled name was barely legible. Figuring Paula had been practicing her "star" autograph, Ethan shook his head and tossed the note aside.

"What difference does a month or so make?" he rhetorically asked the baby lying in the center of his bed, happily gumming the teething ring Ethan had given him.

Keeping an eye on his son, Ethan stripped out of his suit and dress shirt, and into jeans and a cotton pullover. Bobby surely wouldn't miss his mother—if she could even rightly be called that—as she had barely bothered with him.

Bobby began to fret; he lost the teething ring.

"What do you say we go rustle up something for supper, buddy?" he said, scooping the child off the bed and heading for the door. "A nice jar of mixed veggies for you, and a broiled steak for me. How does that sound?"

Apparently it sounded pretty good to the baby, for Bobby stopped fretting and began blowing tiny bubbles through his small, pursed, pink lips.

"Yep, you and I will be fine, son," Ethan continued the one-sided conversation as he descended the stairs and strolled into the kitchen. "I just wish you had a real mother, instead of a paid nanny, pleasant and competent as she is."

An image rose to fill Ethan's mind, torment his senses. An image of a tall, beautiful woman with wild red hair, fantastic eyes, a mouth to drive a man mad with desire, and a lush body to fulfill a man's every fantasy.

Damned how he wished Kate was Bobby's mother.

But life was rarely so accommodating, and a man had to deal with reality. Through his own recklessness, Kate was lost to him, Ethan acknowledged, blowing bubbles back at his son as he settled him in his infant seat.

If Kate were free—now that he himself would be free—but it was not to be.

From what he had observed in the foyer of David's house the day after the funeral, the easy and familiar way Jason Larson had taken Kate into his arms, Ethan halfway expected to hear from his mother any day now that the two were engaged and making plans to marry.

"So, it's just you and me, kid," he chatted on, suppressing a sigh of regret as he twisted the cap off the jar of baby food. "Now, ain't that exciting?"

At dinner time on a Tuesday near the end of May, Mandy came tearing into the house from visiting next door, looking as though she was about to explode with news.

"You'll never guess . . . ," she burst out, coming to a stumbling halt in the kitchen doorway.

"Probably not," Kate agreed, continuing to set the table for dinner.

"And you won't believe it," Mandy went on, with a fair amount of teenage drama.

"In that case, why don't you tell us?" Kate suggested, exchanging a wry glance with Helen.

"Paula has left Ethan to go to Hollywood to be in a TV show," she reported. "They're getting divorced, and he's going to keep the baby!"

Shocked, she stared at Mandy, who had been absolutely correct. Kate would never have guessed such a thing, and she couldn't believe it now. Surely, she thought, her sister had misheard or misunderstood something.

"Mandy, you should not repeat rumors," Kate chastised the girl. "Where did you hear this story?"

"It's not a rumor, or a story, it's true," the girl insisted in self-defense, with a hint of superiority. "Mrs. Winston told me. And I can tell you, she is very upset about it."

"So Paula just left her husband and child to go off to Hollywood to be in a TV show?" Helen asked, as if unsure she had heard right the first time.

"Yes." Mandy's hair bounced with a vigorous nod. "She always wanted to be an actress, you know."

"No, I didn't know," Helen grumbled, turning back to stab a fork into the potatoes cooking on the stove. "And if she always wanted to be an actress," she mumbled on, "why did she get married and have a baby in the first place?"

Because she or Ethan got careless and she got pregnant, Kate thought, feeling sorry for Ethan and his son, but remaining silent on the subject.

"I suppose she was in love at the time," Mandy supplied what to her must have seemed the obvious answer.

"Right," Helen agreed, but in a tone of voice that said just the opposite. She sighed. "Poor Ethan."

Poor Ethan.

The refrain ran through Kate's mind at regular intervals throughout that week and into the next. Raising a child on his own, even with hired help, would not be easy. Kate knew that better than most.

Kate wasn't sure exactly when the idea began to form, but at some point during the following weeks a tiny bud of hope unfurled into a plan, a possible solution for Ethan, and for her . . . if she could work up the nerve to approach him with it, present it to him.

Uncertain, Kate vacillated, and continued to vacillate until she heard again from Mandy via Virginia Winston, that a divorce settlement had been agreed upon, and that Ethan would have sole custody of his son.

Should she? Could she? Dare she?

Those were the questions that kept Kate teetering on the edge of uncertainty.

Ethan had not called her since his breakup with Paula, not even to give her a progress report on David's estate. Was he too busy? Or too distracted by the ramifications of his wife walking out on him, their child, their marriage?

Was Ethan hurt by the loss of his love, much the same way as Kate had hurt when he had walked away from her?

Rather than savoring a feeling of satisfaction over the likelihood that he was suffering the same deep sense of injury and rejection she had experienced,

Kate ached for him, longed to comfort him as he had so often comforted her.

Would he accept comfort from her?

Kate recalled the day after the funeral, when she and Ethan had been alone in David's office. She had been tempted then to take Ethan up on the insinuations he had made . . . or what she had believed were insinuations.

Though his actual remarks were innocuous, his eyes had sent silent, different messages, and he had appeared more interested in her as a woman, a desirable woman, than an old friend and neighbor.

Wishful thinking, then and now?

The school year ended. Carol took Jason home to Hamburg for a two-week visit to meet her family. Mandy and Connie were busy with their friends, and making plans to go to summer camp in mid-July. And Kate found herself with too much time on her hands, time in which to reflect.

If she were to take a chance, meet with him, would Ethan give any credence at all to her idea, or would he instead laugh in her face?

Probably laugh. Or gently mock her, as he had when she was young, forever ago. Or he might simply send her away.

Kate cringed inside at the very real possibility of Ethan responding in any one of those ways.

But still . . . But still . . .

What did she have to lose but her pride? Kate thought. And what was pride compared to the chance, however slim, of being with him, making a life with Ethan?

Whipping up her courage, Kate took the plunge and called him. Her sense of relief at hearing the pleased and surprised tone in his voice was so strong that her knees buckled and she had to sit down.

"How are you, Miss Fuzzywig?" he asked, but before she could respond, he went on, a tinge of concern shading his tone. "Is there a problem? Something with the girls?"

"No . . . no, I'm fine . . . we're all fine," Kate quickly assured him. "But," she rushed on, before her nerve could dissolve, "I would like to see you, to discuss something with you." She gulped a quick breath. "That is, if you can spare the time . . . er, possibly meet me in town for lunch some day?"

Ethan was quiet for a moment, for several long moments. Thinking up an excuse not to meet with her? Kate wondered, beginning to tremble.

"I'd like that," he finally answered. "Are you free this coming Saturday?"

She wasn't. She had made a date to have lunch with a woman she had met in exercise class. "Yes," she said, certain, or at least hoping, the woman would not mind too much rescheduling their lunch date.

"Any place special you'd like to meet?" Ethan asked.

"No. Any place you choose is fine with me." Kate couldn't have cared less, certain she'd be too nervous to eat a thing, anyway. "Any restaurant or fast food place."

"You've really got my interest, Fuzzy," he said, not altogether humorously. He named a restaurant, one of the places where they had dined before his marriage. "Or would you prefer someplace else," he quickly tacked on, as if he suddenly remembered.

"No . . . no, that'll be okay, I liked it there," she assured him. "The food is . . . was . . . always good."

"Twelve-thirty, one?"

"Twelve-thirty," she said before she could change her mind, chicken out.

A time and place agreed on, they said their good-byes. Kate stood by the phone, clutching the receiver for long seconds after disconnecting the line. Then she released the breath she hadn't realized she was holding.

CHAPTER TWENTY-TWO

The morning of the day she was to have her lunch meeting with Ethan, Kate practically emptied her clothes closet, discarding one outfit after another in her search of the perfect dress, skirt, slacks and/or blouse, or pullover to wear.

In the end, fearing she'd be late, she chose a loose and flowing skirt patterned with swirls of spring greens and blues and mauve. With it she paired a darker green overshirt, the tailored ends of which she tied at the front of her waist. The lush green hue of the shirt enhanced the blue of her eyes, which she shadowed with two shades of mauve.

Taming her hair nearly set her into fits; the curly red mop simply would not be brushed and swept into submission. Sighing, she gave up, letting the mass of long spiral curls hang free, over her shoulders and down her back, silently vowing to make an appointment with her hairstylist to have the unruly tresses sheared off to chin length.

Certain she'd be late—what if Ethan thought she wasn't coming and decided not to wait?—she tore out of the house, leaving Helen staring after her in confusion.

"Damn." Ethan winced and stared at the small drop of blood from the wound he just inflicted on his jaw with his razor, his safety razor, safety, that is, when not in the unsteady hand of a man just a mite nervous about a lunch date.

Hearing Ethan's expletive through the open bathroom door, and realizing he wasn't alone, Bobby let out a bellowing demand to be picked up and taken out of his crib.

Doing his best to ignore his son, not easy at the best of times, as the five-month-old had a pair of lungs and a yell that put Tarzan to shame, Ethan managed to finish shaving without cutting his throat.

"It's okay, kid, I'm here, you're not alone," Ethan said in soothing tones as he strode into the bedroom.

Evidently, Bobby was not impressed with the reassurance, nor soothed by his father's crooning voice.

"Oh, give me a break, will you?" Ethan muttered, hopping on the edge of disaster as he stepped first into his briefs, then into casual slacks.

Were the casual slacks the right choice? he asked himself, peering critically at his reflection in the full-length mirror mounted on the closet door. Maybe he should opt for dress slacks to go with the pale blue shirt and navy spring blazer he had decided on. Then again, maybe he should simply pull on a pair of jeans with the shirt and classic blazer, and go for the hip, avant-garde look.

Bobby yelled on.

Heaving a sigh, Ethan dressed as originally planned; casual slacks, pale blue shirt, classic navy blazer. Socks and shoes, keys, money, wallet stashed into the proper pockets, a quick brush of his hair, and he finally quieted Bobby by simply picking him up out of the crib.

Grabbing the overstuffed diaper bag—he subscribed to the theory that too much stuff was better than not enough—certain he had forgotten something, Ethan frowned, glanced around the room, shrugged, and made a beeline for the stairs and the front door below.

He was going to be late, he just knew it, Ethan thought, cautiously backing the car out of the driveway. He still had to drop Bobby off at his parents' house—and he just knew his mother would try to keep him with questions—and get into town in time to meet Kate.

Kate. The mere thought of her name made his gut twist and roll. Kate had been the absolute last person he had expected to hear from the day she called him to ask for a meeting. What did she need from him? Not that Ethan cared, he'd do everything in his power to give her anything she might need . . . advice, money, moral support, whatever.

But first he had to get there, and on time. What if he was late . . . and she didn't wait?

Mindful of his precious son strapped into his car seat, Ethan fought against the urge to press his foot down against the gas pedal.

Kate was early for their appointment.

So was Ethan.

She thought he looked devastatingly attractive.

He said she looked wonderful.

He asked if she wanted a drink.

She declined.

He ordered a beer.

They exchanged the usual banal pleasantries until their lunch orders were taken. He asked about the girls and Helen. She told him they were all well, then asked after Bobby. He said the boy was fine, growing like a weed, and was at that moment with his grandparents, who were probably having a great time spoiling the child.

They laughed, and then silence stretched between them for several taut moments.

Paula's name was not mentioned by either of them.

Kate fiddled with her fork, draped her napkin over her lap, sipped from her glass of ice water.

Ethan finally took the lead. "What was it you wanted to discuss with me, Kate?"

Kate toyed with the stemmed water glass, took a couple more quick sips, then, before her dwindling nerve could desert her altogether, she outlined her idea for him.

It was a simple plan . . . with hidden complexities. She was alone, as he well knew, with the responsibility, however voluntary, of raising two young girls. He also was alone, with a much younger child to raise.

God, she prayed he was still alone, not involved with another woman, a contingency she hadn't considered until that very moment.

She found the nerve to ask.

He answered with a quick, negative shake of his head, a cynical twist tugging on his lips. sigh of relief, and Kate forged ahead. In essence, her plan was for them to join forces. They were friends, old and good friends, were they not?

They were, Ethan acknowledged with a nod, his intent gaze now steady on her, abrading her already ragged nerves.

Kate soldiered on. Why should they not combine their resources, make one family out of good friends?

"Marriage?" Ethan asked, cutting straight to the heart of her plan. "By 'joining forces' you are suggesting we marry, aren't you?"

"Yes," Kate answered, somehow managing to preserve a calm tone, while a storm of emotions raged inside.

"What about Jason? I thought you and he . . . ," he began.

She cut him off with a sharp shake of her head, and a quick and less than clarifying explanation. "We were . . . I mean, we had planned to . . ." She paused, drew a breath, and blurted out, "He fell in love with another woman . . . my close friend Carol, as a matter of fact."

Just then, the waiter arrived with their lunch orders.

Ethan was quiet, apparently chewing on her proposal, and subsequent explanation, along with his food.

"Okay, we'll talk about it," he suddenly said, brisk and businesslike, shocking her just as she had begun to fear he would flat out refuse.

There were stipulations . . . his and hers.

Candid and forthright, Ethan confessed to being old-fashioned so far as children were concerned.

"I'm dissatisfied with having to depend on a nanny, however professionally trained, to care for my son whenever I have to be away from home, whether during the day while I'm at work or for social occasions, like right now," he bluntly admitted.

Kate nodded her understanding of his feelings; David had felt the same way, even about Helen at first, which was one reason he was so thankful for his stepdaughter.

"At the risk of sounding chauvinistic, I'm going to ask if you would be willing to put your teaching career on hold for a period of time, that is, at least until Bobby is ready to start school or possibly preschool?"

In effect, in Kate's view, Ethan was indicating that while he didn't require a wife, he preferred a mother in the home.

"In other words, and remembering that this was your idea to begin with," he went on when she remained silent, "I'm asking if you'd be willing to not only put your career on hold to be a full-time homemaker, but to care for and be responsible for another woman's child. Would you also take on the role of wife to me?"

Kate gave his stipulation, or more accurately, request serious consideration. She loved teaching . . . but in truth, she had also always firmly believed that guiding a child through the early, formative years of life was the most important teaching career of all So, in that sense, she was as old-fashioned as he. Besides, he was right, the idea for them to join forces had been hers.

Still, before she rushed into agreement, Kate thought it vital to put forth her own primary stipulation.

"I have a very strong desire for a child of my own," she confessed with matching candor. "So, if *you* are willing to father and accept parental as well as financial responsibility, *I* will agree to put my career on hold, be a stay-at-home mom, raising and mothering both your child and mine, should I be lucky enough to have one, along with my sisters."

Ethan was quiet for long moments, studying her. "Then you weren't proposing a platonic marriage of convenience," he said with careful precision. "You are proposing a true . . . union, in every sense of the word?"

Kate felt herself grow warm with embarrassment. Hearing him put it like that, it sounded brash, brazenly aggressive. Would he now change his mind if she answered in the affirmative? Only one way to find out.

"Yes," she boldly replied, suddenly dying for a cigarette after weeks of abstinence.

Ethan didn't hesitate. He agreed at once.

The preliminaries over with, a deal was struck. All that had to be ironed out were the details. Ethan's divorce was not as yet final. He expected the decree to be handed down in approximately two months. He suggested they use those months as a period of dating ... courting, so to speak, utilizing that time to make their plans.

Kate voiced concern about the brief amount of "courting" time, and a sudden marriage between them on the very heels of his divorce.

Ethan, claiming a pressing desire to get his son settled in a family atmosphere, managed to convince her that they could pull it off.

Afraid the arrangement might fall apart if she hesitated, Kate conceded to his preference for the short, two-month waiting period.

Ethan mentioned a tentative wedding date of one month after his divorce became final, subject, of course, to the decree being handed down as expected.

Excited, and scared to the point of actually feeling sick, Kate agreed.

Then they both agreed to shelve the details until another time, and apply themselves to the meal both of them had been merely playing with up till then.

Still feeling slightly ill, Kate nevertheless forced the food down her throat, determined to show him a serene acceptance of their arrangement.

Over the following weeks, Kate and Ethan began to date on a regular basis. No one, either in her family or his thought it unusual. They were old friends, weren't they?

On their first date, Ethan brought his son to the house before taking him next door for his parents to babysit. Kate immediately fell in love with the boy, not only because he was almost the mirror image of his father, but for his own sweet self. The girls and Helen were equally infatuated.

In reality, when they were alone, no mutual friends or family members around, their times together were so businesslike, Kate felt herself skating on the edge of despair . . . but not enough to change her mind.

Her twenty-sixth birthday passed with a small family celebration. Ethan presented her with a delicate watch, which reminded Kate of the ticking of her biological clock.

Summer held sway with the usual Philadelphia weather, hot and humid, with an occasional, brief spell of cool air from a summer rainfall or thunderstorm.

During that first month of evenings and a few afternoons out, they firmed up their plans, ironed out the details.

The first item on the list was living arrangements.

"While my townhouse is roomy, it's not big enough to accommodate a family of six, including Helen, never mind a seventh if or when you conceive," Ethan said, apparently not noticing the color tingeing Kate's cheeks. "I think we're going to have to look for a bigger place."

Growing warm at the very idea of being pregnant with his child—never mind the act necessary to achieve that state—Kate put forth another suggestion.

"Why don't you and Bobby just move in with us? The house is certainly large enough, as you know, and I really prefer not to put Mandy and Connie through the trauma of relocating, leaving the only home they've ever known, especially so soon after their father's death.'' She paused, drew a deep breath, then forged ahead. ''The master bedroom has its own bath and it's not been used since . . . ,'' she broke off, swallowing.

Ethan nodded in understanding. ''Are you certain you won't mind sleeping in that room?''

''Yes, I'm certain.'' She smiled. ''It holds good memories. David and my mother were very happy in that room. Mandy and Connie were conceived there.'' She felt the warmth of color flare again in her cheeks, and shrugged. ''We could have the room redecorated. There's time.''

Immediately seeing the wisdom of her suggestion, Ethan agreed. ''Okay . . . on the condition that my bedroom furniture moves in with me.'' He grinned. ''I have a king-sized bed that I absolutely refuse to give up.''

''Of course,'' Kate agreed, secretly relieved at not having to sleep in David and Maureen's bed. ''Mandy has always coveted my bedroom, and now she can have it,'' she went on. ''Her room will be perfect for Bobby, since it is the room right next to the master bedroom.''

''Very well, I'll either sell or rent out the town-house,'' Ethan said, going on to bemoan the very real possibility of his son being spoiled rotten not only by the grandmother next door, but by Kate's sisters and Helen, as well.

The following evening, Ethan had been invited to the house to join the family celebration of Mandy's fourteenth birthday. After dinner, when Mandy blew out the candles on her cake and opened her gifts, Kate and Ethan, hands deliberately clasped like a real couple, seriously in love, told Mandy, Connie, and Helen about their intention to marry.

"Congratulations!" Helen exclaimed, beaming.

"That's terrific!" Mandy cried, running to Kate, then Ethan, to give them hugs. "The best birthday present of all."

"Radical!" Connie whooped, following her sister for a round of hugs. "Does that mean Bobby'll be our brother?"

Kate looked at Ethan.

He grinned, as if delighted by Connie's enthusiasm, the hopeful lilt in her voice. "Would you want Bobby to be your brother?"

"Oh, yes!" Connie sang out. "I always wanted a baby brother. Didn't you, Mandy?"

"Yeah." Mandy nodded. "Or another baby sister."

Ethan slid a quick glance at Kate. "Well . . . maybe a sister some day, but until then, you can treat Bobby as if he were your real brother. Okay?"

The girls agreed and Kate was just starting to catch the breath she had lost as a result of Ethan's sly reference to a future sister—only to lose it again over the next few which words came out of Connie's big mouth.

"If you two are engaged," she said, squinting at Kate's left hand, "where is your engagement ring?"

"Connie!" Kate and Helen scolded simultaneously. Mandy giggled.

Ethan didn't look at all perturbed. "As a matter of

fact," he said, reaching into his jacket pocket and withdrawing a small black velvet box with a domed lid. "I brought it with me to give to Kate here, after the birthday celebration."

"Ethan . . . I . . . you didn't . . . ," Kate began, thinking she should tell him a ring wasn't necessary under the circumstances, but he silenced her with a shake of his head.

Beginning to tremble, she watched, mesmerized, as Ethan flipped open the lid and handed the box to her.

"Woweee!" Connie yelped.

"Oh my gosh," Mandy murmured in awe.

"Holy mackerel," quoted Helen.

Kate was speechless herself. Eyes wide, she gazed at the rather large pear-shaped diamond solitaire set in a platinum mounting with two diamond baguettes on either side.

It was . . . gorgeous, absolutely gorgeous.

"Do you like it?" Ethan asked in anxiety-ridden tones when she didn't say anything, just staring at the ring.

"Like it?" Blinking, Kate looked up at him, her eyes cloudy with bemusement. "It's beautiful . . . but . . ."

"No," he interrupted. "Don't say any more." Taking the box, he removed the ring, handed the box to a very bright-eyed Mandy, and slipped the ring onto Kate's engagement finger. "There are two matching platinum bands to go with it."

"Two?" Kate repeated, surprised, because she had

never expected, never even dreamed, of asking him to wear a wedding ring.

"Two," Ethan said, his voice firm, determined.

Kate was still slightly dazzled by the beauty of the ring, the size of the stone, and still a bit surprised by Ethan's decision to wear a wedding band, a short time later, when they went next door to announce their engagement and show the ring to his parents.

To Kate's amazement, Virginia and Mark appeared every bit as delighted by the news as her sisters and Helen had been. But Virginia went into a tizzy when Ethan told them he and Kate planned to marry a month after his divorce was granted.

"You've set a date for two months from now?" Virginia asked in panicked tones.

"Yes." Frowning in confusion, Ethan mentioned the date they had agreed on, cautioning, "If the decree is handed down when expected."

"It will be," Mark inserted. "Even if I have to pull a few strings, call in a few favors."

Ethan grinned. "Thanks, Dad."

Always correct, rather formal, Mark inclined his head in a silent response.

"Two months," Virginia said distractedly. "It can't be done in two months time."

"What can't be done, Mother?"

"A wedding," she cried. "I can't possibly plan a decent wedding to take place in two months time."

"We don't want any fuss," Kate was quick to insist. "Do we, Ethan?"

"No." He shook his head. "A quiet civil ceremony."

"I won't hear of it," Virginia protested. "Katelyn deserves a lovely wedding. A civil ceremony is out of the question."

"But I don't . . . ," Kate began in denial.

"You're quite right, my dear," Mark blandly interrupted. "Katelyn does deserve a lovely wedding." He turned a cool, forbidding look on his son. "Doesn't she?"

"Actually, yes, she does." Ethan stunned Kate by agreeing with his father.

"But, Ethan . . . ," she tried again. No luck.

"But we won't change the date," he interrupted as blandly as his father had. "You're going to have to come up with something lovely . . . but simple, if you can, Mother."

"Oh, your mother can," Mark said, startling Kate with the look of complete adoration he gave Virginia. "Your mother can work wonders if she puts her mind to it."

CHAPTER TWENTY-THREE

Virginia Winston's mind proved capable of producing the most lovely mid-September wedding anyone could ever imagine, and in her very own backyard, at that.

"It's so pretty, isn't it, Kate?"

Standing inside the French doors leading to the lush gardens, her stomach in nervous knots, Kate managed a smile for Connie, nodding in agreement.

The deep yard and gardens beyond the doors were more than pretty, they were beautiful. Mounds and mounds of various shades of pink hothouse flowers were banked strategically around tall shade trees near a white gazebo draped with white satin swathes, the support posts festooned with bouquets of white roses and trailing ribbons.

Folding chairs were set in neat little rows to either

side, forming an aisle from the house to the gazebo. The chairs were swiftly filling up with guests.

Within the next few minutes, Kate knew someone would press a button on a CD player, the deep voice of an organ would boom forth, and Connie, the bridesmaid, pretty in lavender and Mandy, her maid-of-honor, looking grown-up and lovely in mauve, would precede her down that aisle to her groom.

Her nerves getting tighter by the second, Kate smoothed a hand down the skirt of her tea-length, cream-colored silk dress.

"Oh, doesn't Ethan look handsome," Mandy breathed as Ethan and his two groomsmen took up their positions to one side of the opening into the gazebo.

Eyes only for Ethan, Kate barely looked at the groomsmen, friends of his from their college days, both of whom she vaguely recalled meeting years ago at some Winston function.

To her mind, and heart, Ethan looked more than handsome in his formal dark suit and stark white shirt. He looked perfect, beautiful, wonderful.

The organ blared out. The doors were swung open by two other young men posted outside, and like a proper lady, Connie began her stately pace down the aisle. Mandy followed after a brief interval.

"Ready, Katelyn?" Mark Winston asked, smiling as he presented his crooked arm to her.

"Yes." Grateful for his offer to stand in for David and escort her down the aisle, Kate returned his smile and placed a trembling hand on his arm.

Moments later, when Mark transferred her hand

into the care of his son's, Kate experienced a weakening clutch of panic. Her mind whirled with questions.

Was she doing the right thing in marrying Ethan? Could she go through with . . .

"Dearly beloved."

The soft intonation of the pastor's voice cut through the questioning noise inside Kate's head. After that, she only caught bits and pieces of the ceremony. She heard Ethan make his responses, and gave hers in the correct places.

"I now pronounce you husband and wife."

Kate heard those words loud and clear.

"You may kiss the bride."

Kate felt thrilled at the tender, too brief touch of Ethan's mouth on hers.

The rest of the day was a blur for Kate.

As the reception was to be held in the yard, the folding chairs were put away. Off to one side, a large white tent had been erected by the caterers. Food was laid out in long tables draped in white cloths. A bar had been set up at the end of the food table.

The champagne flowed like wine.

Following tradition, the first dance was reserved for the bride and groom. Kate and Ethan dance with Bobby cradled between them.

Kate then danced with her new father-in-law. She danced with the groomsmen. She even danced with Sharon's docile husband, Charles. She danced until she thought she'd drop. Her feet hurt. Her jaw ached from smiling. She felt strangely like she wanted to cry.

At last, at last, Ethan grabbed her hand to lead her toward the house.

"Let's get out of here."

Kate didn't argue . . . even though she was fraught with trepidation about the night ahead of her.

They didn't bother changing out of their wedding clothes. At the last minute, just as Ethan was heading for the car, Kate took his hand and ran back to the yard, to give hugs to Mandy, Connie, Helen, Virginia, and even Mark, and a special big hug to Bobby. And then, leaving the sleepy-eyed child in the competent care of his grandparents, she finally allowed Ethan to take her away.

They spent their wedding night in one of the newer center city hotels, in a luxurious suite. Kate, stiff with nervous tension, barely noticed the elegant decor, the enormous bouquet of flowers on one table, the silver tray with an assortment of cheeses and fruit, a bottle of champagne chilling in a silver bucket set out on a table near the wide window.

"Are you hungry?" Ethan asked, as he reentered the sitting room after depositing their cases in the bedroom.

"What?" Distracted, nervous about sharing a bed with him, her body with him, her life with him, Kate blinked and looked at him blankly.

He smiled. "I asked if you were hungry?"

"No." She shook her head, feeling empty but positive she wouldn't be able to swallow a thing. "Are . . .

are you?" She immediately wondered if that was a
loaded question . . . or if his had been.

"Yes, actually I am," Ethan answered, strolling to
the table. "I didn't eat very much at the house, so I
think I'll sample the cheese and have a glass of wine,"
he said, oh so casually, lifting the bottle from the
bucket. "Can I pour a glass for you?"

"Er . . . no, thank you," Kate said, inching back
toward the bedroom. "I . . . ah . . . think I'll have a
shower."

A suspicious-looking smile twitching at the corners
of his lips, Ethan murmured, "Take your time. I'll
probably be a little while."

It wasn't until later that Kate realized Ethan very
likely wasn't hungry at all, as he hardly touched either
the food or the wine, but had thoughtfully left her
alone in the bedroom to undress and use the bathroom in privacy.

It wasn't as though they had never been intimate,
Kate lectured herself all the while she undressed with
trembling fingers, took a quick shower, brushed her
teeth. They had been lovers, for goodness sake.

Surely, she could carry this night off with . . . Oh,
God! Shaking all over, Kate returned to the bedroom,
turned off all but one dim light, and jumped into
bed, pulling the covers up to her neck . . . while calling
herself a dim wit.

Why the heck was she shivering like a leaf in a wind
storm?

Well, the air conditioner did have the room pretty
cold, she thought, cowering beneath the blankets as

Ethan entered the room and went straight to the bathroom.

Kate was cold, certain she was freezing . . . until Ethan doused the light, slid into the bed next to her, and drew her trembling body to him, to the warmth and hardness of his body.

Taking a deep breath, Kate drew in the arousing scent of him, activating memories of their times together before . . . well, before. She shivered for different reasons when his hand traced the curve of her breast, then closed around it. She sighed when his breath feathered her lips as he lowered his head.

"Oh, Kate," he murmured against her mouth. "I want you so very much."

In place of Paula? Unbidden, the thought snaked into her mind. Kate bit down on the inside of her lip to keep from crying out.

Murmuring his need for her, Ethan formed his lips to hers, speared his tongue into her mouth in search of hers. His scouring tongue laved the tiny bite she had made, soothing the soreness from the sensitive flesh.

Undone, as she always had been by his kiss, his touch, Kate banned all negative thought and trepidation—and abandoned herself to the pleasure of making love with Ethan.

With slow thoroughness his hands trailed along the curves of her body, over her hips, down the outside lines of her legs to her knees, then up, up the insides to the apex of her quivering thighs.

Kate gasped when his hand cupped her, stroked that most sensitive, responsive part of her body.

Ethan caught her gasp inside his mouth, breathed it back into her own and followed it with his plunging tongue.

His teasing fingers set a fire in the core of her being. Her breaths growing labored, ragged, Kate arched against his hand in mute supplication for more, a fuller, deeper possession.

"Not yet . . . not yet," he whispered, gliding his mouth across her cheek to nip her ear, stab it with the tip of his tongue before laving a wet trail down the side of her throat.

The fire below burst into a blaze. Writhing in response to his lips closing around the aching tip of one breast, his fingers delving deeper, needing to touch him, all over, she spread her palms over his chest, sliding her fingers through the mat of springy curls to caress his nipples.

Ethan sucked in his breath, then began suckling with greedy hunger at her breast. When he opened his mouth, pulled back, she cried out in protest. Laughing softly, he gently blew on the wet nipple, sending delicious sensations dancing down her spine, before turning to capture the other nipple with his teeth, draw it into the hot moisture of his mouth, suckling with equal vigor.

Making soft moaning sounds deep in her throat, needing, needing, Kate dragged her palms down his torso, over his flat belly. He gasped, went still when she curled her hands around him, began to stroke, caress the fullness of him.

Ethan lay rigid under her ministrations, his breath shallow, and then, as if against his will, he arched his hips high, into the sweet torment of her stroking hands.

"Ethan . . ."

Even as she uttered his name in a whispered plea, he pulled her hands away and heaved his body up and over hers, settling between her parted thighs.

Lowering his head, he crushed her mouth with his, slowly, slowly entering her body, as his tongue invaded her mouth. Her body moved in cadence with his as, gradually, his rhythm gained speed, faster, faster, harder, deeper, until Kate wrapped her arms around his sweat-dampened waist, anchoring herself to him as her climax sent her soaring.

It was wonderful, shattering, and blissful as it always had been . . . and yet, not quite. There was something missing. Kate knew that something was a small portion of herself, the portion containing her love, the love she was afraid to feel, offer freely again to Ethan.

They made love three times more before leaving the hotel suite the next morning. Each time had been as passionate, exciting as before, each shuddering completion as shattering.

But still, Kate retained the essence of herself, that tiny segment that contained her unconditional love.

Their wedding night was followed by a settling-in period of almost too much politeness and consideration on both their parts. But, gradually, with each new passing day, their relationship leveled off, the tension and strain dissipating.

Kate couldn't fault Ethan's behavior . . . not that

she was looking for fault. Although he worked long hours—whether from necessity or escape, Kate didn't know, didn't want to know—when at home, Ethan presented a magazine-perfect picture of the content family man.

He was pleasant and always kind to Helen, teased and laughed with Mandy and Connie, played with and helped care for Bobby, treated her with much consideration, and was more than generous in his praise for the devotion Kate lavished on his son.

And at night, in the privacy of their room, in the comfort of his huge bed, Ethan was always a passionate lover.

And yet, as before, though she never failed to achieve shattering satisfaction, there was that small and vulnerable part of herself Kate held back, away from him.

Maybe it was because she couldn't banish the suspicion that Ethan was holding something back from her.

Since he gave no clues as to what he was thinking, feeling, she naturally concluded that the something he was holding back from her was his willingness to let himself love her . . . simply because his love still belonged to the beautiful and heartless woman who had rejected him and their child.

Still, falling more deeply in love with him with each passing day, Kate persevered, determined to build a solid marriage, in spite of its rocky foundation, while hoping, praying, that someday, someway, Ethan would come to love her, fall in love with her in return.

The girls were back in school. Like other stay-at-home moms, Kate drove them back and forth each day while Helen happily minded Bobby.

Bobby was a good baby, a happy child, and Kate loved him almost as though he were her own. They all loved him, and his father, as well. Mandy, Connie, and Helen treated both males as if they belonged exclusively to them, their family. And, of course, in the most important way, the way of love, Bobby and Ethan did belong to them.

So, for all intents and purposes, Kate was content . . . until she became pregnant four months after their marriage. She was thrilled and excited, and a little scared, too. For several days after having her pregnancy confirmed, Kate kept the news to herself, worried about Ethan's reaction.

What if Ethan wasn't thrilled and excited, despite their agreement? Or, more worrisome still, what if now, after having performed his part of their bargain, his duty, he turned away from her in bed?

What if? What if?

The "what ifs" were driving her crazy. Kate decided she needed a cigarette to calm her nerves down. No! Kate thought. She really must be crazy. Good God! She was pregnant. The last thing on earth she needed was a cigarette.

It was time to tell Ethan.

When, late that night, after the house was quiet, Bobby was settled and everyone else asleep, Kate hesitantly told him about the baby, and Ethan's eyes lit up.

"That's wonderful," he declared, obviously delighted by the news, the prospect of becoming a father again.

Kate's nerves had been so tightly strung by maintaining an appearance of calm contentment, her uncertainties so great, that she reacted to his declaration by collapsing onto the bed in a flood of tears she could no longer repress.

Alarmed, Ethan rushed to her side, drew her up, into his arms. "Kate, what is it? I thought this was what you wanted." His voice grew strained as he continued, "Have you changed your mind? Don't you want your, my, our . . . baby?"

"Not want it?" she cried on a choked sob, resting her head against his chest. "Of course I want it!" In that instant, possibly due to her condition, her misery fled before a surging flare of anger. Pushing herself away from him, she jumped up to pace the room.

"But, then . . . ," Ethan began, his expression a mixture of puzzlement, concern and stark fear. "What's wrong? Why are you so . . . so . . ."

"Miserable? Angry?" Kate asked in a near shout. "I'll tell you what's wrong," she said, storming back to shout right into his face. "I love you, damn you!" she confessed, suddenly so mad she poured her heart out without thinking. "I've always loved you. *Of course I want your baby.*"

Eyes widening, Ethan went absolutely still for what seemed endless moments, then grasping her shoulders almost painfully, he pulled her to him to stare into her anger-flushed face, her tear-blurred eyes.

"Ethan . . . ," Kate choked out, suddenly frightened by his intense look.

He made a sharp movement of his head, as if to both silence her and clear his mind. "You love me?" he repeated, his voice harsh, raw with disbelief. "Not like a best friend . . . or an older brother," he stipulated in ragged tones, "but me, next-door neighbor Ethan? You are *in* love with me?"

"Yes," she admitted, blinking, sniffing, scared as hell, but past the point of lying.

"Damn it to hell!" he exploded, his grip on her shoulders tightening to real pain, scaring her even more. "Why the hell didn't you tell me before?"

The very sharpness of his tone, his curses, banished all traces of tears in her glittering green eyes, stiffened her spine, sent her temper soaring.

"Don't you swear at *me*, Ethan Winston," she shot back at him. "Tell you? Tell you? Why would I tell you?" she demanded. "Why humiliate myself when I knew you were still in love with Paula?"

He actually had the nerve to laugh.

Kate went rigid, the sound of his laughter searing through her like a knife. Tempted to strike him, she shrugged, wanting to pull away from him, put distance between them, but was unable to break his tight hold on her.

"Don't laugh at me." The fight drained out of her, deflating her voice with the sound of defeat. "I don't deserve your ridicule."

"Oh, Kate . . . ," he murmured. "I'm not laughing at . . ."

"And you're hurting me," she cut in, once more shrugging against his hold.

"Oh, God, Kate, I'm sorry," he said, loosening his grip, but not releasing her. "And I wasn't laughing . . . ridiculing you. I wasn't even really laughing . . . it was just better than cursing a blue streak for the waste."

Tired, Kate shook her head. "I don't understand what you're saying."

"I'm saying I'm a fool," he said, caressing her upper arms as if to soothe away the pain, the memory of pain. "All this time, I thought . . . believed you were still in love with Jason," he admitted. "That you came to me because . . . well, because of him and Carol . . . on the rebound, I guess."

"No! Oh, Ethan, no!" Kate cried. "I never loved Jason. Even though I agreed to marry him, he was never more than a dear friend, and he knew it, accepted it. But I quickly realized I couldn't marry him, that it wouldn't be fair to him, or to me." She sighed. "I was going to tell him, but before I could . . . he . . . and Carol . . ."

"Oh Lord, Kate," Ethan cut her off with a groan. "What idiots we both have been, me believing I was a substitute for him, you believing I was carrying a torch for her."

"You . . . you aren't?" she asked, her voice now reduced to the merest whisper.

"No. I never have." He let go of one of her arms to rake a hand through his hair, ruffling the dark waves she loved so much. "I should have told you before, right upfront. I never loved Paula." He brought his free hand to stroke her cheek, drawing a finger over her parted lips. "How could I have loved her, when I've been so much in love with you ever since you were seventeen?"

Stunned speechless, Kate stared at him mutely for several seconds until she found her voice, and it wasn't quiet. "But . . . but . . . then, why?" she cried. "Ethan, I'm not stupid. I know Paula was pregnant when you married her . . . which means, you were seeing her, having sex with her, while you were seeing me, having . . ."

"No, don't say it," he interjected, his voice not exactly quiet either. "You and I never had 'sex,' Kate. We always made love . . . at least, I believed we were making love." Uncertainty flickered in his eyes. "Weren't we?"

"I believed that, too," she said, blinking rapidly against a fresh surge of tears. "But, if that's true, and you were in love with me, then . . . why . . . ?" More confused than ever, she shook her head, dislodging the hand resting against her cheek; "I can see, anybody with eyes can see, that Bobby is your child . . . why?"

Ethan sighed, looking unsure and undecided. Then, seeing the tear that escaped to trickle down her cheek, he smiled and drew her with him to the bed. "Come, you look tired. Sit down here next to me, and I'll explain, tell you the whole stupid and sordid story."

He began with the night of Sharon's wedding reception. Then he explained he could not tell her everything before because he had given Paula his word that he wouldn't. But, on reflection, since Paula had broken their bargain by taking off over a month before the agreed upon date, and faced with Kate's unhappiness, he decided now was the time to confess.

Kate didn't interrupt, though she was tempted to do so more than once. His explanation sounded too much like a Hollywood B movie of the forties to be believed. And yet, *he* sounded so sincere, so remorseful, she felt positive that every word was the plain, unvarnished truth.

"Pretty dumb, huh?" he said with bitter self-derision when he was finished.

"Yes," Kate agreed. "At least the part about you getting drunk and going to bed with Paula because you were jealous over seeing me with another man in what appeared to you as a serious relationship." She frowned at him. "Didn't it occur to you to simply ask me if I was serious about him?"

"I guess I thought it was none of my business, and I had no right to intrude," he said, shrugging.

Kate rolled her eyes. "You were right before. You are a fool," she said, biting on her lip to contain a laugh.

"Oh, really?" he drawled, tugging loose the looped knot on the belt to her robe. "Well, how would you like to find out how a fool in love makes love, my love?" he murmured, sliding the robe down and off, and her nightgown up and off her suddenly overly warm body. "A fool in love can be very ardent, very passionate, you know."

Already quivering in anticipation, Kate raised her hand to unbutton his shirt. "I can't wait," she said in a smoky-voiced purr, reaching for his belt buckle.

"You're not too tired . . . emotionally wrung out?"

he asked silkily, pulling off his shirt, while she tugged at the zipper on his slacks.

"Why don't we investigate the matter," she suggested, tossing back the covers and crawling into the big bed.

Kate giggled with nervous excitement as his shoes hit the floor one after the other, immediately followed by his socks, and then his slacks and briefs.

"Good idea, Sherlock," he said, sliding into the bed next to her. "Exactly how intrepid an investigator are you?"

Snaking a hand under the cover, she found his stiff member and curled her fingers around it.

He groaned.

She gave a tug in a physical demand.

He obeyed at once, rearing up and over her.

"Now, then, my love," he murmured, stabbing his tongue into the corner of her mouth. "What can I give you?"

"A fool in love," she answered, grasping his head to draw his mouth to hers.

"You've got him."

Ethan settled into the cradle of her thighs.

Kate raised her hips to meet his thrust.

It didn't come. Instead, he frowned down at her.

"I won't hurt you, will I?"

Kate narrowed her eyes and frowned back at him. "Did you ever hurt Paula?"

He jerked back, as if she had struck him. "I never touched Paula after that one night."

"Not even after you were married?" Kate asked in patent disbelief.

"No." His tone was adamant, and rang truthful. "Not even when she invited me into her bed."

"But . . . surely you were not celibate that whole time?"

"I was so," he shot back, offended.

"So was I," Kate admitted. "I mean . . . after you."

"Ahhh, my sweet Fuzzywig," he murmured, moving to gently, carefully join them into one. "I adore you." He moved deeper. "I always have." Deeper still. "I always will."

They were well and truly joined. Sighing her pleasure, Kate met and matched his easy rhythm. "And you are my hero. Oh . . ." She gasped as he increased the speed. "You always were. Oh, my . . . ," she moaned, "you always will be." She gripped his hips to ride out the storm of desire.

It was incredible. Fantastic. More thrilling, more earth-shaking than ever before. Drifting back to reality from the ultimate heights of ecstasy, Kate felt completely depleted, completely satisfied, completely loved.

Bearing the weight of Ethan's spent body, she stroked his damp hair, thinking that at last, at long last, all her long-held hopes, her dreams, had been realized.

Ethan stirred, and raised his head to gaze into her dreamy eyes, the light of love alive in his.

"Oh, Kate," he murmured, brushing her moistened lips with his. "I honestly feared I would never live to see this night, hear you say you loved me . . . have you . . ."

"I love you." She interrupted him to say the words.

"Have you for my very own," he finished.

Hearing the echo of her own most fervent wish, Kate stared at him in wonder for a full five seconds. Then she laughed in sheer delight.

CHAPTER
TWENTY-FOUR

"You know, I'm really tired of this." Kate grimaced at the breathless, whiny sound of her own voice.

"Of what?" Carol sounded even more breathless, which was understandable, considering she was carrying more weight. "Of doing these exercises, or being pregnant?"

"Both." Kate grinned around a whooshing exhalation. "As moderate as these exercises are, they are still tiring. As for the pregnancy, I'm not so much tired of that, as I am getting anxious to have the baby, hold it in my arms."

"I know what you mean." Calling a halt to the mild stretching routine, Carol stood still, taking deep breaths as she rubbed one palm over her belly, which was even more extended than her friend's. "But you could be holding yours at almost any time now, with your due date so close."

Kate also gave up on the stretching exercise. "Yes, but you'll likely go into labor before me," she said, mopping her sweat-sheened face with the towel draped around her neck, "even though I became pregnant before you."

"Only if I go into labor early," Carol reminded her. "Besides, who knew that twins ran in Jason's family, and that I'd be the lucky one to carry on the tradition?"

Kate chuckled, still amused by the chain of events leading up to their current situations.

Two months after Kate's pregnancy had been confirmed, Carol had called her up to make a request, and a surprising announcement.

"Kate, Jason and I are getting married," she said in a rush. "Will you be my matron of honor?"

"I'd love to . . . ," Kate answered at once, but felt constrained to add, "That is so long as you don't mind having an obviously pregnant matron of honor."

"It won't be all that obvious yet," Carol said, dry-voiced. "We're getting married in two weeks."

"Two weeks," Kate repeated, laughing in surprise. "What's the hurry?"

Dumb question, as she quickly learned.

"I'm pregnant," Carol shot back. "That's what the hurry is, and I want to get married in the size four dress I worked my ass off dieting and exercising to get into."

"You're pregnant?" Kate couldn't hide the note

of shock in her voice, simply because she couldn't believe her friend had been so careless. "How ... Why ..."

"You know damn well how," Carol interrupted with a soft giggle. "As to the why ... well ... you see, Jason and I were arguing about ...

"Arguing again?" Kate interjected, rolling her eyes.

"Well ... yes ..."

"About what this time?"

"About the video we were watching," Carol answered, laughing aloud.

"For heaven's sakes!" Kate mentally threw up her hands. "But how did you go from arguing to being pregnant?"

Carol burst out laughing. "You won't believe it."

Kate sighed ... noisily. "Try me."

"Weell ... you remember that other time, the time Jason kissed me instead of hitting me?"

"How could I forget?" Kate drawled.

"This time, instead of ... er, no ... while kissing me, he ... we, kinda got carried away and ... well ... one kiss led to another, and they led to ..."

"I've got the picture," Kate said.

And now, here they were, Carol long since out of a size four, both in advanced pregnancy, and both still exercising ... and bitching about it.

"What do you think your chances are of carrying full term?" Kate asked, gently patting her friend's big belly.

"Slim to none," Carol admitted, returning the patting compliment to Kate's protruding but smaller belly. "I know it would be better for the babies if I could carry full term," she said, sighing. "But good grief, as huge as I am now, I'll be as big as a whale if I go full term." She made a face. "And I have to confess, I am growing weary of walking in a tilted-back position."

Laughing at her friend's only slight exaggeration, Kate linked her arm with Carol's as they ambled, waddled actually, to the parking lot and their respective cars.

"So, have you and Ethan got a romantic evening planned to celebrate your first wedding anniversary on Saturday?" Carol asked, before attempting to shimmy behind the wheel of her car, a new bigger vehicle than the small sporty job she used to dash around in.

"We're going out to dinner," Kate said. "But . . . romantic? How can anyone get romantic in this condition?" She heaved a sigh. "Honestly, Carol, I can hardly stand looking at myself in the mirror any more."

"I know." Carol echoed the sigh. "Boy, do I know."

"And yet, Ethan insists I look glowing and beautiful, believe it or not."

"I believe it . . . because Jason tells me the same thing."

"They lie." Kate's lips twitched in a smile.

"Yeah." Carol grinned. "And don't we love 'em for it?"

"Like mad," Kate agreed, her smile brilliant as she

slid behind the wheel of her own newer, bigger car.
"See you later, and give my love to Jason."

"Will do," Carol called back, firing the motor.
"And my love to Ethan and the rest of your crew."

The anniversary dinner turned out to be as romantic as any woman, pregnant or not, could wish for.

Kate had woken that Saturday morning feeling good, and the feeling lasted throughout the day. After feeding and bathing Bobby, Mandy and Connie took over baby-sitting, freeing Kate to have a long bath before dressing.

Later, while preparing for the big night out, she stood before her mirror and decided she looked pretty good in the cleverly designed maternity dress, not nearly as large as the two car garage.

"You look beautiful," Ethan murmured, coming up behind her to encirle her nonexistent waist with his long arms, and nibble on her earlobe with his strong teeth.

"And you look handsome," she said, shivering with delicious tingles within his embrace. "But then, you always do." It was true. In her eyes, there was no man more handsome than he.

During dinner, Ethan was attentive and sweet, even more so than usual. Instead of champagne, he plied her with lavish compliments, delicious food, and for dessert, he clasped a diamond tennis bracelet around her wrist.

By the time they returned home, Kate was not only still feeling good, but as though she were walking on air. Then, her spirits were lifted even higher by the surprise anniversary cake and gifts the girls and Helen had waiting for them.

They were laughing, everybody talking at once when the phone rang.

"I'll get it," Mandy offered, jumping up to run for the wall-mounted instrument.

Though the rest lowered their voices, they continued to chatter away, until . . .

"You're kidding!" Mandy exclaimed, gaining their silence and attention. "Hey, guys, it's Jason. He's at the hospital. Carol just had the twins. . . .

"What are they?" Kate asked, aware that, like herself, Carol had not wanted to know the sex of her babies.

"Boys!" Mandy said, nearly dancing with excitement. "And he says they're small but okay, and really beautiful."

"Tell Jason we're on our way," Kate directed, every bit as excited as Mandy.

"Kate, are you up to it?" Ethan asked, a line of concern scoring his brow. "It's been a long eventful day for you."

"I feel wonderful," Kate said, taking his hand to tug him to the door. "Of course I'm up to it." She laughed. "I wouldn't miss seeing Carol's new sons for the world."

"Can we go, too?" Connie pleaded. "We'll be good."

"Well . . . ," Kate began, uncertain, looking to Ethan for guidance.

It came, not from Ethan, but from the eldest member of the group.

"Not tonight, girls," Helen decreed. "It's already after ten, and Carol is probably exhausted." She held up a hand for quiet when the girls started to protest. "No arguments, now. The three of us will go tomorrow."

The hospital was quiet when Kate and Ethan arrived even on the maternity floor. Standing at the viewing window, Kate's heart melted on sight of the two tiny infants inside the incubators.

"Oh, Jason," she murmured, as it afraid she'd disturb the sleeping babies. "You were right, they are beautiful."

"Congratulations," Ethan said, extending his hand to shake Jason's. "You're a lucky man. Two sons on the first try."

Jason agreed, laughing in delight.

Kate felt a little twinge inside at the sudden realization that, like most men, Ethan obviously wanted another son. As neither one of them had wanted to know the sex of their child, they had not stated a preference, either, both claiming only to want a healthy baby.

But, secretly, in her heart of hearts, Kate longed for a daughter. Now, desiring Ethan's happiness above her own, she ran a hand over her belly and hoped for a boy.

Kate and Ethan peeked in on Carol before leaving, to kiss and congratulate her.

Tired, but beaming with pleasure and pride, Carol teased, "I beat you to the starting gate, Kate."

"You certainly did," Kate agreed, laughing. "And, now, Ethan and I are going to beat a retreat, so you can rest." She grinned. "With two to take care of, you're going to need all the rest you can get."

"And all the help," Carol said, grinning back at her.

Later that night, after the house was quiet and they were in bed, Ethan placed his palm on Kate's belly, waiting for the thrill of feeling his child move.

"Soon, love," he murmured against her cheek. "I love you so very much. I can hardly wait for our baby to be born."

"Me, either," she whispered, content to snuggle closer to his warmth.

And, amazingly, Kate was still feeling wonderful, except for a tiny sense of disappointment about Ethan wanting a son, and the tiny ache in her lower back.

But, what was a tiny disappointment, a mild ache, when she had everything she had always wanted . . . Ethan, and his child safely tucked inside her.

EPILOGUE

The very next day, bright morning sunlight washed the pastel painted walls and glinted off the window pane.

Standing at the foot of the hospital bed, Mandy and Connie on one side, Helen on the other, Ethan stared in joyous wonder into the beautiful face of his daughter, Emily, cradled securely in his arms. He had brought Kate to the hospital when she had finally wakened him at four that morning.

His daughter.

Swallowing rapidly, blinking suspiciously, he glanced up, into the watchful, fantastic blue eyes of his pale-faced wife.

"Thank you, my love," he said, then cleared his throat to ease the hoarse sound. "How did you know I secretly wanted a daughter?"

"You did?" Her eyes flew wide and she gazed at him in astonishment. "So did I," she confessed, laughing.

Turning, Ethan carefully settled his daughter in Helen's waiting arms, then walked to the bed to take his smiling wife into his own.

"I love you, my love," he whispered against her lips.

"I love you back, my own," Kate whispered, sealing her vow with a kiss.

Please turn the page for
an exciting sneak peek
of Joan Hohl's newest
contemporary romance

I DO

coming from Zebra Books
in December 2001!

CHAPTER ONE

"In the name of the Father, the Son, and the Holy Spirit. Amen."

The solemnly intoned benediction seemed to hang like a pall on the chill March air long seconds after the pastor closed his prayer book. A muffled sob shattered the silence, and, as if the cry had been a signal, the large crowd around the grave site began to move in a slow, unsure manner.

Some distance off to one side, in a small, sparse stand of trees, a tall man stood, unobserved by the group of mourners. Hands thrust inside the deep pockets of a hip-length sheepskin jacket, broad shoulders hunched, wide collar flipped up against the cold, damp air, all that was visible of his head and face was a shock of sun-gold hair and a pair of amber eyes, narrowed and partially concealed by long, thick, dark brown lashes. At the moment, the eyes were riveted on the flower-draped brass casket suspended over the open grave.

The figure remained still as a statue, but the eyes, cold and unemotional, shifted to the source of the low sobs. A small, fair-haired woman, dressed entirely in black, stood unsteadily, supported on both sides by two tall, slender, fair-haired young men who wore the same face. The cold eyes flashed for an instant with cynicism, gone as fast as it came, then moved on to rest on the face of a younger woman, also dressed in black, standing close to one of the young men. There was an oddly protective attitude in her stance, although she was much smaller than the man. The amber eyes grew stormy as they studied the small, pale, wistfully lovely face, the soft, pure lines set in fierce determination. The lids dropped, and the eyes again became clear and cold and moved on to briefly scan the crowd before once again coming to rest on the coffin, gleaming dully in the gray, overcast morning light.

"I loved you, you old bastard."

The softly muttered words bounced off the warm fleece of the collar; then the man turned sharply and strode through the trees to the road some yards away and a sleek black BMW parked to the side.

Anne rested her head against the plush upholstery of the limousine, eyes closed. She was tired and the day wasn't half over. There would be a lot of people coming back to the house and she'd have to act as hostess, as her mother obviously wasn't up to it. The soft weeping coming from the seat in front of her gave evidence of that. Not for the first time Anne wished she'd known her father, for she surely must have inherited his character. For although except for hair color she resembled her small, fragile mother, beyond the surface features there was very little comparison. Her mother was gentle natured but had always been high-strung and of delicate health, whereas Anne had enormous stamina and strength for such a small woman. About the only thing she and her mother shared by way of emotions was the gentle nature. Anne was a pushover for any hard-luck or sob story and had been taken in by and involved with so many of her friends' problems she had finally had to harden her heart in self-defense.

Taking advantage of the drive back to the house to relax, Anne's mind was going over what still had to be gotten through that day when a disturbing thought pushed its way forward: he didn't even come to his father's funeral. Her head moved restlessly; her soft lips tightened bitterly. For days now, ever since her stepfather's death, she had managed to push away all thoughts of her stepbrother, but even so she had felt sure he would be at the funeral. Of course it had been ten years, but still, he had been notified and the least he could do . . . She felt the car turn into the driveway and, opening her eyes, sat up straight, pushing the disquieting thoughts away.

During the next two hours Anne was kept too busy to do any deep thinking, but still her eyes went to the door each time the housekeeper opened it to admit yet another friend offering condolences.

When finally the door was closed after the last well-wisher, Anne sighed deeply before squaring her shoulders and walking to the door of the library. With her hand on the knob she paused, her gaze moving slowly around the large, old-fashioned foyer. The woodwork was dark, gleaming in the light of the chandelier that hung from the middle of the ceiling. The furnishings could only be described as heavy and ornate. Anne didn't really care too much for the house, yet it had been the only home she'd ever known, as Judson Cammeron, Sr. had been the only father she'd ever known. Sighing again, she turned the knob and entered the room.

Mr. Slonne, the family attorney, sat dwarfed behind her stepfather's massive oak desk, hands folded on the blotter in front of him. He was speaking quietly to her mother, who was sitting in a chair alongside the desk. As Anne gently closed the door he glanced up and asked, "Everyone gone?"

Smiling faintly, Anne nodded and moved to the chair placed at the other side of the desk. As she sat down, her eyes scanned her mother's face.

"How are you feeling now, Mother?"

Margaret Cammeron smiled wanly at her daughter, her eyes misty. "Better, dear." Her tremulous voice had a lost, childlike note. "I don't know how I'd have managed to get through this without you and your brothers." Her breath caught and her hand reached out for, and was grasped by, that of her son who leaped from his chair and came to stand beside hers.

"Well, you don't have to get through anything without us, ever." Anne spoke bracingly, her eyes going to first one, then another, set of matching blue eyes, in the faces of her identical-twin half brothers.

Like a small mother hen, Anne was proud of her younger brothers. Usually carefree and unhampered by responsibility, due to too little discipline and too much indulgence, their conduct the last few days had been faultless. At twenty-one and in their last year of college, Troy and Todd Cammeron had never done a full day's serious work. They had inherited their mother's sweet nature and their father's quick temper, but little of his iron will and tenacity. They were good-looking and well liked and too busy having a good time to worry about the future. Their father was rich and they had known they would go to work in his business when they left school. Meanwhile they had been busy with girls and cars and girls and fun and girls. Their father's sudden death had shocked them, as it had everyone, but they had rallied well in support of their mother. Although only four years their senior, Anne also admitted she had had as much of a hand, if not more, in their spoiling as anyone.

Mr. Slonne glanced at his watch then cleared his throat discreetly. "I think we had better begin, Mrs. Cammeron. The time stated was two o'clock and as it is now two-fifteen I—"

He stopped, startled, as the library door was thrust open and Anne felt the breath catch in her throat as her stepbrother walked briskly into the room. He paused, his eyes making a circuit of the room, then proceeding to her mother.

"Sorry I'm late, Margaret, I stopped for something to eat and the service was lousy."

Anne shivered at his tone. So unfeeling, so cold, could this hard-eyed man be her stepbrother?

Margaret raised astonished eyes to his face, murmuring jerkily, "That—that's all right, Jud. But you—you should have come home to eat."

His smile was a mere twist of the lips before his head lifted to turn from one then the other twin, standing on either side of her chair.

"Troy, Todd, still the same bookends, I see."

Their faces wore the same strained expressions, but both stretched out hands to grasp the one he had extended. He nodded to the lawyer, murmured, "Mr. Slonne," then turned to Anne. She felt a small flutter in her chest as he walked to the chair next to hers.

"Anne."

His tone was low, but so coolly impersonal that Anne again felt a shiver go through her. Was it possible for a man to change so much in ten years? Apparently it was, for the proof of it was sitting next to her.

He had left home a charming, laughing, teasing young man and had walked through that door a few minutes ago with the lazy confidence of a proud, tawny lion. And tawny was the only way to describe him. The fair hair of ten years ago had darkened to a sun gold, and his skin was a burnished bronze. His features hadn't changed, of course, but had matured, sharpened. The broad forehead now held several creases as did the corners of his eyes. The long nose that had been perfectly straight now sported a bump, evidence of a break surgically corrected. The once firm jawline now looked as if it had been cut from granite. The well-shaped mouth now seemed to be permanently cast in a mocking slant. And the once laughing amber eyes arched over by sun-bleached brows now held the mysterious, wary glow of the jungle cat. Incredibly he seemed to have grown a few inches and gained about thirty pounds and he looked big and powerful and very, very dangerous.

With a feeling of real grief Anne felt a small light go out inside for the death of the laughing, teasing Jud Cammeron she'd known ten years before.

Mr. Slonne lifted the papers that had been lying on the desk and with a sharp movement Jud lifted his hand.

"If you'll be patient just a few more minutes, Mrs. Davis is bringing me something to drink." Then he turned to Margaret. "I hope you don't mind."

Her still lovely face flushed, Margaret whispered, "N—no, of course not."

At that moment the library door opened and the housekeeper, her face set in rigid lines of disapproval, entered the room carrying a tray bearing a coffeepot, cups, sugar bowl, and creamer. Mrs. Davis had been with the Cammerons only six years and she obviously looked on this new arrival as an interloper. Placing the tray, none too gently, on a small table beside Jud's chair, she turned on her heel and marched out of the room. Hearing him laugh softly, Anne thought in amazement, *He's enjoying her discomfort. No, he's enjoying the discomfort of all of us.* And for the third time she felt a shiver run through her body.

Mr. Slonne waited patiently while Jud filled his cup and added cream. Then he began reading. The atmosphere in the room grew chill then cold as he read on. Anne, her hands gripping the arms of her chair, couldn't believe her ears. Her mother's face was white with shock. The twins wore like expressions of incredulity. Jud sat calmly sipping his coffee, his eyes cold and flat as a stone and his face a mask. When the lawyer's voice finally ground to a halt, the room was in absolute silence. After a few long, nerve-racking minutes Jud's unemotional voice broke the silence.

"Well, then, it seems, in effect, he's left it all to me."

"Precisely."

Mr. Slonne's clipped corroboration brought the rest of them out of their trance.

"I—I don't understand," Margaret wailed.

Mr. Slonne hastened to reassure her. "There is no need for concern, Mrs. Cammeron, you've been well provided for. Indeed you've all been well-provided for. It is just that Mr. Cammeron, young Mr. Cammeron, will have control of the purse strings, so to speak. In effect, he will be taking over where your husband left off."

"You mean I'll have to ask Jud for everything?" she cried.

Before Mr. Slonne could answer, Jud rapped, "Did you have to ask the old man for everything?"

Margaret winced at the term "old man," then answered wildly. "But you've been away for ten years. Not once have you written or called. It was as if you'd died. He never mentioned your name after you left this house. Why should he do this?"

Jud's eyes went slowly from face to face, reading the same question in all but Mr. Slonne's. Then with cool deliberation he said, "Maybe because the business that made him so wealthy was started mainly with Carmichael money. My mother's father's money. Maybe because he was afraid there was no one here who could handle it. And just maybe because he trusted me. Even after ten years."

He paused as if expecting a protest, and when there was none he continued. "Don't concern yourself, Margaret. You're to go on as you always have. I will question no expenditures except exceedingly large ones. This house is as much your home as it ever was. I have no intention of interfering with its running."

"You are going to live here?" Dismayed astonishment tinged Margaret's tone and one not-quite-white eyebrow arched sardonically.

"Of course. At least for the next few months. As you said, I've been away for a long time. I'll have to familiarize myself with the company, its management. Perhaps make a few changes."

Anne didn't like the ominous sound of his tone or the significance of his last words. Incautiously she snapped, "What changes?"

She realized her mistake as he turned slowly to face her. He didn't bother to answer her, he didn't have to. His eyebrows arched exceedingly high, the mocking slant of his hard mouth said it all loud and clear: *Who the hell are you to question me?* Anne felt her cheeks grow warm, heard him laugh softly when her eyes shied away from his intent amber stare.

"Now, then." The abrupt change in his tone startled Anne so much she actually flinched. "Mr. Slonne, thank you for your time and your assistance. You will be hearing from me soon." The lawyer was ushered politely, but firmly, out of the room. Margaret was next. In tones soothing but unyielding, Jud saw her to the door with the opinion that she should rest for at least an hour or so.

When Jud turned back to face Anne and her brothers, she felt her palms grow moist, her heart skip a beat. In no way did this man resemble the Jud she remembered. The Jud she had known ten years ago had had laughing eyes and a teasing voice. This man had neither. His eyes were alert and wary, and his voice, so far, was abrupt and sarcastic. This man was a stranger with a hard, dangerous look that spoke of ruthlessness.

"Now, you three," Jud said coolly. "I think we had better have a small conclave, set down the ground rules as it were."

Troy was the first one to speak. "What do you mean ground rules? And who the hell are you to lay down rules anyway?"

"I should think the answer to that would be obvious, even to you, Troy." Completely unruffled, Jud moved around the desk, lazily lowering himself into his father's chair.

"Sit down," he snapped. "This may take longer then I thought."

"I prefer to stand."

"So do I," Todd added.

The twins then began to speak almost simultaneously. Beginning to feel shaky with the premonition of what was coming, Anne was only too happy to sink into the chair she had so recently vacated. Jud pinned her there with a cold stare.

"I'll get to you shortly."

He turned the stare to the twins and his voice took on the bite of a January midnight. "I will tell you exactly who I am. As our father saw fit to leave me in control, from now on I'm the boss. And there are going to be a lot of changes made, starting with you two earning your keep."

"What do you mean?"

"In what way?"

He silenced them with a sharp, slicing move of his hand.

"From today on every free day you have, except Sundays, will be spent at the mill learning the textile business from the ground up, starting with the upcoming Easter vacation."

"But we have plans made to go to Lauderdale at Easter," Troy exclaimed angrily.

"*Had* plans," Jud stated flatly. "There will be no romping on the sands for you two this year."

"We're over twenty-one," Todd sneered. "You can't make us do anything."

"Can't I?"

Anne felt her mouth go dry at the silky soft tone. Her eyes shifted to the twins' faces as Jud continued.

"Perhaps not. But I can stop your allowances. I can neglect to pay your school fees for the final term. I can demand board payment for living in this house— my house."

White-faced, Troy cried, "We still have our income from the business."

"Wrong," Jud said coldly. "You heard the terms of the old man's will. Unless I choose to sign a release, every penny of that income goes into a trust fund until you are twenty-five. I'm the only one who can draw on that fund for your maintenance. Now, unless you want to be cut off without a penny for the next four years, when I say jump, the only question I want from either of you is: How high?"

Anne closed her eyes to shut out the glazed expression of shocked disbelief on her brothers' faces. With a tingling shiver she heard Jud coolly dismiss them with the advice they attend their mother; then her eyes flew open at his crisp, "Now you."

"You can't frighten me, Jud. You have no control over me whatsoever. I have simply to pack my things and walk out of this house to be away from your—control."

Anne felt an angry flush of color flare in her face as he studied her with amused insolence, his eyes seeming to strip her of every stitch of clothing she was wearing.

"That's exactly right," he finally replied silkily. "But you won't. The old man was no fool. His plan was beautifully simple. He knew full well the sons of his second marriage were incapable of taking over, while at the same time he wanted to insure their future, so he split up forty-five percent of the company stock between them but left me in control of the actual capital. At the same time he knew I could handle the business and the twins, and that I would. But he wanted a check rein on me, too, so he only left me forty-five percent. That leaves you, right in the middle, with the other ten percent."

"To do with as I please," she inserted warningly.

"But of course," he countered smoothly. "But as I said, the old man was no fool. He was reasonably sure you would not surrender your share to me, thus giving me full control. On the other hand he could also feel reasonably sure you would not throw in with the twins, as you are as aware as he was that they would probably run the company right into the ground. Does it give you a feeling of power, Anne?"

"You can't be sure I won't sell or give my share to Troy and Todd." Very angry now, she lashed out at him blindly. Everything he'd said was true, and she hated his cool smugness.

"Right again," he mocked. "But, like the old man, I am reasonably certain, and being so, I'll call the shots. And I'll give you one warning: if you decide you can't hack it, and to hurt me you sign over to the twins, I'll ruin them—and I can easily."

Wetting her lips she stared at him in disbelief. He mean it.

"But you'd be destroying your own interests as well."

Mocking smile deepening, he shrugged carelessly. "I'll admit that I want it, but I don't need it to survive. The twins do. And don't, for one moment, deceive yourself into thinking I won't do it. I will."

She believed him. He wasn't just bluffing or trying to scare her, though he did. He meant it. Confused, frightened for her brothers, she cried, "Why are you taking this position? Do you hate us all so much?"

"Hate? The twins?" Again the brows rose in exaggerated surprise. "You forget, the twins are my brothers, too. I'll be the making of them."

The fact did not escape her that he referred to Troy and Todd only. Shocked by a pain she had thought long dead, she argued. "You're being too hard on them."

"Hard?" He gave a short bark of laughter, shaking his head. "You call it hard to expect them to learn a business they have almost a half interest in? Good grief, they are twenty one years old and have never done a full day's work. Do you know how old I was when I went to work for my father?"

Subdued by his sudden anger, Anne shook her head dumbly.

"I was fourteen. Fourteen." His tone hardened on the repeated word. "And how old were you? Don't answer, I know. You've had almost sole care of those two ever since you were six. You've cared for, protected, and played general guard dog to them from the time they could say your name. How old were you when you went to work in the old man's office?"

"Eighteen."

"Eighteen," he repeated softly. "No carefree college days for Anne."

"I wasn't his daughter," she protested. "I never expected—"

"No, you weren't his daughter," he interrupted. "You were, for all intents and purposes, his slave."

"He was very good to me." She almost screamed at him.

"Why the hell shouldn't he have been?" he

shouted. "You never made a move he disapproved of."

Anne drew deep breaths, forcing herself to calm down. This was proving nothing. Her voice more steady, she said quietly, "I won't argue anymore about this, Jud. If there is nothing else you want to discuss I'll go up to Moth—"

"There is," he cut in firmly. "If you have any papers or anything else pertaining to the office here at home, I'd like you to get them together. My secretary will be in the office tomorrow and it will be easier for her if—"

Now it was Anne's turn to interrupt. Her voice hollow with shock, she cried, "Your secretary? But that's my office."

Even though his voice was bland, it chilled her.

"I don't need you in that office, Anne; that's what I pay my secretary for. So if there's anything here, collect it before tomorrow. Now if you'll excuse me, I have some phone calls to make."

Turning quickly, Anne left the room. She heard him dialing as she closed the door. Then she stood staring at her trembling hands. That easily, that coolly, she had been dismissed, not only from the room but from the office as well. Fighting tears, she ran upstairs to her bedroom. What was she supposed to do now?

CHAPTER TWO

Anne paced the deep rose carpet in her bedroom, Jud's words still ringing in her ears. If she wasn't to go to the office and he didn't want her to move out of the house, what was she to do? Get another job? Work for a rival company? That didn't make much sense. Maybe he meant her to stay at home, run the house, live the kind of life her mother did. Women's clubs and bridge games and shopping week in, week out. Anne shivered. She would go out of her mind. Maybe if the twins were still small enough to keep her running, but not now. She was too used to the office. Tears trickling down her face, she riled silently. Didn't he realize she knew almost as much about the managerial end of the business as his father had? She could be of help to him while he was familiarizing himself with it. Why had he turned her out? Did he hate her that much?

In frustration she flung herself onto the bed and stared at the ceiling. He had changed so drastically. Uninvited and unwelcome, a picture of him as he was the last time she saw him formed in her mind. How young she had been then. Young and naive and so very much in love. Anne's face burned at the memory of how very gullible she had been at fifteen.

It had been Jud's twenty-fifth birthday and Anne had waited with growing impatience for him to come home to dinner. She felt her spirits drop when her stepfather came home alone and when he told her mother that Jud would not be home for dinner as he had a date, her spirits sank completely.

The hours had seemed to drag endlessly as Anne, unable to sleep, sat in her room, ears strained for the sound of his car on the driveway. On the table beside her small bedroom chair lay a tiny birthday present, its fancy bow almost twice the size of the package. At intervals Anne touched the bow gently, lovingly. She had saved so long to buy this gift, had been so eager to give it to him. Eager and also a little nervous. It was not quite a year since she had first seen the brush-finished gold cuff links and she had known at once she wanted to give them to him. At first she had thought of giving them to him at Christmas but she had not been able to save enough money. So she had taken the money she had and had talked to the store manager. He in turn had removed the links from the display window, put her name on them, and had set them aside for her. She had made the last payment on them the previous week. Now, staring at the small, wrapped box, she saw the matte surface of the gold ovals, could see the initials engraved on them. J.C.C., Judson Carmichael Cammeron. How she loved him. And how she prayed he'd like her offering.

The slam of the car door startled Anne out of a daze. The front door being closed brought her fully aware. She heard him come up the stairs, pass her door, and close his own door farther down the hall. What should she do? It was past two-thirty. Would he be angry if she went to his room now? Should she wait until morning?

Anne hesitated long minutes. Then she thought fiercely, *No, it won't be the same. By morning his birthday will be truly over.* Without giving herself time to change her mind, she slipped out of her room and along the thickly carpeted hall on noiseless bare feet. She tapped on his door softly then held her breath. It seemed to take a very long time for him to open the door, but when he did she knew why at once. He had obviously just come out of the shower, as his hair was damp and he was wearing nothing except a midcalf-length belted terry cloth robe. At the sight of him Anne felt her resolve weaken, but before she could utter an apology or whisper good night, he caught her hand and said with concern, "Anne! What is it? Is something wrong?"

Her voice pleading for understanding, Anne shook her head quickly and answered softly, "No, nothing. I'm—I'm sorry to disturb you. I'm silly. I wanted to give you your birthday present and I couldn't wait till morning."

Jud sighed, but his voice was gentle. "You're right; you are silly." He paused, then chided, "Well, where is this present you couldn't wait to give me?"

Flushing, Anne slid her hand into the pocket of the cotton housecoat she'd slipped the gift into before leaving her room. As she withdrew the gift, he gave a light tug on the hand he was still holding and murmured ruefully, "You had better come in. We don't want to wake the household for the event of giving and receiving one gift."

She stepped inside and he reached around her to close the door before taking the small package from the palm of her hand. Silently he removed the wrapping and silently he flipped the case open and stared a very long time at the cuff links. When he raised his eyes to hers they were serious, questioning. Fear gripped her and she blurted breathlessly, "Don't you like them, Jud?"

"Like them? Of course I like them, they're beautiful. But, chicken, they must have cost a bundle. Why?"

More nervous than before, Anne plucked at the button on her robe.

"I—I saw them in the window and—and I wanted to buy them for you."

"When was this?" he asked softly.

"Almost—not quite a year ago."

"And you've been saving all this time?" His voice was even softer now and Anne shivered. His tone—something—was making her feel funny.

"Are you angry with me, Jud?"

"Angry? With you? Oh, honey, I could never be really angry at you."

"I'm glad," she whispered. "I wanted to give them to you tonight so badly. I could have cried when you didn't come home for dinner."

His beautiful amber eyes seemed to flicker, grow shadowed and he carefully laid the jeweler's box on the night table by his bed, then brought his hand to her face. Again a tiny shiver went through her as his fingers lightly touched her skin. Now his voice was barely above a murmur. "And do I get a birthday kiss, too?"

"Yes." A mere whisper broke from a suddenly tight throat.

His blond head descended and then she felt his lips touch hers lightly and tenderly. The pressure on her lips increased and then he groaned softly and pulled his head away with a muttered growl. "You had better get out of here, Anne."

She felt stricken, shattered, and as he turned away she cried, without thinking, "Jud, please, I love you. What have I done wrong?"

He swung back, his eyes filled with pain.

"Wrong? Oh, chicken, you've done nothing wrong. Don't you see? Can't you tell? I want to kiss you properly and you're so young. Too young. I think you'd better get out of here before I hurt you."

His eyes burned into hers, and with a feeling of fierce elation she couldn't begin to understand running through her, she pleaded, "Oh, Jud, please don't make me go. Tell me, show me, what to do, please."

He moved closer to her, his eyes searching hers as if looking for answers. Again his hand touched her face lightly, then his forefinger brushed, almost roughly, across her lips. Her lips parted fractionally in automatic reaction and leaning closer he whispered, "Like that, honey." Again his finger brushed her mouth, this time the lower lip only, and she could hardly hear his murmured, "Part your lips for me, Anne," before his lips were against hers. She obeyed him and felt a shock of mingled fear and joy rip through her as his mouth crushed hers. Never could she have imagined the riot of sensations that stormed her senses.

When his mouth left hers, she gave a low "no" in protest, and grasping her arm, he whispered, "Come."

He led her to the side of the bed, sat her down, then sat down beside her. Cupping her head in his hands he stared broodingly into her face a long time before saying quietly, "Sweetheart, if you're at all frightened, tell me now while I can still send you back to your room."

Her eyes clear, she faced him without fear. "I could never be afraid of you, Jud. How could I be? I told you. I love you."

"Yes, you told me," he groaned. Then he was on his feet, moving away from her. "But, honey, I'm not talking about brother-sister love. You know the facts of life?"

She looked up indignantly at the sharp question. "Yes, of course I do."

His tone lost none of its sharpness. "Then you know what I want?"

Unable to voice the answer, Anne lowered her eyes, nodded her head.

"Honey, look at me."

Some of the edge had left his tone and in relief Anne looked up.

"Ever since the day you first came to this house, I loved you. Like a brother with a small sister, I loved you, wanted to protect you. A little over a year ago, some months after your fourteenth birthday, I began to feel different." Anne felt a pain twist at her heart and she would have cried out but he held up his hand to explain. "Suddenly one day I realized I did not love you as a brother loves a sister. I was in love with you, the way a man loves a woman." His eyes closed but not before Anne saw the pain in them.

"Jud." She made to get up and go to him.

"No." It was an order. Anne stayed where she was. His eyes were again open. His voice wracked with torment, he went on. "I don't know how. I don't know why. But, dear God, Anne, I love you and you are too young. Get out of here, chicken. Go back to your room while I can still let you go."

"No."

"Anne."

"No, Jud," she repeated firmly then more softly, "Jud, please. I don't want to go. I want to stay with you."

In three strides he was back beside her, his hands again cradling her head. "You are a small, beautiful fool. And I will very likely burn in hell, but, honey, I need you so, want you so."

This time when his mouth touched hers she needed

no prompting. Eager to experience again that wild riot of sensations, her lips parted beneath his searching, hungry mouth. His hand dropped to her shoulders then moved down and over her back, drawing her slight, soft body against his large, hard one.

Slowly, reluctantly, his lips released hers, moved over her face and she felt her breath quicken as he dropped featherlight kisses across her cheeks, on her eyelids, and along the edge of her ear. Breathing stopped completely for a moment when his teeth nipped gently on her lobe and he whispered urgently, "Anne, I want you to touch me. Put your hands on my chest, inside the robe."

Her hands had been lying tightly clasped on her lap and at his words she relaxed them, brought them slowly up. Slowly, shyly, she parted the lapels of his robe, then placed her palms against his hair-roughened skin. Enjoying the feel of him, she grew braver and slid her hands across the broad expanse of his chest. He shuddered, then moaned deep in his throat when her fingertip brushed his nipple. Made still braver by his reaction to her touch, she whispered. "Do you like that, Jud?"

"Like it?" he husked. "Lord, sweetheart, I love the feel of your hands on me. I just hope you enjoy the feel of my touch half as much." His hands moved to the buttons of her robe, unfastening them quickly. His lips close to hers, he murmured, "I don't think we need all this material between us."

He slipped the robe off then gathered her close against him, his mouth driving her to the edge of delirium as he explored the hollow at the base of her throat. Anne stiffened with a gasp when his hand moved caressingly over her breasts, his touch seeming to scorch her through the thin cotton of her short nightie, but the heady excitement his gently teasing fingers aroused soon drowned all resistance. His mouth sought hers over and over again becoming more urgently demanding with each successive kiss and Anne felt desire leap and grow deep inside.

She felt a momentary chill when his arms, his mouth, released her and he leaned away from her. Dimly she was aware of his movement as he shrugged out of his robe and tossed it aside. The flame inside her leaped higher when he pulled her close against his nakedness. Afire with a need she didn't fully understand, inhibitions melting rapidly in that flame, she slid her hands along his body, loving the feel of his smooth warm skin. When she ran her fingers up and over his rigid, arched spine, he shivered and groaned against her mouth. "I could kiss you forever but, Anne, baby, it's no longer enough. Raise your arms."

She obeyed at once and sat meekly as he tugged her nightie up and over her head. When she was about to drop her arms, he caught her wrists in one of his hands and pulled them high over her head then forced her down against the bed. Stretched out below him, she felt her cheeks go pink as his eyes went slowly, burningly, over her body. Her color deepened when his hand followed the route his eyes had mapped out and her eyes closed with embarrassment when, without conscious thought, her body moved sensuously under his fingers.

"Open your eyes, Anne," he ordered softly, and when she did she found herself staring into warm liquid amber.

"Don't ever be embarrassed or ashamed with me. From tonight on, you are mine. You belong to me. No, we belong to each other, for I am surely yours. There's no reason for you to be shy with me. You are beautiful and I love every inch of you. Do you understand?"

Unable to speak around the emotion blocking her throat, Anne nodded. He kissed her hard then whispered, "Tell me again that you love me, Anne."

"I love you, Jud, more than anything or anyone else on this earth."

Anne heard his breath catch and then his head lowered and his mouth followed the path of his eyes and hands, branding her with his ownership. They were both breathing heavily, almost painfully, when his hard body moved over hers and between short, fierce kisses, he vowed, "I love you, Anne. I'll always love you."

Neither one of them heard the door open and they both went rigid when Jud's father said coldly, "Get away from her, Jud."

Jud hesitated a second then through clenched teeth spat out, "Get the hell out of here, Dad."

"I told you to get away from her and I mean it. Now, move."

Judson Cammeron had not raised his voice, but there was an icy, angry command in his tone. Overwhelmed with disappointment and shame, Anne moaned softly, "Jud, please."

Jud remained still, every muscle in his body tense with anger; then he moved, slowly, pulling his robe over her body as he went.

Shaking with reaction, Anne lay listening to the silence crackle angrily between father and son. Her stepfather finally broke the silence. "Haven't you had enough with all the girls you've had in the last year? Must you bring your appetite home? Use your stepsister? Good God, man, she is little more than a child."

Jud started tightly, "Dad, you—" His father cut him off. "I'm taking Anne to her room, but I'll be back." He tucked the robe around her shaking body, then lifted her in his arms. At the door he paused, his voice thick with disgust. "Get some clothes on."

He carried her to her room, laid her on the bed, then turned his back to her, saying, "Put on a nightgown and get into bed. I'll be back. I'm going to get you something to help you sleep."

Tears running down her face, she leaped off the bed the minute he closed the door. With jerky movements she pulled a clean nightie over her head, crawled back into bed, turned her face into her pillow, and sobbed brokenly.

By the time he returned she was shaking so badly he had to help her sit up and hold the glass for her while she chokingly swallowed the two pills he handed her.

"Don't cry so, Anne, you'll make yourself ill. I don't blame you in this, you're too young to understand."

"Mother?" Anne sobbed.

"She's asleep and I give you my word she, or anyone else, will not hear of this."

He left her and slowly, as the pills, whatever they were, took effect and she grew drowsy, the sobs subsided.

It had been late when Anne woke the next morning. A beautiful Saturday morning that didn't fit at all with her depressed state. Feeling hurt, uncertain, very young, Anne showered and dressed, afraid to think about Jud and what had happened. She felt ashamed that her stepfather had found them the way they were, but she felt no guilt. She loved Jud and he said he loved her and their lovemaking, aborted though it had been, was a natural outpouring of that love. Things might be uncomfortable for a while, but somehow she felt sure Jud would make it right. On that thought she had squared her shoulders and gone downstairs.

The twins were nowhere around, but her mother and stepfather were having midmorning coffee in the living room. Anne started into the room, then stopped, a finger of fear stabbing her heart at their expressions. Her stepfather's face was set, stony. Her mother looked upset, near tears. Fearfully Anne asked, "What happened? Is something wrong?"

Judson opened his mouth, but before he could speak her mother cried, "Oh, Anne, it's Jud. Sometime during the night he packed his bags and left. He left no word of where he was going or when he'd be back, nothing."

Feeling her knees buckle, Anne dropped into a chair.

"But—"

The sight of her stepfather's eyes dried the words on her lips, for although his face was set, his eyes were filled with disappointment and despair. When he spoke, his voice was cold and flat.

"Margaret, I don't want his name mentioned in this house ever again, do you understand?"

"Judson!" her mother's voice mirrored her astonishment.

"I mean it," he went on in the same flat tone. "Talk to the twins; make them understand. Not ever again. Anne, do you understand?"

Anne had nodded her head bleakly, not understanding at all.

Anne, coming back to the present, stirred restlessly on the bed, eyes closed against the tears and pain that engulfed her. She had thought she had left the pain behind a long time ago. At first she had waited hopefully for a phone call or a letter. But as the weeks became months the hope died, only the pain went on. As one year slipped into two, then three, the pain dulled, flaring at intervals as word of him began to reach them.

He had come into a sizable inheritance from his mother's estate the same day he left and he had used it well. Jud had always had a flair for the use of fabrics in clothes and he used that flair by opening an exclusive menswear shop. Somewhere he had run across two budding but avant-garde designers and he hired them. They had obviously worked well together, for by the time Anne and his father heard of it, he had expanded to four stores in key cities. The first contact between Jud and his father had been made through Jud's assistant four years before.

Anne would never forget the look on Judson Cammeron's face the day he had called her into his office and silently handed her a letter. It had been a request for an interview to discuss the possibility of the production of a particular fabric and it had been signed by a John Franks, assistant to Judson Cammeron of Cammeron Clothiers. The only word that could describe her stepfather's expression was stunned.

Maintaining a rigid control she had asked quietly, "Will you see this John Franks?"

He had hesitated, then replied heavily, "We may as well, Anne. If we don't, they'll only go to the competition. Besides which, I'm curious to know what he has in mind for this fabric." He, of course, being Jud.

The meeting was held, a deal was struck, and they had been supplying Jud with special fabrics off and on ever since. But never at any time had personal contact been made between father and son. And at no time did Jud's name pass his father's lips although Anne knew by his attitude that he was pleased by even this small contact.

At last report Jud's stores numbered eight and he was reputed to be becoming a very rich man. The word that had filtered down to them was that there were some very wealthy men who bought almost exclusively from Jud and that their numbers were growing by the week.

And now, Anne thought, he would have it all. The

company that produced the fabric, the designers who whipped up the original clothes, and the stores where they were sold. *Not all,* Anne corrected herself, *not if I can help it.* She had no right to any part of the company, but Troy and Todd did, and somehow she had to make sure they got it.

Suddenly Anne realized that her train of thought, the last few minutes, had alleviated, to a degree, her pain and shock. The tears were gone, replaced by determination. She had taken care of the twins since they were toddlers. Her protective, mother's instinct was to the fore replacing the hurt, humiliated feeling of that long-ago fifteen-year-old girl.

Her lips set in a determined line, Anne slid off the bed and walked to the window. The light was gone from the day that had never brightened above gray. Anne's room was on the side of the house and below, some distance beyond, the bright lights above the doors of the triple garage lit the surrounding area in an artificial glare. Eyes bleak as the weather, Anne studied the dark tracery of bare, black tree limbs. The stark branches in that eerie light had the effect of many arms raised in supplication to the heavens.

Restlessly she turned from the harsh etching, her eyes moving slowly over the muted pinks of the room bathed in the soft glow of the bedside lamp. She had felt a measure of security in this room the last few years, had thought her shattered emotions healed, her heart becoming free once more. Now she felt scared, vulnerable, not unlike that tree outside with limbs lifted as if in yearning. She knew a longing deep inside that had to be quickly squashed.

Moving with purpose, she slowly undressed. One could show no sign of weakness with Jud, for if she did, she was sure he'd trample her as completely as would a wild, fear-crazed mob. She had allowed, no, invited, his trampling before. She wasn't sure she could survive it a second time.

Anne's head came up in defiance and her spine went taut with determination. She may have allowed him to hurt her, but she would not let him hurt her family. The thought that they were his family, too, was dismissed out of hand. He had disclaimed all rights to any of them ten years ago. The clock could not be turned back.

ABOUT THE AUTHOR

Joan Hohl lives with her family in Pennsylvania and is currently working on her next Zebra contemporary romance, I DO. Joan loves to hear from readers and you may write to her c/o Zebra Books. Please include a self-addressed stamped envelope if you wish a response.

BOOK YOUR PLACE ON OUR WEBSITE AND MAKE THE READING CONNECTION!

We've created a customized website just for our very special readers, where you can get the inside scoop on everything that's going on with Zebra, Pinnacle and Kensington books.

When you come online, you'll have the exciting opportunity to:

- View covers of upcoming books
- Read sample chapters
- Learn about our future publishing schedule (listed by publication month *and author*)
- Find out when your favorite authors will be visiting a city near you
- Search for and order backlist books from our online catalog
- Check out author bios and background information
- Send e-mail to your favorite authors
- Meet the Kensington staff online
- Join us in weekly chats with authors, readers and other guests
- Get writing guidelines
- AND MUCH MORE!

**Visit our website at
http://www.zebrabooks.com**